"Does it fit?" she asked anxiously. "Can you get it in there?"

It was too much to expect Dane's mind not to head straight for the gutter, not with her seductive heat seeping into his bones. He cleared his throat. "It should be fine," he managed thickly.

"Let me help you," she offered.

He was beyond help. "It'll fit, don't worry." His voice was a low, rough growl he hardly recognized as his own.

Mistaking the reason for his tone, Solange backed away. He didn't know whether to be relieved or disappointed. "Sorry," she said sheepishly. "I packed the car myself before leaving Haskell, so I have a pretty good idea how and where everything should go."

Dane had a few ideas of his own that had nothing whatsoever to do with maneuvering boxes around the backseat of her car. In fact, right now he could think of far better uses for the backseat in question.

Books by Maureen Smith

Kimani Romance

A Legal Affair
A Guilty Affair

Kimani Press Arabesque

With Every Breath
A Heartbeat Away

MAUREEN SMITH

is the author of nine novels and one novella. She received a B.A. in English from the University of Maryland, with a minor in creative writing. As a former freelance writer, her articles were featured in various print and online publications. Since the publication of her debut novel in 2002, Maureen has been nominated for two *Romantic Times BOOKreviews* Reviewers' Choice Awards and nine Emma Awards, and has won Romance in Color Reviewers' Choice Awards for New Author of the Year and Romantic Suspense of the Year.

Maureen currently lives in San Antonio, Texas, with her husband, two children and a miniature schnauzer. She loves to hear from readers and can be reached at author@maureen-smith.com. Please visit her Web site at www.maureen-smith.com for news about her upcoming releases.

A RISKY AFFAIR

Maureen Smith

KIMANI™
ROMANCE

 KIMANI PRESS™

ISBN-13: 978-0-373-86059-3
ISBN-10:   0-373-86059-5

A RISKY AFFAIR

Copyright © 2008 by Maureen Smith

www.kimanipress.com

Printed in U.S.A.

Dear Reader,

After I finished writing *A Legal Affair*, I realized that Crandall Thorne, despite his past sins, deserved to find closure with his old flame Tessa. I could think of no better way to bring these two star-crossed lovers together than to bless them with a granddaughter who would help heal the wounds of the past and give them hope for the future. Solange Washington proved to be a willing vessel, although she had no idea what she was getting herself into when she agreed to work for Crandall. As a reward for putting up with her grandfather's mercurial ways, I gave Solange a man like Dane Roarke—fun, irresistibly sexy and intensely passionate.

I hope you enjoyed getting to know Dane and Solange as they put aside their mutual fears and took a chance on love. Although their story officially concludes the "Affair" series, I might decide to revisit the Roarke and Thorne families sometime in the future. So stay tuned!

I love to hear from readers! Please e-mail me at author@maureen-smith.com, and visit my Web site at www.maureen-smith.com for news and updates on my upcoming releases.

Until next time, happy reading!

Maureen Smith

For Maravia and Jared,
because children are precious gifts from God

Chapter 1

"Please don't die on me, please don't die on me," Solange Washington muttered under her breath as the ancient Plymouth she was driving lumbered up a steep hill blanketed in the deep green of pine trees.

"If you get me to the interview in one piece," she continued her plea bargain, "I *promise* to put you out of your misery once and for all. You have my word." Her fingers were crossed because junking the Plymouth and buying a new car weren't in her plans—nor in her budget.

Unless, of course, she landed the job with Crandall Thorne.

She felt a surge of excitement at the thought. Three weeks after being contacted by Thorne's secretary, Solange still couldn't believe the incredible opportunity she'd been given. Crandall Thorne, a wealthy criminal defense attorney, was one of the most powerful men in Texas. Solange knew many people—not just aspiring lawyers like herself—would give their eyeteeth for the chance to work for him. He'd probably been inundated with hundreds of résumés from people vying to become his new personal assistant. And out of those many applicants, Solange was the only one who'd been invited for an interview.

She couldn't believe it. What were the odds?

Don't question your good fortune, she told herself, as her mother had been fond of saying. *Just focus on convincing Crandall Thorne that you're the best candidate for the job!*

Solange grimaced as the old Plymouth lurched and groaned in protest. Too bad Thorne had insisted on conducting the interview at his remote ranch tucked deep in Texas Hill Country. She'd expected to be interviewed at his downtown law firm, and was surprised to be informed that she would meet Thorne at his home instead.

She glanced at the directions his secretary had faxed to her and wished for a landmark—a Whataburger, a bank, a gas station—*anything* to reassure her that she was going the right way. But all she could see for miles was an endless stretch of road that wound through the lush foothills of a mountain range.

And then, suddenly, a hacienda-style ranch house perched high on a bluff came into view. As Solange gazed upon the house, she realized the glossy photographs she'd seen in an old issue of *Architectural Digest* had not done the property justice. No photograph, professional or not, could capture the way the sprawling house sat proud and erect on a hilltop, framed against a vivid blue sky and reigning above a lush green valley that stretched against the backdrop of vast, rugged mountains.

With a mixture of excitement and nervousness, Solange steered the car uphill and through a heavy iron gate bearing the name C&C Ranch. She drove past several barns and outbuildings and a large roping arena before reaching the main house. She parked in one of the three detached garages as she'd been instructed and turned off the ignition. The Plymouth shuddered and groaned loudly, as if heaving its last breath.

"God, I hope not," Solange muttered, reaching over and grabbing a battered leather briefcase from the passenger seat.

She didn't have time to dwell on the fate of the old car. In five minutes she'd be late for the interview, and based on everything she'd read about Crandall Thorne, he wouldn't tolerate tardiness from a prospective employee—or anyone else, for that matter.

Clutching her attaché case, Solange hurried across the manicured ranch yard toward the rambling two-story house that boasted a red-tiled Spanish roof and a wide, curving porch that beckoned visitors.

The tall, handsome woman who answered the door beamed a smile at Solange that was equally welcoming. "Why, hello," she said in warm, lilting tones that whispered of a Southern accent. "You must be Crandall's three o'clock appointment."

Solange smiled. "Yes, that's right. My name's Solange Washington."

The woman, who appeared to be in her midsixties, arched a finely sculpted brow. "Solange? What an unusual name. I imagine you must hear that all the time, though."

Solange chuckled softly. "Yes, ma'am, I do. I think my mother wanted to name me something different, something unique. Either that, or she just ran out of ideas and thought she was making up something."

The woman's smile widened with pleasure. "A sense of humor. Good. You'll need it if you want to work for Crandall Thorne." At Solange's mildly alarmed look, the woman laughed and swung the door wide to usher her inside the house.

"Goodness, where are my manners?" she exclaimed as Solange paused to glance around the wide, spacious foyer. "Been working for Crandall too long. Thirty-three years, to be exact. My name is Rita Owens."

"Nice to meet you, Ms. Owens," Solange said, shaking the woman's warm, slightly calloused hand. Work hands, like her mother's had been.

"May I offer you something to drink, Miss Washington?" Rita Owens asked. "Some coffee, tea or hot chocolate? It *is* December, though it doesn't quite feel like it. Are you from Texas?"

"Yes, ma'am. Born and raised."

"Then you're already used to our unseasonably warm winters. Let me take you on back to Crandall before he thinks you're running late. He doesn't like to be kept waiting."

Solange nodded. She'd already figured as much.

The entryway spilled into a large living area that boasted the finest in contemporary furnishings, a far cry from the worn, shabby furniture that had filled the tiny farmhouse Solange had grown up in. Tall glass windows soared to cathedral ceilings, and custom ceramic tile floors gleamed beneath her feet as she followed Rita Owens down a wide hallway with archways on both sides that opened into several spacious rooms, each show-casing the work of a very talented—and no doubt expensive—interior designer.

"Did you find the ranch with no problem?" Rita asked over her shoulder.

"Yes, thank you," Solange said, silently wishing she'd re-membered to buy self-adhesive pads for the new black pumps she'd gotten on sale at JCPenney. The smooth, slippery soles were no match for the polished floors of Crandall Thorne's home.

As they reached the end of the hallway, Rita stopped and rapped her knuckles lightly on a closed door. "Your three o'clock appointment is here," she announced.

After another moment, a deep, gravelly voice called, "Show her in."

Rita smiled at Solange before opening the door and guiding her into a room that smelled of leather, ink and freshly polished wood. It was a large, richly appointed suite that boasted a twenty-foot ceiling and mahogany-paneled walls lined with rows and rows of books, more than Solange had ever seen outside an actual library. The upper rows of bookshelves were accessible by a pair of ladders on wheels.

A tall, broad-shouldered man stood beside one of these ladders, thumbing through a thick leather-bound book. He wore a crisp white shirt over impeccably tailored coffee-brown trousers and dark Gucci loafers that had probably cost more than everything in Solange's closet.

As she stepped into the room, the man lifted his head from the book he'd been perusing and slowly turned. Behind a pair of rimless glasses perched on the bridge of a strong, aristocratic nose, eyes the color of bittersweet chocolate landed on Solange—and widened in surprise.

"This is Miss Solange Washington," Rita announced.

Crandall Thorne didn't move or utter a word. Instead he continued staring at Solange in a way that knotted her stomach. Did he hate her gray pinstriped skirt suit? Or did he hate her patent-leather shoes? Could he tell she'd bought them on sale at a department store? Was he already dismissing her as an unsuitable candidate simply because of the way she looked?

Mustering a polite smile, Solange crossed to him with an outstretched hand. "It's an honor to meet you, Mr. Thorne," she said briskly, just as she'd rehearsed on the way over. "Thank you for giving me this wonderful opportunity to discuss my skills and qualifications in person."

When Crandall's mouth twitched, she inwardly cringed. Had she overdone it? Had she come across sounding too eager, too brown-nosey?

Crandall's large, elegant hand swallowed hers in a firm handshake. "A pleasure, Miss Washington," he drawled in a voice that resonated with authority. At sixty-six years old, Crandall Thorne was even handsomer than he'd appeared in the newspapers, with salt-and-pepper hair, deep brown skin, dark, piercing eyes and a neatly trimmed mustache that framed firm, no-nonsense lips. According to the articles Solange had read, Thorne's deteriorating health over the past three years had forced him to take a backseat role in the multimillion-dollar legal empire he'd built with his own two hands. He'd retreated to his secluded estate in the Hill Country and was seldom seen at the power luncheons and lavish galas he'd once headlined.

But as Solange stood in his library that warm winter afternoon, she realized there was nothing frail or feeble about the man before her. With little or no effort, Crandall Thorne exuded the confidence and power of a man who knew he was—and always would be—a force to be reckoned with. She doubted he ever took a backseat role in anything, much less the running of his own company.

"Please have a seat, Miss Washington," Crandall said, gesturing toward a pair of oxblood leather chairs opposite a mahogany island of a desk.

As Solange moved to claim one of the chairs, Rita Owens asked, "Would either of you care for something to drink?" When both declined, she slipped out of the room and closed the door behind her.

Solange folded her hands neatly in her lap and watched as Crandall returned his book to the shelf and walked toward her with a relaxed, unhurried pace that told her he rushed for no one.

"Now then," Crandall began once he was seated behind the large, gleaming desk. "Why are you here?"

Solange sat up straighter in her chair, confused by the question. "I was referred to you by—"

Crandall shook his head. "I didn't ask *how* you got here, Miss Washington. I'm well aware of those details. I asked *why* you're here. Why do you think you're the best person for this job?"

"I have the skills and qualifications you're looking for," Solange replied. "I have eight years of combined experience as a secretary and paralegal at the oldest family law firm in Haskell, Texas. I'm very familiar with the legal system, possess excellent research and investigative skills, and I've prepared written reports, legal arguments, draft pleadings, motions and a number of other important documents that were used in court. I'm smart, conscientious, trustworthy and a hard worker, whether I'm preparing a contract or running errands for you."

Crandall nodded slowly, those shrewd, dark eyes narrowed on hers. "It would seem to me, Miss Washington, that your next move should be applying to law school." When Solange said nothing, he continued flatly, "When I first advertised for this position, I received hundreds of résumés, from established attorneys to third-year law students wanting to secure a job before graduation. I dismissed them all. Do you know why?"

Solange shook her head, though she already had an inkling.

"I dismissed them because I'm not looking for a lawyer to fill this position, and quite frankly, I'm skeptical of anyone who would put themselves through the rigors of law school only to settle for a job as a personal assistant. If you have any aspirations of becoming a lawyer, Miss Washington, and you're hoping to use this position as an opportunity to 'learn from the best,' then I'm afraid you're wasting your time—and mine. It's been years since I took it upon myself to mentor anyone, and I don't intend to start now."

Solange swallowed, keeping her expression carefully neutral. "With all due respect, Mr. Thorne, I'm not looking for a mentor, although I'd be lying if I said the opportunity to learn from you *wasn't* one of the main things that attracted me to this position."

Crandall regarded her in thoughtful silence for a moment. "Contrary to what you may have read in the papers or heard about me, Miss Washington, I'm still very active in the daily operations of my corporation. I'm looking for an energetic, highly capable professional to handle my scheduling, correspondence and travel needs—at any and all hours of the day. That means when I say 'Jump,' you not only ask 'How high?' but you demand perfection of yourself in carrying out the task. I'm looking for someone who can represent me well at any business, political or social function I deem important. Discretion and integrity are not optional character traits in the individual I'm seeking—they're *mandatory*. I don't want to spend time worrying about my personal assistant leaking sensitive information about me, my company *or* my family to the media or to competitors."

"I understand that, sir," Solange said. "I can assure you that this wouldn't be an issue with me."

He appeared vaguely amused. "Talk to me after you've been approached by someone offering you thousands of dollars for confidential information about my financial or medical status. You'd be surprised how often it happens," he added grimly at Solange's disconcerted look. He studied her another moment, then said, "Ted Crumley spoke very highly of you. He said you were one of the best paralegals he'd ever hired."

Solange couldn't stop the wry smile that curved her lips. "Makes you wonder why he was so willing to part with me then, doesn't it?"

Crandall chuckled dryly. "Not at all. When I told him about the position and asked if he could recommend anyone, he indicated that you, out of all his employees, would benefit the most from a change of scenery." He paused for a moment, then added soberly, "Allow me to express my condolences on the passing of your parents."

Solange nodded. "Thank you."

With his elbows braced on the desk, Crandall steepled his fingers in front of his face and quietly studied her. "Ted tells me you grew up in Haskell."

"Yes, that's right."

"Not much to do in a small town like that, I would imagine."

Solange bristled. "Depends on what you're looking for," she said archly. "I liked my small town just fine."

"Touché," Crandall murmured, his mouth twitching. "I never meant to imply otherwise, Miss Washington. Were you born there? In Haskell?"

Solange hesitated. "Yes, I believe so."

Crandall raised an eyebrow. "You don't know for sure?"

"I was adopted as a child. Some of the details of my past are a bit, um, fuzzy to me." Eager to change the subject, she said, "I assume you've had a chance to review my résumé. Are there any questions you'd like to ask about my employment history?"

Crandall gave her a long, assessing look. "As you can imagine, I have a vast number of resources at my disposal. For this position, I could have selected a qualified candidate from a pool of prescreened applicants courtesy of an executive search firm. But I decided to cast my net wider and open the search to the general public, in the hopes of finding someone truly extraordinary. A diamond in the rough, if you will." He paused, his eyes narrowing on her face. "What can you tell me to persuade me you're that diamond, Miss Washington?"

Solange smiled. "One of my college English professors always lectured me on the importance of showing, not telling, in my writing." She reached inside her attaché case and withdrew a laptop computer containing the PowerPoint presentation she'd prepared for the interview. "Rather than *tell* you why I'm the best person for this job, Mr. Thorne, I'll *show* you."

Crandall leaned back in his chair with a coolly amused expression. "You have my undivided attention."

When Solange left the ranch house forty minutes later, she honestly believed she'd seen the last of Crandall Thorne.

He'd remained mostly silent throughout her presentation, watching her with an impassive expression that made her wonder what he was thinking. Nothing seemed to impress him—not her beautifully designed PowerPoint slides detailing her skills and qualifications, nor had she impressed him with her demonstrated knowledge of the law or her recitation of the facts surrounding his very first court case.

To make matters exponentially worse, as she was escorted to the front door following the interview, Solange had lost her footing on the slippery tile floor and would have landed squarely on her butt if she hadn't reached out quickly and grabbed the first thing she could—a fistful of Crandall's shirt. He'd kept her upright, but at the expense of several buttons, which popped free and scattered across the floor. With her cheeks flaming with embarrassment, Solange had apologized profusely to her frowning host and left as gracefully as she could.

As she slid behind the wheel of her car and cranked the engine, Solange grimaced, thinking back to the conversation she'd had with her former boss three weeks ago.

She'd been having a bad day. Not only was she appallingly behind on a report, but earlier that morning she'd sent one of the attorneys to court with the wrong affidavit, then she'd misfiled an important case document that had taken several hours to track down. When Ted Crumley appeared at the entrance to her cubicle and asked to see her in his office, she just knew he was going to fire her. Ted was the managing partner at the small law firm where she'd worked for eight years. At sixty-six, he was medium height, thin, with silvery brown hair that receded from his broad forehead, and a reddened, bulbous nose that gave him the appearance of having a perpetual cold. His suits, though not as expensive as anything worn by Crandall Thorne, were always neatly pressed, his worn, sensible loafers still polished to a high gloss. He took as much pride in his appearance as he did in the daily operations of the family law practice he'd helped to establish thirty years ago—which was what made Solange so nervous about his request to see her.

She needn't have worried.

Instead of firing or even reprimanding her, he'd offered her something else, something she'd never expected but had been secretly longing for.

The chance to start a new life.

"Have you ever heard of Crandall Thorne?" he'd asked.

Solange stared at him. Of course she'd heard of Crandall Thorne! Any aspiring attorney worth her salt had heard of the man, and she said as much.

Ted chuckled. "Well, it just so happens that Thorne and I attended law school together at UT. We've kept in touch for a while, and he recently called to tell me about a position he was hiring for. He needs a personal assistant, preferably someone who doesn't have any ties to San Antonio politics or media, and someone who would be interested in relocating."

"And…and you thought of me?" Solange didn't know whether to be flattered or offended that her boss seemed so willing to relinquish her to another employer.

A soft, rueful smile lifted the corners of Ted's mouth. "I thought of you because you haven't been the same ever since your parents died almost a year ago. I know that grief and the stress of settling their estate have taken a serious toll on you, even if you're too proud to admit it. I thought of you because you've never ventured beyond Haskell, and even a small-town lawyer like me can recognize what a travesty that is. I thought of you because it would have been selfish of me to deny you such an incredible opportunity simply because I didn't want to lose the best paralegal this firm has ever had."

Tears had welled in Solange's eyes, blurring her vision.

Blinking and swallowing hard, she'd whispered, "Crandall Thorne is a very rich, powerful man. What if he doesn't think I'm good enough to be his personal assistant?"

"I don't think you have to worry about that," Ted said with a gentle smile. "If Crandall is the excellent judge of character I still remember, he'll realize within minutes of meeting you how lucky he'd be to have you working for him."

Solange had thanked him and left his office before she embarrassed both of them by bawling like a baby. She'd needed less than a day to reach a decision, and within a week she'd loaded all her worldly possessions into the clunky old Plymouth, kissed her friends goodbye and headed out of town, leaving behind the only home she'd ever known.

She'd told herself that even if Crandall Thorne didn't hire her, she was doing the right thing by moving to San Antonio and starting anew. But now that the much-anticipated interview was over, and she faced the very real possibility that she wouldn't get the job, Solange wondered if she'd been too hasty in her decision to leave home. Crandall Thorne had hated her on sight, and unless her instincts were completely off base, she had probably seen the last of him.

Which meant she might have upended her life for nothing.

After Solange Washington's ignominious departure, Crandall changed his ruined shirt, then returned to his study and closed the door. His hand shook slightly as he dialed the number of his executive secretary, Arlethia Cunningham, at the downtown law firm where she'd worked for over twenty years.

"My three o'clock appointment just left," Crandall said without preamble.

"Oh? And how did it go?" Arlethia asked warily.

Crandall lifted Solange Washington's impressive résumé from his desk, gazed at it for several moments then set it aside and leaned forward in his chair. A solitary vein throbbed at his temple. "I want you to call Miss Washington. Call her first thing in the morning and offer her the job."

"Sir?" Arlethia made no attempt to hide her surprise. "Are you sure? She's the only candidate you've interviewed—"

"I know that," Crandall snapped. "Tell her the offer is contingent upon her passing a complete background check, which is to be administered through Roarke Investigations." After rattling off a series of instructions, Crandall hung up the phone and scrubbed a hand wearily over his face.

The reason he'd told his secretary to call Solange Washington in the morning was to give him time to change his mind. But, of course, he knew he wouldn't. Once he reached a decision about something, he rarely, if ever, reversed it. He'd built his reputation on being steadfast and resolute in his decision-making, both in and out of the courtroom. He'd also survived by keeping his friends close and his enemies closer.

In the case of Solange Washington, he'd need to keep her as close as possible.

Suddenly restless, Crandall rose from his chair and wandered over to a pair of French doors that overlooked a small courtyard, the stucco walls covered with a network of vines that were dry and brown this time of year.

A moment later, the door opened and Rita Owens—his longtime housekeeper who'd never believed in knocking—stepped inside the room. "Was that your only appointment of the day?"

Crandall glanced over his shoulder at her. "Yeah. So what?"

Rita shrugged, folding her arms across her chest. "I just wondered, that's all. I was thinking about catching a nap before dinnertime, and I wanted to make sure you weren't expecting any more visitors. Though I certainly wouldn't mind if they were anything like Miss Washington. She was something, wasn't she? So sweet and well-mannered. You can tell she had a good upbringing." Rita paused, her lips pursed thoughtfully. "You know, she kinda reminded me of someone. Someone I once knew."

"Me, too," Crandall said softly, remembering Solange Washington's clear, golden-brown skin, shoulder-length hair, big dark eyes and enchanting smile. His chest tightened painfully. He turned away from Rita, adding in a raw whisper, "You have no idea how much."

Chapter 2

Two days later, Solange stepped through the double-glass doors of Roarke Investigations, a private-detective agency housed in a single-story brick building located ten minutes away from the hotel she'd called home since arriving in San Antonio.

Her days at the Alamo City Inn were numbered, according to Crandall Thorne's secretary, who'd called Solange with the unexpected job offer. Solange had been scouring the Help Wanted ads when she received the phone call, and two days later, she was still in shock. Not only would she get the coveted opportunity to work for Crandall Thorne, but she'd do so while residing at his sprawling country estate, with its breathtaking views of the surrounding valley and mountains.

All she had to do was pass a background check, and then she'd be on her way to achieving her goals.

Finding no one behind the large oak desk or seated around the brightly furnished reception area, Solange ventured farther into the office. From somewhere down the narrow corridor, she could hear voices, male and female, and what sounded like the rapid clicking of a camera.

"Hello?" she called out.

There was no answer. She hesitated a moment, wondering if

she should just wait for someone to emerge from the back to assist her. But then she heard the low, husky rumble of masculine laughter, and she found her legs moving of their own accord, drawing her toward the owner of that voice.

The first thought that occurred to her when she reached the open doorway at the end of the corridor was that she'd made a wrong turn somewhere and wound up at the wrong building. The large conference room had been converted into a photography studio. In the center of the room, a slender, twenty-something Asian woman wearing baggy jeans and a blunt pageboy haircut was crouched on the floor, snapping photographs of a man who stood against a white canvas backdrop with his back to her. Solange's mouth went dry at the sight of him. He was tall, at least six-three, with skin the color of mahogany, broad shoulders and hard, sculpted muscles that bunched and flexed beneath a pair of suspenders. Charcoal trousers hung dangerously low on lean hips and hugged a firm, muscled rear end you could bounce quarters off. He was stunningly, brutally masculine—so potently male he stole her breath. Solange couldn't tear her gaze away.

He wore a black fedora, the kind sported by ace private detectives in the hard-boiled mysteries of old. With his face averted and the hat slanted low over his eyes, Solange had only a teasing glimpse of his profile—the ruthlessly square jaw and sensual mouth were enough to whet her appetite for more.

And then, suddenly, she got her wish.

At the photographer's flirtatious coaxing, the man slowly turned and flashed a dazzling white grin that set off a flurry of flashbulbs—and jack-hammered Solange's pulse. Before she could catch her breath, he noticed her standing in the doorway. Beneath the low brim of his fedora, the killer smile wavered and a pair of black, piercing eyes locked with hers.

If Solange thought she'd had trouble looking away before, it was now an impossibility. The stranger's heavy-lidded eyes probed hers with searing intensity, trapping the air in her lungs. He was as darkly handsome as his profile had suggested, with razor-edged cheekbones, a strong, masculine nose and those full, sensuous lips that ought to be registered somewhere as a lethal weapon.

As Solange stared at him, his gaze slid down her body as if he could see through her creamy silk blouse, through her tan slacks, her mismatched lace underwear, right down to the quivering flesh beneath.

To show him she could, she returned his bold appraisal, letting her eyes trace the wide expanse of his shoulders and the hard, sinewy muscles carved into his chest and abdomen. Without warning, she envisioned herself standing before him and dragging the suspenders off his shoulders, then lowering her head to flick her tongue over one flat dark nipple. She imagined taking it into her mouth and gently suckling, teasing and pleasuring him. The thought was enough to make her shiver.

When one corner of the man's mouth lifted, Solange was surprised to find her own lips curving in response.

A movement to her right caught her eye, and she suddenly remembered there were two other occupants in the room, including the photographer, who had followed the direction of the man's stare and was now looking at Solange with a mixture of curiosity and amusement.

"I'm sorry," Solange murmured, stepping into the room. "I didn't mean to interrupt. I must be at the wrong address. I'm looking for Roarke Investigations."

"You've found it." The sexy stranger came toward her, moving with the fluid ease and grace of a panther. As he drew nearer, Solange didn't know whether to look at his face or his bare chest—both were equally riveting.

"Dane Roarke," he introduced himself, wrapping his big, warm hand around hers. Tingles of awareness swept through her body. Their eyes held.

Solange's mind went completely blank.

"You must be from the temp agency," he said. His deep, resonant voice brushed across her awakened nerve endings like a slow, hot caress. "We've been expecting you."

She swallowed hard, and shook her head. "No, actually, I'm

not from the temp agency. I have an appointment with you this morning. My name's Solange Washington." She glanced around the room at the camera tripod, lighting equipment and the young woman who was now packing up her supplies with the help of her assistant. "Did I catch you at a bad time?"

"Not at all. In fact, you rescued me," Dane Roarke confided with a chuckle, and her stomach bottomed out at the low, sexy rumble. He was wrong—*she* was the one in desperate need of rescuing.

"Hey, I heard that," the photographer retorted as she approached them. Smiling easily, she passed a business card to Solange. "Hi, I'm April Kwan. I'm shooting a calendar featuring twelve of San Antonio's hunkiest men in law enforcement. Dane graciously agreed to be Mr. January."

"I don't know about the 'gracious' part," Dane grumbled. "My cousins didn't exactly leave me much of a choice, telling me at the last minute that their wives wouldn't allow them to pose for the calendar and volunteering me instead."

April grinned. "Well, thanks for being such a good sport about it. And remember that all proceeds from the calendar will benefit breast cancer research and education in San Antonio, so your willingness to be photographed half-naked was for a good cause. The women of San Antonio will thank you." Her dark eyes danced with mirth as she looked at Solange. "I'm taking orders, if you're interested. These calendars are gonna sell like hotcakes."

Solange could definitely believe it, especially if the rest of the models looked anything like Dane Roarke. Before she could respond to the girl's inquiry, Dane said, "I'll send her an autographed copy," and proceeded to usher Solange from the room.

"Sorry to keep you waiting," he said, his warm breath fanning the nape of her neck as he guided her down the hallway with a hand at the small of her back. She could feel the heat from his body and wondered if he'd forgotten he was shirtless. She certainly hadn't. "The photo shoot ran a bit longer than I'd expected."

"That's all right," Solange said. "I was a little early."

"The early bird gets the worm," Dane murmured whimsically.

He stopped outside a small, windowless office dominated by a large wooden desk and black metal filing cabinets along one wall.

"Have a seat," he said, waving her into one of the visitor chairs.

As she sat, he rummaged through the clutter on his desk until he located a manila file folder labeled with her first and last names. He opened the folder and pulled out a small sheaf of papers, which he passed to her, along with a pen and clipboard. When their fingers brushed, a melting warmth spread through her veins. Their eyes met for a prolonged moment.

"These are some forms for you to fill out and sign," Dane said softly. "I'll be back in a little while."

Solange nodded wordlessly, waiting until he'd closed the door behind him before drawing a deep, calming breath. She couldn't remember the last time, if ever, she'd been so fiercely attracted to a man, so acutely aware of him. Not even her former boyfriend Lamar Rogers had elicited such a response from her in the three years they'd dated. It was crazy. Sure, Dane Roarke was good-looking, virile and incredibly appealing, but that didn't mean she had to lose her mind. She'd always been a smart, savvy, cool-headed woman when it came to dealing with members of the opposite sex. But there was nothing remotely *cool* about her hot-blooded reaction to Dane Roarke.

Relax, girl, she told herself. *After today, you'll probably never see him again, anyway.*

She frowned, unsure whether that was a good or bad thing.

Shoving aside the unsettling thought, Solange started on the paperwork Dane had given her, which included detailed questionnaires about her employment and educational history, a drug-testing consent form, as well as a confidentiality agreement. She'd heard that Crandall Thorne had been involved in the hiring of every employee at his law firm since its inception. Considering that Solange, as his soon-to-be personal assistant, would be privy to sensitive information about him, she fully expected to undergo a background check comparable to those administered by the FBI.

Dane returned to the office as she was completing the last

form. When Solange glanced up and saw that he'd put on a shirt, she didn't know whether to be relieved or disappointed.

"All finished?" he asked briskly.

Solange nodded, passing him the paperwork attached to the clipboard.

He leafed through the forms as he rounded the desk and sat. While he was preoccupied, she covertly studied him. Without the fedora, she saw that his black hair was cropped close to his scalp, matching the smooth texture of his heavy eyebrows. Those piercing onyx eyes were rimmed with thick lashes, long enough to touch his cheeks as he looked down. His big hands were liberally sprinkled with black hair, his fingernails short and clean. Her gaze lingered on his left hand, searching his dark skin for traces of a wedding band, inexplicably relieved when she found none.

"No middle name?"

His deep voice jerked her to attention. Her eyes snapped to his face and found him looking at her. Her face heated with embarrassment at the realization that he'd caught her checking him out. "I'm sorry. What did you say?"

His mouth twitched. "I asked if you have a middle name."

She shook her head. "No. Just Solange." She waited for him to comment on how unusual her name was, or to ask her if she knew she shared her name with a popular singer's sister, but he merely nodded and continued his perusal of her paperwork. After another moment, he gave a satisfied nod and set aside the clipboard.

Leaning back in his chair, he regarded her with lazy indulgence. "So you're going to be working for Crandall Thorne, huh?"

"It appears so."

Dane shook his head slowly at her. "Brave woman."

She let out a startled laugh. "What's that supposed to mean?"

Dane chuckled softly. "You're new in town. I'll let you find out on your own."

Solange gave him a wry smile. "How well do you know Crandall Thorne?"

"Well enough. His son is married to my cousin Daniela, so we're practically related. Not to mention the fact that Crandall's one of our biggest clients. We do all of the employee background checks for his company."

Solange arched a teasing brow. "Aren't you afraid I'll go back and tell him you were badmouthing him?"

"Nah," Dane drawled lazily. "You don't strike me as the type to stab a man in the back like that."

Solange grinned. "I'll take that as a compliment."

"Oh, it was." His hot, possessive gaze roamed across her face, making her pulse quicken. "One of many compliments I could pay you, Miss Washington."

Her belly quivered, and she felt a thrill of pleasure at his words. Clearing her throat, she said, "I have a lot of errands to run this morning. Was there anything else you needed from me?"

"Actually, there is." Dane paused for a moment, watching her carefully. "Mr. Thorne asked me to invite you to take a polygraph test."

Solange stared at him in dumbfounded silence. She couldn't have heard right. "A *polygraph test?* He wants me to take a lie-detector test?"

"Only if you're willing to," Dane said mildly.

Solange shook her head in disbelief. She'd fully expected Roarke Investigations to conduct a thorough background check on her, but this was going overboard. "I'm sure you and Mr. Thorne are aware of the Employee Polygraph Protection Act of 1988, a federal law that prohibits employers from requiring employees to take lie-detector tests."

Dane inclined his head. "I'm aware of it, as is Mr. Thorne."

Solange said coolly, "That means employers are prohibited from even *suggesting* that an employee or applicant take a lie-detector test, nor can they decline to hire an applicant who refuses to take one."

A soft, enigmatic smile quirked the corners of Dane's mouth. "You're very familiar with the terms of the law. I'm impressed, Miss Washington. Rest assured that Mr. Thorne has no intention of withdrawing the job offer should you decide not to take the test."

"But he still wants me to do it, even though it's illegal. Is that what you're telling me?"

Dane's expression remained deadpan. "It's entirely up to you, Miss Washington."

Her eyes narrowed on his face. It was some kind of test. It had to be. She didn't believe for one second that a prominent, successful attorney like Crandall Thorne would expose himself to an unnecessary lawsuit by forcing a prospective employee to submit to a polygraph test. Time and again, he'd defeated his opponents in court by knowing the law better than their attorneys, even some judges. Asking Solange to take a lie-detector test—or *inviting* her, as Dane had so eloquently phrased it—was risky business.

What was Crandall Thorne up to?

A number of possibilities ran through her mind. He was trying to gauge how badly she wanted the job and what she was willing to do to secure it. Or maybe this was the first of many "tests" he would put her through to see how she performed under pressure. Or maybe he genuinely wanted her to undergo the polygraph test and was arrogant enough to believe he could get away with violating the law.

"Miss Washington?"

Solange met Dane's steady gaze with a subtle challenge in her own. "All right, Mr. Roarke. I'll play along. I'll take your lie-detector test. After all, I have nothing to hide."

His eyes glinted with satisfaction. "Give me a few minutes to set up."

Chapter 3

Ten minutes later, Solange was having serious doubts about her decision to take the lie-detector test—and that was before the actual questions began.

When she'd agreed to be tested, she hadn't counted on how nerve-racking the setup process alone would be. It was pure torture to hold herself perfectly still in a chair while Dane connected a series of tubes and wires to her body, explaining the purpose of each device in that deep, hypnotic voice that poured over her like dark honey. She struggled valiantly to pay attention, every nerve ending in her body tingling from the touch of his hands—beneath her breasts, around her stomach, between her trembling fingers as he attached finger plates that would monitor her electrodermal activity.

By the time Dane sat behind the computer monitor to begin the exam, her blood-pressure was off the charts, if the pounding of her heart was any indication.

"Relax," Dane murmured.

Solange shot him a freezing look. His answering chuckle whispered across her skin, soft as a lover's caress. She wanted to cross her legs, but remembered his instructions to keep both feet planted firmly on the floor.

"Are you qualified to administer these tests?" she demanded, more out of frustration than anything else.

The amused glint in his eyes told her he knew it, too. "I've received some training," he said vaguely.

"Where?" When he didn't immediately answer, she said crisply, "I have a right to know if the person giving me a lie-detector test—*illegally,* I might add—has the proper credentials and qualifications. So where did you receive your training, Mr. Roarke?"

He hesitated for a moment. "From the Federal Bureau of Investigation."

Solange stared. "You were an *FBI agent?*"

"Once upon a time." A shadow crossed his face, disappearing so swiftly she might have imagined it. "Shall we begin?"

She hesitated. There was a story behind his cryptic response, but she didn't have the time—or right—to explore it. Slowly she nodded.

"I'm going to ask you eleven questions," Dane explained. "Please indicate your responses with a yes or no. You don't have to elaborate on anything. Just yes or no. Do you understand?"

Solange nodded. "Go ahead."

"Is Solange Washington your real name?"

"To my knowledge."

"Yes or no," he reminded her.

"Yes."

"Are you twenty-nine years old?"

"Yes."

"Have you ever falsified information on an employment application?"

"No."

"Have you ever used illegal substances?"

"No."

"Have you ever been convicted of a felony?"

"No."

"Have you ever been arrested?"

Solange hesitated, biting her bottom lip. "Well…"

Dane's gaze shifted from the computer monitor—where

digital algorithms recorded her physiological responses—to her face. "Yes or no, Miss Washington." His tone was neutral, but there was a glimmer of interest in his dark eyes.

"Yes, but it wasn't my fault. I was thirteen, and they were going to bulldoze our farmhouse. I had to do *something*. They're lucky I didn't blow up their—" At Dane's arched brow, she broke off and grinned sheepishly. "Sorry. I know you told me not to elaborate. What was the next question?"

"Are you married?"

"God, no."

"Miss Washington—"

"Sorry. The answer is no. Just plain no."

He nodded, mouth twitching. Then, as if unable to resist, he looked at her again. "What do you have against marriage?"

Solange let out a startled laugh. "*Excuse me?* Is that one of the questions?"

Dane chuckled, shaking his head. "No. Just me being nosy." His expression sobered as he turned back to the monitor. "Are you a registered voter?"

"Yes."

"Have you ever been terminated by an employer?"

"No."

"If you knew another employee was stealing from the company you worked for, would you report that employee?"

Solange shifted slightly in her chair. "Depends."

"Yes or no."

"It depends on what the person is stealing. If we're talking about a few pens and notepads, then I wouldn't report him. But if he's stealing large sums of money, then yes, I would turn him in."

"So your answer is yes."

"Okay. Yes."

"Have you ever accepted a bribe?"

"Yes." When Dane paused, she added demurely, "Not the kind of bribe you're referring to, I assure you. This was strictly of a personal, altruistic nature."

His gaze returned to her face, tracing her eyes and lingering on her mouth in a way that made her pulse accelerate—which was picked up by the polygraph machine. They stared at each other for several charged moments.

"Are you seeing anyone, Miss Washington?" Dane asked huskily.

Her lips curved in a softly chiding smile. "That's the twelfth question," she said. "I'm afraid our time's up, Mr. Roarke."

Dane stood at the window in the reception area, hands thrust into his pockets as he watched Solange Washington climb into an ancient blue Plymouth that had seen better days a lifetime ago. He found himself willing her to look back at him, to give him some sign that he hadn't imagined the chemistry between them. But after revving up the old engine, she drove out of the parking lot without so much as a backward glance.

Dane chuckled quietly to himself. He didn't need any last, lingering looks between them to know he hadn't imagined her attraction to him. He'd seen it in her dark, exotically tilted eyes whenever she looked at him, heard it in her soft, breathless voice, felt it in the way her body trembled as he'd prepped her for the polygraph test. He'd administered the exam countless times before; today was the first time he'd ever been so aroused by a subject he could hardly remember which tubes and wires went where. He'd wanted nothing more than to run his hands along the lush, inviting curves of her body, kiss her plump, bow-shaped lips, wrap a fistful of her chestnut-brown hair around his hand and pull back her head, exposing the slender column of her throat to his hungry mouth.

Dane heaved a deep sigh, his body thrumming with desire. He'd even been deprived of the pleasure of removing the tubes and wires from her body following the test. She'd managed the task on her own while he was on the phone with a client.

Dane scowled. He knew he shouldn't have taken that damn call.

The front door opened, and a tall, dark-skinned man entered the building balancing a leather briefcase and a large, expensively gift-wrapped box. At the sight of Dane standing at the window, Noah Roarke made a face. "Thanks for helping with the door."

Dane grinned, still a little dazed from thoughts of Solange Washington. "Is that for me?" he teased, nodding toward the heavy package in his cousin's arms. "Aw, man, you shouldn't have."

"I didn't," Noah muttered, glancing at the empty reception desk as he walked past. "Where's the temp?"

"On her way. Called to say she got stuck in traffic." Dane followed Noah down the hallway to his office, then watched from the entrance as Noah placed the gift-wrapped box inside the small closet and shut the door.

"Let me guess," Dane drawled, propping a shoulder against the doorjamb. "Riley's figured out all your hiding places at home."

"Unfortunately," Noah admitted, setting down his briefcase on a desk that was as littered with files and paperwork as Dane's own desk down the corridor. Noah shook his head with a grin. "I swear she's like a kid around Christmastime, shaking presents under the tree to see if she can guess what's inside, dropping sly little hints to trick me into telling her what I got for her. She really knows how to wear a man down."

Dane chuckled dryly. "And you love every last second of it."

Noah shrugged, not even bothering to deny it. Everyone knew how much he adored his wife, Riley, whom he'd married three years ago in a big, festive ceremony that was still talked about in coffee shops and bars frequented by local cops. Noah, a former homicide detective, had been secretly in love with his best friend's girlfriend for years. Even after Trevor Simmons died tragically in the line of duty, it had taken Noah another three long, torturous years to confess his feelings to Riley—which, luckily for him, she happened to return. Nearly every cop in the city had attended their summer wedding, which had included a police-escorted motorcade fit for royalty.

"So what'd you get her for Christmas?" Dane asked, hitching his chin toward the closet.

"No way. I'm not telling you," Noah said with an emphatic shake of his head as he sat.

Dane laughed. "Why not? I can keep a secret."

Noah shot him a wry look. "This is your first Christmas with us since Riley and I got married, so I'll explain to you how things work. For the past three years, Riley has done her best to convince someone in the family to give up the goods on her Christmas presents. She's hit up everyone—Mom, Daniela, Caleb, Mama Florinda, Janie, Kenny, even the *twins.* She's relentless, man, and downright sneaky. So this year I'm playing it safe. I figure if no one else knows what I bought for her, then no one can be tricked or even *tempted* into spilling the beans."

"Smart man."

"I have to be, to keep one step ahead of that lovely wife of mine. You'll see someday," Noah told Dane with a sly grin.

Dane snorted rudely. "When hell freezes over." Even as the words left his mouth, he heard Solange Washington's response to his question about her marital status. *God, no,* she'd said without hesitation. Which pretty much summed up *his* feelings on the matter.

So why had he found her vehement denial so unsettling?

Noah shook his head at him. "You can run, but you can't hide forever."

"We'll see about that," Dane countered, straightening from the doorway. "Between you buying presents for Riley almost an entire month before Christmas, and Kenny working from home this week to nurse Janie through the flu, I definitely don't think I'm cut out for marriage. It requires too many selfless acts of kindness."

Noah smiled slowly, as if at some secret amusement. "Never say never, my friend. Never say never."

Chapter 4

Dane was still at the office late that evening when the front buzzer rang, announcing a visitor. Setting aside the case file he'd been reviewing, Dane rose from his chair and took a moment to stretch the cramped muscles in his back before heading out of the room to answer the door.

The reception area was empty and mostly dark, save for a softly burning lamp perched on the reception desk. The temp had gone home at six, Noah shortly afterward, citing a "hot date" with his wife. Dane chuckled to himself, shaking his head at the memory of his cousin abruptly ending a conversation with him, striding to his office to grab his briefcase and hightailing it out of there with a grin and a wave. Once upon a time, Noah had been a notorious workaholic, habitually pulling all-nighters to catch up on paperwork or carry out surveillance assignments. But that was *before* he'd married Riley Kane and discovered a reason to rush home every night. It wasn't that he was any less committed to the detective agency and their clients; he'd simply realigned his priorities and come up with a better way to balance them, and he made no apologies for either.

As Dane approached the front door, the buzzer sounded again. He knew who the late-night visitor was even before he unlocked the door and saw Crandall Thorne standing there. Wearing a silver-gray Stetson and an expensively tailored cashmere suit, Thorne was the epitome of the urbane, wealthy gentleman who'd graced countless magazine covers, including a recent issue of *Black Enterprise* that anointed him one of the most influential businessmen in America.

Without a word, Dane stepped aside and opened the door wider to let in the old man, who entered the building the same way he did everywhere else—as if he owned the joint.

Stopping in the center of the dimly-lit reception area, he swept an appraising glance around, taking in the rustic pine furniture, leafy potted plants and papaya-colored walls as if seeing the room for the first time, instead of just two days ago. At length his dark gaze came to rest on Dane.

"Burning the midnight oil, Roarke?" he intoned dryly.

"Something like that." Dane locked the door behind him. "You didn't have to come all the way out here in the middle of the night. I could have stopped by the ranch first thing in the morning."

"No need. I was in town visiting Caleb and Daniela, anyway."

"How're they doing?" Dane asked, moving around the room as he turned on more lights. He'd decided against inviting Crandall Thorne back to his office. If they stayed in the reception area, maybe Thorne would keep the visit short—although Dane knew the old man wouldn't leave until he'd gotten the information he came there for.

"They're doing well," Crandall answered, settling on the turquoise sofa Daniela had insisted upon purchasing when she'd redecorated the reception area four years ago. The sofa, like the rest of the furnishings, complemented the Southwestern theme she'd worked so hard to create.

"Caleb's still happy at the university, and Daniela's still complaining that she doesn't look like a woman in her third trimester of pregnancy," Crandall said with a low chuckle. There was no mistaking the way his voice softened whenever he spoke of his only son and daughter-in-law. His love for and devotion to Caleb had enabled him to embrace Daniela as if she were his own flesh and blood. No one was more excited than Crandall when the couple announced earlier in the summer that they were expecting their first child. It was the consensus that the old man was going to spoil his first grandchild rotten, although—as Crandall himself liked to point out—Caleb had had to work his butt off for everything he ever received from his father.

"Daniela was complaining that she hasn't seen you in a while," Crandall continued, a hint of reproach in his eyes as he regarded Dane from beneath the brim of his Stetson. "She said you've missed the last three Sunday dinners with the family."

"I know," Dane said guiltily. "It couldn't be helped. Work was calling. But I already got an earful from Aunt Pam *and* Daniela, so I'll make every effort to be there this Sunday."

Crandall gave an approving nod. "Don't let this—" he gestured smoothly to encompass the silent building "—keep you from realizing the important things in life. *Family* is important. Everything else is secondary."

Dane had to swallow back a laugh. It was one thing to receive advice about his personal life from Noah, with whom he'd grown up and who genuinely cared about him. But to receive such counsel from Crandall Thorne was an entirely different matter. The man had spent over half his life pouring blood, sweat and tears into building a legal empire—at the expense of his marriage and his relationship with his son. As far as Dane was concerned, Thorne was the last one to lecture anyone about putting family first. His very presence at the agency at ten o'clock that evening was proof that business matters still ranked high on his list of priorities.

"Now then," Crandall began, dispensing with the small talk in order to get to the purpose of his visit. "How did everything go with Miss Washington this morning?"

Dane sat down on one of the straight-backed chairs that lined the walls of the reception area and stretched out his long legs. "What exactly do you want to know?"

Crandall slowly removed his hat and set it on the small table beside him, next to a stack of glossy magazines and a glass bowl filled with pine potpourri that perfumed the air with a fresh, earthy scent.

Turning back to Dane, he inquired, "How did she react to being asked to take the polygraph test?"

Dane chuckled dryly. "She wasn't too happy about it, I can tell you that. She kindly referred me to the Employee Polygraph Protection Act of 1988."

"Like a good little lawyer." A sardonic smile curved Crandall's mouth. "How did she perform on the test?"

"What makes you so sure she agreed to take it?"

Crandall gave him a don't-insult-my-intelligence look. "I've been around a long time, son. Long enough to cultivate certain instincts about people. Miss Washington is a very smart woman, as I'm sure you realized within minutes of speaking with her. As you pointed out, she knew her legal rights concerning the polygraph exam, which means she knew I couldn't decide not to hire her based on the test results. I believe she guessed—correctly—that it was more about testing her reaction to the request than actually determining whether she would pass the test. And, of course, I'm sure she wanted to prove to me she had nothing to hide."

"She may have mentioned something to that effect," Dane said wryly.

"So, are you going to show me the test results?"

"Not a chance."

"I didn't think so." Crandall sent him an amused, knowing smile. "Mighty protective of her, aren't you? That didn't take very long."

Dane shrugged, crossing his booted feet at the ankles. "If anyone needs protection, it's you," he said idly. "We both know Miss Washington could cause trouble for you if she decided to challenge the legality of your request in court."

Crandall shook his head with a faintly mocking smile. "She's not interested in causing me trouble," he said so softly he might have been talking to himself.

Not for the first time since starting the background check on Solange Washington, Dane wondered about the *real* reason behind Thorne's preoccupation with her. He'd arrived at the office two days ago and specifically requested Dane, bypassing Noah and Kenneth Roarke, who'd established the private-detective agency.

Once Dane and Crandall were behind closed doors, Thorne had proceeded to tell him about the woman he planned to hire as his personal assistant. He'd asked Dane to conduct a thorough background check on her, comparable to the screenings he performed for senior executives at the law firm. Now, two days later, Dane wasn't buying the old man's explanation that Solange warranted the same level of intense scrutiny because she'd have access to his personal information and material belongings, which included expensive jewelry, priceless heirlooms and a rare art collection. Dane had been with Roarke Investigations for a year, and in that time he'd never known Crandall Thorne to ask a prospective employee to submit to a polygraph test. This was also the first time Crandall had ever shown up at the office in the middle of the night to check on the status of an employee background investigation.

He could deny it all he wanted, but Dane knew there was more at stake than Crandall hiring the most trustworthy personal assistant. The old man was hiding something, and Dane intended to find out what it was.

Crandall was watching him expectantly. "Do you have some information for me?"

Dane studied him in silence for several moments. Thorne's expression was mildly inquisitive, his posture relaxed, but there was an alertness about him, a taut energy that thrummed in the air around him like an invisible force field. He was practically waiting with bated breath to hear what Dane had discovered about Solange Washington.

"At the age of three," Dane began, "she was adopted by George and Eleanor Washington, a middle-aged African-American couple from Haskell, Texas. They had already lost a child—a teenage son—and were unable to conceive any more children. They came to San Antonio hoping to adopt a child, preferably another boy. They found Miss Washington through a local adoption agency that has since closed down. She spent the first three years of her life in the foster care system. By the time she was adopted by the Washingtons, she'd lived with no less than ten different foster families. Thankfully, according to my source, she showed no visible signs of abuse or neglect. She simply hadn't found a permanent home yet."

He delivered the news matter-of-factly, but the truth was he'd been moved with compassion and anger when he learned about Solange Washington's past. He'd tried hard not to imagine the cherubic, frightened toddler she must have been, bounced around from one foster home to the next, wondering why no one wanted to keep her. It was a lousy way for any child to start a life, and it made him that much more grateful for the loving, nurturing home he'd been raised in.

"What about her parents?" Crandall demanded gruffly. "Where were they? *Who* were they?"

Dane grimaced slightly. "That's where it gets a little tricky. Her birth records are sealed."

"Oh, you could get around that," Crandall said with an impatient wave of his hand.

"I could," Dane slowly agreed, "but it would take more digging than usual. Her records are sealed tighter than any I've ever encountered."

Crandall frowned. "What are you suggesting, Roarke?"

"I'm saying that someone went to a great deal of trouble to conceal the details of Solange Washington's birth. Someone wanted to make sure the identities of her birth parents remained a secret from everyone—the adoption agency, George and Eleanor Washington, even Solange herself. Someone who had not only the means, but the motivation to make a child's birth simply disappear like a puff of smoke from public record." Dane paused, his eyes narrowed on Thorne's stony face in silent appraisal. "Why do you suppose anyone would go to such extreme lengths?"

Crandall lifted one broad shoulder in a shrug that struck Dane as a bit too cavalier. "People seal birth records for any number of reasons," he replied blandly. "The main reason, of course, is that they don't want to be contacted by the adoptive parents or the child. That's probably what we're dealing with in this particular case."

"Probably." Dane offered a tight, grim smile. "At the very least, we can assume that one, or both, of Miss Washington's parents were wealthy and powerful enough to call in such a big favor. It was either a birth parent—or an interfering, overprotective grandparent."

Crandall nodded slowly, then reached for his Stetson and settled it atop his head before rising from the sofa. "Thanks for your time, Roarke. I appreciate the information you've provided."

Dane stared at him. "That's it? You don't want me to dig deeper to learn the identity of her birth parents?"

Crandall frowned. "There's no need to further invade her privacy. As long as Miss Washington isn't a criminal or working as a double agent for the government, I have no reason to continue probing into her background. You've satisfied my need to ascertain that she's a safe hire."

Dane inclined his head. "Then I guess our business here is finished."

Crandall chuckled on his way to the door. "Don't sound so relieved, Roarke. You're not getting rid of me that easily. I enjoy working with you. You're sharp, efficient and tenacious to the bone. Rest assured I'll be sending more jobs your way in the future."

"Not too many," Dane drawled humorously, "or my partners will get jealous."

Crandall laughed, framed in the open doorway. "Nothing wrong with a little healthy competition between partners. It's good for business." Tipping his head to Dane, he turned and sauntered into the dark night, looking, Dane thought, like a huge weight had been lifted from his shoulders.

Dane wondered, once again, what the old man was hiding.

Comfortably ensconced in the backseat of his Rolls Royce limousine a few minutes later, Crandall Thorne felt the tension slowly ebb from his body.

He was immensely relieved to know that Dane Roarke's investigation had not yielded the identity of Solange Washington's biological parents. Not that Crandall needed the private detective's help to find out what he already knew.

Twenty-four years ago, Crandall had been stunned to learn that the illegitimate daughter he'd once given up for adoption had become a mother at the age of fourteen. When Melanie, who'd been bounced around the foster-care system all her life, had discovered she was pregnant, she was terrified. After delivering a premature infant girl, she'd panicked and abandoned the baby at the hospital, fearing she'd get in trouble if her foster parents at the time found out about the birth.

Solange, like her teenage mother, had become a ward of the state. But unlike Melanie, she'd eventually found a permanent home with what appeared to be a good, loving family.

By the time Crandall learned about her existence, after Melanie's untimely death, Solange was already five years old—a happy, precocious little girl who was the apple of her parents' eyes, according to the private investigator Crandall had hired to find her. Over the next twenty-four years, he'd kept close tabs on her, content to watch her grow from afar. When George and Eleanor Washington died, he assumed it was only a matter of time before she'd attempt to locate her biological parents, which could lead her straight to his doorstep. Rather than take that chance, he'd continued monitoring her for several months while devising a scheme that would bring her to San Antonio.

How fortuitous for him that her employer, Ted Crumley, happened to be a fellow law-school graduate, and that he'd thought nothing of Crandall seeking him out at the class reunion they'd attended in Austin during the summer. Ever the strategist, Crandall had befriended him over the next six months, so that by the time he contacted Ted to ask him to recommend candidates for a personal assistant position, he knew the benevolent country attorney would consider it his duty to hand over his best employee to someone who could offer her better career opportunities. He'd gambled on a hunch that Solange, still mourning the loss of her parents, would be ready for a change of scenery.

His gamble had paid off.

Solange had taken the bait, never suspecting that her new employer was the grandfather she never knew existed.

It had been downright risky to ask Dane Roarke to conduct a thorough background check on her, but Crandall knew it was the only way to find out if the measures he'd put in place all those years ago to conceal the truth about the past withstood scrutiny. They had. Not even Roarke—a highly trained, seasoned investigator—had been able to crack the code to uncover the identity of Solange's biological parents.

But Crandall was nobody's fool. He knew that with a little more time and effort, and with the right incentive, Roarke could expose the truth about everything.

He couldn't let that happen.

Not until he'd gotten to know Solange better, to determine whether she could be trusted to be part of the family, to uphold the Thorne legacy.

And not until he'd gotten his one true love back into his life.

Hiring Solange as his personal assistant had been the first step. Setting up a meeting with Tessa Philbin would be the next.

If all went according to plan, Crandall would not only have a chance to right past wrongs. He'd have a chance at something that had eluded him for decades: happiness.

Chapter 5

It was after 10 p.m. by the time Solange let herself into her room at the Alamo City Inn. Balancing a taco takeout dinner with a laundry basket teeming with freshly washed clothes, she bumped the door shut with her hip and crossed the room to deposit her meal on the living room table. It was a short walk from there to the queen-size bed, where she dumped the contents of the laundry basket on top of the floral-patterned spread. She knew if she left the clothes in the basket overnight, she'd procrastinate about folding and packing them away until the last minute. After a day spent running errands and waiting for hours in a crowded clinic to take a drug test, she wanted nothing more than to soak in a long, hot bath and go to bed. But she had too much packing to do, and Saturday—the day she was to report to Crandall Thorne's ranch—was right around the corner.

With a deep sigh, Solange toed off her low-heeled pumps, pinned up her shoulder-length hair and returned to the seating area, where dinner awaited her.

She'd just bitten into a hot, spicy beef taco when her cell phone rang. She quickly fished it out of her purse and smiled at the familiar number displayed on the caller ID screen.

"Hey girl," she answered around a mouthful of food.

She was greeted by the warm, vibrant laughter of her longtime best friend Jill Somerset. "Hey yourself. Kinda late to be eating dinner, isn't it?"

Solange grinned. "When has that ever stopped me? Besides, it couldn't be helped this time. I've been running around all day trying to get things in order before I start my new job."

"When do you start?" Jill asked.

"Monday, officially, but I move on Saturday." Taking another bite of her taco, she glanced around the cramped suite she'd called home for the past week. With its dated yellow wallpaper, drab window treatments, cheap paintings and timeworn furniture, the extended-stay hotel room—while far from luxurious—had served its purpose. And, more importantly, it had been affordable. "Call me crazy," Solange said with a wry smile, "but I think I might actually miss this place."

Jill snorted loudly. "*Puh-leeze.* You won't think twice about that dump once you're comfortably situated in your boss's lavish country estate. Girl, I read the article about him in *Black Enterprise,* and the way his ranch was described made *me* want to pack up and move to San Antonio to try and get a job with him. Does he need another housekeeper or personal assistant?"

Solange snickered, taking a sip of her Coke. "You know your family would have a royal fit if you even thought about leaving Haskell. And they'd blame me for putting the crazy idea in your head, just like they blamed me when you broke up with Wyatt, the man everyone expected you to marry and have ten children with."

"You've got a point there," Jill agreed, and Solange could almost see the rueful, dimpled grin on her friend's gently rounded face. "They did blame you for the breakup—like it was *your* fault I walked in on Wyatt and that little hussy he'd been seeing behind my back for months. If you hadn't canceled our dinner plans in order to work late that night, I wouldn't have gone over to Wyatt's house and caught him red-handed. So *I* thank you for being a workaholic, even if my family didn't see it that way at the time. And it was *eight* children they expected us to have, not ten."

Solange chuckled dryly. "I stand corrected."

Jill laughed, sobering after another moment. "Seriously, though, Solange. Is Crandall Thorne's ranch as beautiful as it was described in the magazine article?"

"Definitely. And I can say that without having seen every room in the house. But before you even reach the property, the scenery alone takes your breath away."

Jill heaved a long, wistful sigh. "You are so lucky, having an opportunity to live in a place like that. Maybe I'll come for a visit during Christmastime."

"I wish you would," Solange murmured. "The holidays won't be the same without you around—and my parents, too. I miss them so much."

"I know," Jill said quietly.

A mournful silence fell between the two women. It had been almost a year since Solange's parents were killed in a fire that swept through their farmhouse late one night while they were sleeping. The arson investigator had ruled the fire an accident, caused by a leak in the gasoline generator they'd been using to heat the old house that chilly January evening. If Solange had not been out of town on a business trip that week, she, too, might have died in the inferno that claimed the lives of George and Eleanor Washington and reduced her childhood home to a blackened, burned-out shell. The fact that she'd escaped the horrible tragedy haunted her every day of her life, along with memories of her adoptive parents. After their funeral, she'd moved in with Jill and her older sister Theresa, who'd always treated Solange like a member of their large, boisterous family. She honestly didn't know how she could have survived those dark, devastating days without the friendship and support of the Somerset sisters.

"They would have wanted you to move on," Jill said gently, rousing Solange from her painful reverie. "They would have approved of your decision to leave Haskell and start a new life someplace else. You know that, don't you?"

"I think so." Solange swallowed past the tight ache in her throat and blinked back tears. Suddenly she had no appetite for the half-eaten taco dinner on the table before her. Not for the first time since arriving in San Antonio a week ago, she wondered if she *had* done the right thing by leaving her hometown and all that was familiar to her. San Antonio was a big, bustling city, nothing at all like the small, quiet town to which she'd grown accustomed, where everyone knew their neighbors by first name and traffic was considered an urban legend.

"How long do you think you'll have to work for Crandall Thorne to save up enough for law school?" Jill asked curiously.

Solange began packing away her unfinished meal. "Two years, ideally. He's paying me sixty thousand dollars, plus providing room and board, so that should really cut down on my expenses and allow me to save plenty of money. I've been doing some research on the law programs at St. Mary's University here in town and UT in Austin, and they're both pretty expensive. But I'd be happy attending either school."

"I read that Crandall Thorne's son teaches at St. Mary's, so maybe you'd be better off going there so he could take you under his wing and show you the ropes."

"That might not be a bad idea." Solange chuckled dryly. "Assuming I ever get a chance to meet him, that is. The way Crandall Thorne described the position to me, come Monday I'll be working so hard this may be the last time you ever speak to me again."

Jill wasn't amused. "Hush your mouth. You already know that's one of my biggest fears, that you'll get so caught up in your new life that you'll forget all about me."

Solange smiled, touched by the trace of vulnerability she heard in her best friend's voice. "You know that could never happen," she said softly. "Not after all we've been through together. Hell, if I could've knocked you over the head and dragged you to San Antonio with me, I would have."

Jill laughed. "That would have been a great way to start your new life—as a fugitive of the law."

"Hmmm. And speaking of the law," Solange murmured, an image of Dane Roarke's sexy face filling her mind, "you'll never guess what happened to me today."

Jill listened with rapt absorption as Solange relayed the morning's events to her, starting from that first electrified moment when she and Dane locked gazes across the conference room, to the nerve-racking experience with the lie-detector test.

"I've never been so *distracted* by a man in my life," she admitted, settling back against the sofa cushions and drawing her knees up to her chin. "Girl, I couldn't think straight. All I wanted to do was jump his bones."

"No wonder," Jill said with a lascivious chuckle. "He sounds downright delicious. Tall, dark and sexy—just the way you like them."

Solange laughed. "Yeah, but I can tell you there's *nobody* like Dane Roarke in Haskell. Before today, I honestly didn't know God made 'em that fine." Just thinking about the man was enough to heat the blood in her veins and quicken her pulse.

"Maybe Dane is just what the doctor ordered," Jill suggested, adding quietly, "You know, to help you get over Lamar."

Solange stiffened at the mention of her ex-boyfriend, a man she'd once thought she would marry. A lieutenant colonel in the army, Lamar Rogers was ten years older than Solange and a lifetime more experienced. He'd lived in Germany, Korea and Italy, and had traveled to numerous exotic locales, while Solange had never ventured outside her small hometown until a week ago. His worldliness was one of the main things she'd found so attractive about him. That, and the way he looked in uniform.

They'd met at the annual county fair, where Solange was selling fresh produce from the farm, as she did every year. Lamar, on leave from the military, had wandered over to her table and struck up a seemingly innocuous conversation about the "inferior" quality of goods being sold by her competitors at the fair. She'd found him clever, charming and good-looking, with a warm, gentle smile, beautiful brown eyes that crinkled at the corners when he laughed, and skin the color of the caramel apples on display at a neighboring booth. By the time her mother returned from judging the apple pie contest—another annual tradition—Solange had given Lamar her phone number and agreed to a date that very same evening.

It became the first of many.

After he returned to Germany, they'd kept in touch via e-mail *and* postal mail, because, as Lamar often told her, seeing her handwriting and being able to hold her letters in his hand assured him that she was real and not a figment of his imagination. Solange had never been with a man who wasn't afraid to express his feelings so openly and earnestly. She'd soaked it all up like a sponge immersed in a bucket of water. When Lamar returned home in six months, they'd picked up right where they'd left off, rediscovering the best restaurants in town, visiting the local Civil War museum like a pair of tourists, picnicking by their favorite lake. For almost three years they'd been inseparable.

Until Lamar grew bored with her.

Unlike Jill's ex-boyfriend Wyatt, Lamar hadn't cheated on Solange. He'd simply lost interest in her. And the pain of his desertion, the confusion and rejection she'd felt even before he ended their relationship, had taken a long time to get over.

"I saw him at the bank today," Jill said softly, breaking into Solange's painful reverie. "He asked me how you were doing, wanted to know if you'd found a job yet. I think he was hoping I'd tell him no, that you regretted your decision to leave home and were thinking about returning."

Solange traced a pattern on the worn sofa. "Why would he hope to hear something like that?" she murmured.

"You know very well why. Because he misses you."

Solange gave a derisive snort. "Girl, you always *were* a hopeless romantic. Lamar Rogers doesn't miss me. If he did, he sure had a funny way of showing it. I can count on one hand how many times I've seen or heard from him since my parents' funeral."

"That's because you didn't want to see or hear from him," Jill gently reminded her. "After he told you he needed space, *you* told him to take all the space he needed—permanently. Or have you forgotten that?"

"Of course not," Solange grumbled morosely. She'd had some other choice words for Lamar as well, but they didn't need to rehash that. As far as she was concerned, her three-year relationship—and subsequent breakup—with Lamar Rogers was ancient history.

Jill had never paid much attention in history class. "He was half-afraid to attend the funeral," she continued, unwilling to drop the subject. "He was worried you'd have him tossed out of the church."

"Typical, selfish Lamar," Solange murmured with a sad shake of her head. "Always making everything about him. I was too busy saying goodbye to my parents to be thinking about the final argument he and I had. As I told you then, I was glad he showed up to pay his last respects. You know how fond of him my parents were."

"Mine, too. They're always saying what a fine, respectable young man he is, serving his country the way his father, grandfather and great-grandfather did before him. If I didn't know any better, I would think they were trying to marry *me* off to Lamar!"

Solange managed a tremulous smile. "You know I would give you my blessing."

Jill grunted. "Maybe you would, but I have no interest in marrying Lamar or anyone else you've ever dated."

"Why not?"

"Are you kidding? Apart from the fact that I've never enjoyed leftovers, there's that other matter to consider."

"What *other* matter?"

Jill heaved a dramatic sigh. "You've ruined Lamar for all other women, Solange. My mama has been saying so for months now, but I didn't believe her until I saw the look on his face today. Poor Lamar."

Solange nearly leapt from the sofa. "Poor *Lamar?*" she cried, full of righteous indignation. "*He's* the one who suddenly started canceling dates on me with no explanation and stopped returning my phone calls. *He's* the one who assured me nothing was wrong every time I asked him about our relationship. *He's* the one who waited until we were at a New Year's Eve party—and the clock was about to strike twelve—to pull me aside and tell me he needed space. And you're calling *him* poor Lamar?"

"Solange—"

"Do I need to remind you how utterly humiliated I was, standing in that roomful of couples who were kissing, throwing confetti and celebrating the new year after I'd just been dumped by my boyfriend?"

"Of course I remember how awful that was for you! *I'm* the one who left the party I was attending to go pick you up because you refused to let Lamar drive you home. *Humph.* A lesser friend would've made you call a cab."

"I know," Solange snarled. "Which is why I can't understand why you'd even *think* about referring to him as a victim."

"I'm not saying he's a victim. I know how much he hurt you, and I'm not excusing that. But when I saw him at the bank today, I realized he still loves you, Solange. He never stopped."

Emotion clogged Solange's throat, temporarily robbing her of speech.

Taking advantage of the moment, Jill quickly forged ahead. "You should have seen the look in his eyes when I told him you'd landed a good job and probably wouldn't be returning home. He looked crushed, Solange, like a dying man who's just been informed that the kidney he's been waiting for won't be a good match after all. That man still loves you, and I know he regrets messing up the good thing you two had."

"Did he tell you that?" Solange asked, appalled by the glimmer of hope that bloomed in her chest.

Jill faltered for a moment. "Well…no. But he didn't have to. It was written all over his face!"

Solange's heart sank a little. "Whatever you say. Anyway, it doesn't matter. I'm not moving back to Haskell, and I'm not going to waste another minute of my life wondering what went wrong between me and Lamar Rogers. I have to move on."

"You're right," Jill agreed with a long, deep sigh. "And I guess having an affair with a sexy private eye is as good a place to start as any."

Solange chuckled ruefully. "Hate to be the bearer of bad news, but I'm not having an affair with Dane Roarke."

"Why not?" Jill demanded. "Is he married?"

"I didn't see a ring on his finger, but we both know that doesn't mean anything nowadays." Inexplicably, the thought of Dane Roarke going home every night to another woman left a bad taste in Solange's mouth. Or maybe that was the beginning of heartburn, she told herself. After all, she had no reason to care whether or not Dane was married. He was a complete stranger; he meant nothing to her.

"I didn't come to San Antonio to find a new boyfriend," she said resolutely, as much for her own benefit as Jill's. "I came here to find a good job that would enable me to save money for law school."

"I know. You've always accomplished whatever you set your mind to. This time won't be any different." Jill paused. "Do you think you'll ever see him again? Dane Roarke, I mean?"

"Not unless I find myself needing the services of a P.I.," Solange said wryly.

"Well, if you ever decide to try and find your birth parents, maybe you can hire him to help you." Jill yawned. "Well, I'd better say good-night. You've had a long day, and I'm beat from pulling a double shift at the hospital. Call me once you're settled in at Crandall Thorne's ranch."

"I will," Solange promised. "Give Theresa my best."

Long after Solange got off the phone with Jill, her best friend's suggestion lingered in her mind.

In the twenty years she'd known Jill Somerset, Solange had only raised the topic of finding her birth parents once, and that was after she'd had a big argument with her mother. Solange had been a headstrong, temperamental fifteen-year-old in the throes of her first major crush on a senior at the local high school. When Eleanor Washington forbade her from attending the boy's senior prom because she was too young, Solange had stormed off down the road to the neighboring farmhouse of her best friend's family. While ranting and raving to Jill about her unreasonably strict mother, she'd blurted out angrily, "I wish I could find my *real* parents. I bet they're nowhere near as mean as George and Eleanor."

Immediately afterward she'd felt guilty. Her adoptive parents were good, honest, hardworking people who had shown her nothing but love and kindness throughout her life. While they could be rather strict at times, she knew it was only because they wanted the best for her and wanted to protect her from the same terrible fate that had befallen their teenage son, who'd died in a drunk-driving accident caused by his best friend.

She felt like a spoiled brat, an ingrate, for badmouthing her parents to Jill, so she'd never done it again. But she could never take back the harsh words she'd spoken that afternoon, nor could she stop the questions that began whispering through her mind like wisps of smoke from a flame.

At the age of fifteen, twelve years after being adopted by the Washingtons, Solange began to wonder about her biological parents. She wondered who they were, where they lived and what they looked like. And for the first time in her life, she allowed herself to ponder what would happen if she tried to find them. Thankfully, her curiosity had never morphed into an all-consuming obsession. She'd heard countless horror stories of adult adoptees who spent years and thousands of dollars searching for their biological parents, only to be disappointed in the end when their parents turned out to be horrible people. Solange had never felt a burning need or desire to put herself through the emotional roller coaster of trying to locate two individuals who obviously hadn't wanted her. But every now and then, when she least expected it, the curiosity would return, and the same questions would invade her thoughts.

In the aftermath of losing her adoptive parents, the questions had returned with increasing frequency.

Lying in bed that night, Solange stared up at the darkened ceiling, Jill's words echoing through her mind. *Was* it a sign that she'd crossed paths with Dane Roarke, who happened to be a private investigator? Was he meant to help her track down her biological parents?

Solange frowned in the darkness. George and Eleanor Washington had never been entirely comfortable discussing her adoption with her. They'd always told her that the most important thing was that they loved her as if she were their own flesh and blood, and they'd raised her accordingly.

"It's not where you came from, but where you're going," Eleanor had been fond of saying, particularly whenever Solange broached the subject of her adoption.

Unfortunately, their reluctance to discuss the details of her past had left her with more questions than answers about her future. And their untimely deaths had left her with no one in the world other than some distant relatives scattered around the country, whom she hardly knew, anyway. At no time had she felt the full magnitude of this realization more than in the days following the funeral—and now.

She was completely alone.

Maybe it was finally time to rectify that, Solange thought.

Maybe after she'd been working for Crandall Thorne for a while and had earned enough money, she could hire Dane Roarke to help her find her parents.

She felt a twinge of excitement at the thought, and told herself it had more to do with the prospect of eventually locating her birth parents than with seeing the sexy private investigator again.

Closing her eyes, Solange rolled onto her side and let exhaustion tug her to sleep within minutes.

Chapter 6

On his way to the office late Saturday morning, Dane made a slight detour that led him to the Alamo City Inn. He drove around the parking lot until he found Solange Washington's blue Plymouth. Secretly relieved to discover that she hadn't checked out of her room yet, he parked beside the ancient clunker, grabbed a sealed envelope from the passenger seat and climbed out of his truck.

According to the contact information she'd provided, Solange had been a guest of the extended-stay lodge since arriving in San Antonio a week ago.

Dane made his way across the parking lot toward the old, two-story stucco building surrounded by gently swaying palm trees that almost made one forget the hotel's location—smack-dab in the middle of an industrial park. As he strode past an overflowing metal trash bin and a deserted swimming pool littered with brown winter leaves and other suspect debris, he couldn't help but wonder why Solange Washington had chosen to dwell in such a dump, even temporarily. Surely she could've afforded better with the large sum of money she'd received from her parents' life insurance policies. Unless, of course, she'd already run through her inheritance.

Shoving aside the cynical thought—since it was none of his damn business what the woman did with her money—Dane climbed a flight of stairs and strode down the open walkway until he reached room 206. He rapped his knuckles lightly on the door, then waited.

After several moments, the door swung open. "I'm ready now. You can come—" Solange broke off abruptly at the sight of Dane, those dark, thick-lashed eyes that tilted exotically at the corners widening in surprise.

"I'm sorry. I thought you were the maid," she said, her cheeks flushed as if she'd been exercising or lifting heavy items—he guessed the latter. "What are you doing here?"

Dane held up the yellow envelope he'd brought. "I forgot to give these to you on Thursday. Copies of your signed paperwork."

Solange frowned slightly. "You didn't have to come all the way out here," she said, reaching for the envelope.

Dane handed it over slowly, letting his eyes roam across her body from head to toe. With her chestnut-brown hair scooped into a ponytail and wearing a plain white T-shirt and blue jeans that molded long, shapely legs, she was as beautiful as he remembered. And he ought to know. He hadn't stopped thinking about her since meeting her two days ago. Personally delivering the documents to her had given him a legitimate, if somewhat lame, excuse to see her again.

"You could have saved yourself a trip and mailed this to me," Solange gently chided.

"It's no trouble," Dane drawled, propping a negligent shoulder in the doorway. "At Roarke Investigations, we pride ourselves on going the extra mile for our customers—figuratively and literally."

"I see." Those lush, bow-shaped lips twitched with barely suppressed humor, as if she could see right through the bogus explanation. "Well…thank you, I suppose." She sent a brief glance over her shoulder. "I'd invite you inside for a cup of coffee, but I was just about to leave. I have to check out of the room by noon."

"That's right. You're moving into Thorne's ranch today, aren't you?"

She nodded, her mouth curving in a playful smile he could easily become addicted to. "I'm assuming that I passed the background check, otherwise I'd still be looking for employment."

Dane smiled a little. "You passed."

Solange glanced at her watch. "Well, I'd better—"

Dane straightened from the doorway. "I'll help you carry your stuff to the car. Going the extra mile," he reminded her when she opened her mouth to decline the offer.

"All right. If you insist." Smiling, she stepped back and opened the door wider.

As Dane shouldered past her into the room, her fresh scent filled his nostrils—soap and a subtle trace of perfume, something exotic and undeniably feminine, like her. Resisting the compulsion to draw greedy gulps of it into his lungs, he glanced around. On the floor near the door were two large suitcases and four small cardboard boxes. Those items were the only indication that someone was checking out, not checking into the modestly furnished room. The place was immaculate, from the spotless kitchen countertops to the carefully made bed. He wondered half-incredulously what the maid could possibly do to make the room any cleaner, and didn't realize he'd spoken aloud until Solange laughed.

"My mother was a compulsive neat freak," she said ruefully. "I learned from an early age to pick up after myself."

Dane chuckled. "Looks like you did a little more than pick up after yourself. You *do* know that the maids are paid to clean the rooms after each guest leaves?"

"Of course." Solange gave a dismissive shrug. "No harm in making their jobs a bit easier, though. And they're not paid *nearly* enough. Take my word for it." Sidestepping him, she walked over to one of the suitcases and knelt down to unzip it and place the envelope he'd given her inside.

He was transfixed by a sliver of smooth golden-brown skin revealed above the waistband of her low-rise jeans. Almost at once, he saw himself standing behind her and slowly, deliberately, raising her T-shirt over her flat belly and past her rib cage

until her high, round breasts—braless in this particular fantasy—
sprang free, filling his eager hands. He imagined kneading and
caressing them, then brushing the pad of his thumbs across her
nipples until they tightened in response and a breathless moan
of pleasure escaped from deep in her throat. He imagined
pressing his lips to the fragrant nape of her neck, grinding his
body against the lush, curvy roundness of her bottom and—

"All set," Solange announced, interrupting his lustful
daydream as she straightened from her kneeling position.

Dane quickly schooled his features into an impassive expression that belied the throbbing ache in his groin. "Do you have
everything?" he asked huskily.

She nodded, gesturing to indicate the suitcases and cardboard
boxes. "This is it. All my worldly possessions." Her voice held
a trace of sadness that tugged on his heartstrings, and he remembered that she'd lost most, if not all, of her belongings in the
house fire that had killed her parents nearly a year ago. She must
have had to start all over again when she moved in with her childhood friend.

Not wanting to arouse her suspicions by letting on how deep
he'd dug into her background, Dane said, "Well, from what I
understand, you'll be well provided for at Thorne's ranch. So not
having a lot of stuff actually works to your advantage."

She flashed him a grateful smile. "You're right."

He answered with a slow, lazy grin. "I usually am."

She laughed, that soft, smoky sound that sucker-punched him
in the gut. "I'll try to remember that, Mr. Roarke."

"Dane."

"Hmmm?"

"Call me Dane," he told her. "Mr. Roarke is my father, who
doesn't tolerate being called anything else."

Solange gazed at him for a moment, then nodded. "All
right…Dane."

"Much better." He picked up both suitcases as if they were
weightless, showing off just a little for her benefit. "Shall we go?"

In no time at all, he and Solange had carried everything down to the parking lot and began loading up her car. Although it was old and rust-stained, the interior of the Plymouth was as tidy as the hotel room she had just vacated. No loose change, discarded paper cups or fast food wrappers on the floor to speak of. Dane didn't know whether to be impressed or appalled.

Before he could decide, he was distracted by the warmth of her body as she hovered behind him, watching as he arranged one of the cardboard boxes on the backseat.

"Does it fit?" she asked anxiously. "Can you get it in there?"

It was too much to expect his mind not to head straight for the gutter, not with her seductive heat seeping into his bones. He cleared his throat. "It should be fine," he managed thickly.

"Are you sure?" She pressed closer, the soft, enticing fullness of her breasts grazing his back. Dane closed his eyes as a fresh wave of arousal swept through him, making him grow instantly hard.

He must have grunted or made some other inarticulate sound. "Let me help you," she offered.

He was beyond help. "It'll fit, don't worry." His voice was a low, rough growl he hardly recognized as his own.

Misreading the reason for his tone, Solange backed away. He didn't know whether to be relieved or disappointed. "Sorry," she said sheepishly. "Didn't mean to imply you couldn't handle it on your own. It's just that I packed the car myself before leaving Haskell, so I have a pretty good idea how and where everything should go."

Dane had a few ideas of his own that had nothing whatsoever to do with maneuvering boxes around the backseat of her car. In fact, right now he could think of far better uses for the backseat in question.

"Why don't you go check out while I take care of this?" he suggested. "It's almost twelve."

"Okay. I'll be right back."

Her absence bought him time to load everything into the Plymouth and, more to the point, get his raging libido under control. When she returned from the lobby a few minutes later, he stood holding the car door open for her.

Solange beamed a smile at him that made him feel absurdly heroic. "Thanks so much for all your help, Dane," she said warmly.

"No problem."

As she slid behind the wheel of the car, he closed the door and took a step backward, already thinking ahead to the cold shower that awaited him when he got home later—if he could hold out that long. Never before had another woman wreaked such havoc on his senses, making him feel as horny and restless as an adolescent boy. And yet, Dane wanted nothing more than to prolong his time with her. He knew once she drove out of that parking lot, there was a very good chance he would never see her again. With her tucked away in Crandall Thorne's remote, secluded ranch, buried deep in the Hill Country, Dane wouldn't be able to just drop by unannounced, claiming he was "in the neighborhood." And even if he tried, Thorne would probably have him tossed out on his ear, the irascible old bastard.

Solange rolled down the window to look at him. Wisps of dark hair had escaped from her ponytail to frame her exquisite face. "Well, I guess I'd better hit the road," she said, and he wondered if he'd only imagined the trace of reluctance in her voice. Was it possible she shared his desire to prolong their time together? "Mr. Thorne's expecting me by two."

Dane inclined his head. "Drive carefully," he murmured.

"I will. Thanks again for everything."

"My pleasure."

What occurred next could only be interpreted as divine intervention.

When Solange turned the key in the ignition, nothing happened. She frowned, trying to crank the engine a second time.

Nothing. Not even a single click. Just dead silence.

Solange groaned loudly, leaning her head back on the headrest and closing her eyes. "I was afraid this was going to happen sooner or later," she grumbled. "Why couldn't it have been *later?*"

"Pop the hood so I can take a look," Dane instructed.

Even before he checked the transmission fluid, timing belt, battery connections and starter, Dane knew what the problem was. He'd diagnosed it often enough as a part-time mechanic in his father's auto repair shop back in Houston. And he couldn't help feeling a perverse surge of pleasure, as if he'd been given a rare, unexpected gift at someone else's expense.

Solange climbed out of the car and slowly skirted the fender to stand beside him. "What's the verdict?" she asked warily.

Dane straightened from leaning over the engine and gave her a slight, grim smile. "Do you want the good news or bad news first?"

"Start with the bad, I guess."

She looked so forlorn that he felt guilty for thinking only of himself a moment ago—well, almost. "The bad news is that you need a new engine. The one you have has finally given up the ghost."

She nodded, closing her eyes as she wearily pinched the bridge of her nose between her thumb and forefinger. "Don't keep me in suspense. What's the good news?"

If she'd been looking at him, she would have seen the wicked gleam of satisfaction in his eyes as he answered, "The good news is that after your car has been towed, I'll drive you to Thorne's ranch myself."

Chapter 7

"Are you absolutely sure I'm not keeping you from important business at the office?" Solange asked as she and Dane headed out of town in his black Dodge Durango, which had accommodated all of her belongings with room to spare. By the time the tow truck had arrived, nearly two hours had passed.

Dane slanted her an amused sidelong glance. "For the last time," he drawled, "you're not keeping me from important business. It's Saturday. The only thing I was going to do at the office was catch up on some paperwork. Quite frankly, taking a scenic drive through the country sounds far more appealing."

"If you're sure…."

A half smile quirked the corners of his mouth. "There you go again."

"Sorry," Solange said with a rueful grin. "Another bad habit I picked up from my mother—being overly considerate of other people's time."

Dane shook his head slowly. "One thing you'll learn about me," he said silkily, "is that I rarely, if ever, do anything I don't want to. Always remember that."

His words, like a seductive promise, sent a shiver through her.

"Now stop worrying," he said, "and just relax and enjoy the ride. It's a beautiful day, isn't it?"

Solange had to agree. The sun shone brightly against a cloudless, vivid blue sky. There was only a slight nip in the air to remind them it was December, not September. On the stereo, Nat King Cole crooned the timeless lyrics to "The Christmas Song," evoking her favorite childhood memories of decorating the giant spruce tree with her mother and baking homemade apple cobblers her father would exclaim over. To her surprise, remembering her parents didn't make her sad, as it had every other day for the past eleven months. And despite everything that had happened with her car that morning, Solange felt a sense of peace wash over her.

She turned her head to study Dane Roarke beneath her lashes. She was struck once again by how handsome he was, how powerfully male. He wore a black T-shirt, dark jeans that clung to the strong, corded muscles of his thighs, and a pair of black Timberland boots that looked enormous. She'd been utterly shocked to open her door that morning and find him standing there, especially since she'd spent the past two days trying—unsuccessfully—not to think about him. She had no intention of becoming involved with him. She was on a mission to get her life back on track, to save enough money to realize her dream of attending law school. Romance did not factor into her plans, and a man like Dane Roarke would prove to be way too much of a distraction. Beneath his dark good looks, sinfully sexy smile and raw animal magnetism beat the heart of a dangerous man, the kind Eleanor Washington had always warned her about. Dane would never have to go out of his way to hurt any woman. He'd break her heart in the time-honored way preferred by most gorgeous, charming men: by simply being unattainable.

Solange had no wish to become one of his hapless victims. God knows she'd had more than enough of unavailable men. Yet she hadn't put up too much of a fight when Dane had insisted on driving her to the ranch. Against her better judgment, she'd wanted to spend more time with him, to explore the heat and attraction that had sizzled between them from the moment they met. She blamed it on hormones. It had been a while since she'd had sex.

"How do you know so much about cars?" she blurted, shoving aside the unwelcome reminder of her prolonged sexual drought. "The mechanic who arrived with the tow truck agreed with your assessment about the engine."

Dane sent her a crooked smile. "You sound surprised."

"I guess I am, a little," Solange admitted. "Not too many men nowadays know about cars and things like that. At the first sign of trouble, they run to the nearest dealership for help." She made a face. "Most guys I know haven't the faintest idea how to change the oil, let alone how to diagnose a bad engine."

Dane chuckled softly. "Maybe you don't know the right men, Solange," he said, sliding her a heavy-lidded look that made her pulse quicken. It was the first time he'd spoken her name, and hopefully it wouldn't be the last. The way he said it in that deep, intoxicating voice of his made it sound like the sexiest, most exotic name in the world.

He was right. She *didn't* know the right men. She'd definitely never encountered one like him before.

"Is that important to you?" Dane asked idly. "Being with a man who knows about cars?"

"I don't know." Solange frowned, giving the matter careful consideration. "I'm not saying he has to know the latest advances in fuel injection systems, but if we're out on a date and we get a flat, he should at least be able to change the tire without requiring my assistance—especially if I'm wearing an expensive dress and three-inch heels."

Dane threw back his head and roared with laughter. The deep, rumbling sound was so pleasant, so downright infectious, that Solange found herself joining him. And it felt good, really good. She hadn't had much to laugh about since her parents died. It didn't occur to her to question why it felt so natural to rediscover her sense of humor with Dane Roarke, a virtual stranger.

When their laughter finally subsided, Dane looked over at her and shook his head, dark eyes glittering with mirth. "Not exactly a feminist, are you, Miss Washington?"

She grinned unabashedly. "Hey, I'm as independent as the

next gal, but I make no apologies for having certain basic require-
ments of the men I'm dating." She lifted one shoulder in a
careless shrug. "What can I say? I grew up on a farm where, like
it or not, the division of labor was largely determined by gender.
That means on any given day, my father might have been out in
the field tending the crops while my mama and I fed the horses,
washed laundry and prepared dinner."

As she spoke, Dane's dark, intent gaze roamed across her face.
Afraid that she'd turned him off with all her farm talk, she started
to say something clever, something hip, when he murmured, "So
you're just a simple country girl at heart." There was no mistaking the appreciation in his voice, the quiet sense of wonder, as if
he thought she was a breath of fresh air.

Solange warmed with pleasure at the unspoken compliment. "I
guess you could say I am." She shot him a look of mock severity,
adding in an exaggerated country drawl, "But that don't mean I'm
a wide-eyed innocent, sport for you fancy city folk. Don't ever try
to pull a fast one on me jes 'cause you think I'm gullible enough
to fall for it. You'll rue the day you was born, y'hear?"

Dane grinned. "I'll consider myself forewarned."

Solange smiled, enjoying the teasing banter between them—
perhaps a bit *too* much.

Soon they were heading down an endless stretch of highway
flanked by lush, green pastures dotted with grazing cattle and
horses. These were familiar sights to Solange, not like the
bustling freeways and urban sprawl they'd left behind in the city.
She knew she'd feel right at home at Crandall Thorne's country
estate. She hoped so, anyway.

"My father owns an auto repair shop," Dane said suddenly,
out of the clear blue. "I worked there during the summers when
I was in high school and college. That's how I know so much
about cars, to answer your previous question." His mouth
twitched. "So I have an unfair advantage over all those poor men
you were berating earlier."

Solange laughed. "You don't give yourself enough credit.
Some of those very same men I was talking about had fathers,

brothers and uncles who were mechanics, and they *still* knew absolutely nothing about cars."

He chuckled low in his throat and shifted in his seat, heightening her awareness of him. She drew in a breath of his clean-scented male warmth and struggled to keep her eyes off the way his jeans molded the hard, sculpted muscles of his thighs.

"Where are you from?" she asked, as much to distract herself as to learn more about him.

"Houston. Born and raised."

She nodded. "What brought you to San Antonio?"

"I used to visit all the time when I was growing up."

"You have family here?"

He nodded. "An aunt and three cousins. My cousins—Kenneth, Noah and Daniela—are actually the owners of Roarke Investigations. I've only been there a year."

"Where did you work before?" When he sent her a bemused sidelong glance, she said quickly, "I'm sorry. Was that too personal?"

He shook his head, but a solitary muscle tightened in his jaw. "I worked out of the FBI field office in Philadelphia."

Solange waited, brows arched expectantly. When he offered no more, she tipped her head thoughtfully to one side and studied him. "You don't like to talk much about yourself, do you? That's very interesting coming from a man who makes a living investigating the lives of others."

"I don't mind talking about myself," Dane countered evenly. "But some things are more personal than others."

Solange got the message loud and clear. Whatever had caused him to leave the FBI was not open for discussion—not with her, anyway. She told herself she was crazy for feeling a sharp pang of disappointment.

"Are you going to buy a new car?" Dane asked, deliberately changing the subject.

Solange sighed heavily. "I don't know. The Plymouth is way too old to pour any more money into."

"I wouldn't recommend it," he agreed. "Besides, you might

not need your own vehicle. Unless I'm mistaken, one of the perks of being Crandall Thorne's personal assistant is unlimited use of a company car."

Solange brightened. "I hadn't even thought of that. It would certainly make things a lot easier for me."

Dane's mouth twisted sardonically. "Considering what that man is going to put you through, providing transportation is the *least* he can do."

Solange huffed out an indignant breath. "That's it, mister. No more rude comments about my new boss, or my first order of business will be to find a new private detective agency for him to work with."

Dane chuckled. "Touché."

Thirty minutes later, Dane steered the truck through the heavy iron gates of Crandall Thorne's property. As the sturdy rig climbed uphill, the grind of wheels upon the gravel path sent clouds of dust through the open windows, but Solange was too riveted by the sight of the sprawling country estate to notice or care. Situated atop a five-hundred-foot bluff that boasted panoramic views of the surrounding valley, the Spanish-style ranch house was as impressive as she remembered, and now that she knew it would be her home for at least the next year, she felt even more awed.

As Dane nosed the truck into one of the three detached garages, a tall, brown-skinned woman in a sunny yellow dress emerged from the house and made her way over. Solange immediately recognized her as Rita Owens, her friendly hostess from her previous visit to the ranch.

Rita beamed a warm, welcoming smile as Solange and Dane spilled from the truck. "Why, ain't this a wonderful surprise?" she exclaimed, her eyes landing on Dane first. "I haven't seen you around here in ages. What have you been doing with yourself, Dane Roarke?"

He winked at her, grinning mischievously. "Nothing you'd approve of, Ms. Rita."

She laughed, reaching up to give his lean cheek an affectionate pat. "I don't doubt it for one second."

Her smile widened with pleasure as Solange appeared beside
him. "Why, hello, Miss Washington," she said, stepping forward
to clasp both of Solange's hands in the warmth of her own. "It's
so good to see you again. I can't tell you how pleased I was when
Crandall told me he'd offered you the job. I had a very good
feeling about you."

Solange gave her a grateful smile. "Thank you, Ms. Rita. I
hope I won't disappoint you."

Rita waved a dismissive hand. "Nonsense, child. You have
nothing to worry about. Now then, let's get you settled into your
room. Crandall had to go into town, but he promised to return
before nightfall. In the meantime, the two of you can join me for
dinner. Don't look so surprised. We always eat dinner earlier on
the weekends. Gloria is putting the finishing touches on her
award-winning lasagna."

"Sounds good," Dane said, "but I should probably get back—"

"You'll do no such thing," Rita said with an adamant shake
of her head. "It's Saturday—whatever you need to do at the
office can wait. From what I hear, you spend too much time there,
anyway. I won't take no for an answer," she doggedly continued
when Dane opened his mouth to protest the accusation. "You're
joining us for dinner, young man, and that's all there is to it.
Besides, you brought Miss Washington all the way out here. The
least I can do is feed you."

Chuckling, Dane held up his hands in surrender. "Yes, ma'am.
I'm not going to argue with you."

"Why, I think that's the smartest thing any man has ever said
to me," Rita quipped with a teasing wink at Solange. "By the way,
what happened to your car, baby?"

Solange heaved a deep, mournful sigh. "The engine died on me."

Rita nodded sympathetically. "Figured as much. That old
clunker reminded me of a cantankerous fella I once dated.
Humph. *He* wasn't built to last either."

"Men," Solange pronounced in mock disgust.

"Hey!" Dane protested, feigning insult as he glowered at each woman in turn. When they merely laughed, he shook his head and turned toward the Durango to open the trunk, grumbling over his shoulder, "Why don't you two head on inside while us 'men folk' unload the truck?"

"Thank you, Dane," Solange said sweetly, to which he muttered something unintelligible that made Rita cackle with amusement.

Inside the spacious foyer of the house, a giant cornucopia overflowing with silk flowers, pinecones and a lovely assortment of fruit adorned the glossy mahogany sideboard. Rita made a right turn and guided Solange past a curving staircase that swept upward to the second floor. They passed a large great room, a cheerful sunroom and continued down a wide expanse of corridor that eventually led to the guest wing of the house.

The moment Solange crossed the threshold of the bedroom suite, an audible gasp escaped her lips. The room was exquisitely furnished with a Chippendale armoire, dresser and desk carved in cherry. The antique four-poster bed sat high off the floor and was covered with a thick satin duvet that promised a heavenly night's sleep. The walls were a soft, muted shade of honey that beautifully complemented the ceramic-tile floors. In a separate seating area, a suede chair, sofa and chaise longue in cream and rust were arranged around a wood-burning fireplace that added a cozy, inviting warmth to the room. Little touches of holiday cheer were interspersed throughout—a bowl of Georgian silver filled with pinecones and flanked by white candles, and poinsettias in a pair of gilt-trimmed pots perched at opposite ends of the window seat.

The pièce de résistance was a private terrace that boasted a stunning view of the lush green valley below. With a soft cry, Solange hurried toward the tall French doors and flung them open, unable to resist the lure of that view.

Behind her, Rita Owens took in her reaction with a quiet, knowing smile. "Well? Think we can convince you to hang around for a while?"

Solange laughed, the buoyant sound carrying on the cool

breeze that caressed her upturned face. "I definitely think that's a safe assumption, Ms. Rita."

Rita chuckled warmly. "Glad to hear it."

Solange breathed deeply, filling her lungs with the scent of pine and earth from the distant mountains. *I can get very used to this,* she thought. Thankfully, she had no other choice.

Smiling, she turned and stepped back into the room as Dane entered and carried her two suitcases over to the bed. As he set them down on the floor and straightened, he swept an appraising glance around and grinned. "I recognize Daniela's handiwork."

Rita nodded, beaming with pleasure. "I was just about to tell Solange that your cousin graciously volunteered to redecorate the room in anticipation of her arrival. This used to be where Caleb Thorne stayed whenever he visited his father," she explained to Solange. "Now that Caleb is married, he and his wife, Daniela, sleep in one of the second-floor bedrooms whenever they come for a visit. You'll meet them both soon enough."

Solange nodded, grinning easily. "I'm looking forward to that. If Daniela's anywhere near as wonderful as her decorating skills, I'm going to love her."

Dane turned from studying a gilt-framed oil-on-canvas painting that captured a stunning West African sunset, to gaze at Solange. "I think the feeling will be mutual," he said softly.

Solange gave him the shy smile of a teenager who'd just received an unexpected compliment from her secret crush. "Thanks, Dane."

He inclined his head, then turned and started toward the door. Solange watched him leave, admiring once again the way he walked—shoulders and back straight, long legs moving in those relaxed, powerful strides.

Unbeknownst to her, Rita had followed the entire exchange with a speculative gleam in her dark eyes, which slid away when Solange finally looked at her. A hint of a smile curved the woman's mouth. "I'm going to check on dinner," she announced. "There's a private bathroom straight through that door, in case you want to freshen up. Make yourself at home."

"Thank you, Ms. Rita."

After her hostess left, Solange took another slow turn around the room, lightly running her fingertips across the glossy surface of a side table, bending to sniff an assortment of fresh-cut flowers arranged in a crystal vase. The contrast between this elegant suite and the drab accommodations she'd called home for the past week was as dramatic as the difference between night and day. She also realized that this room, with its priceless antiques and original oil paintings, was nothing like the small, simply furnished bedroom she had grown up in. George and Eleanor Washington had worked hard to keep a roof over her head and food on the table, but their modest income hadn't allowed for much else. Their livelihood had depended on the land yielding a large crop every season, and when that didn't happen, money could be very tight. Solange had learned from an early age how to be frugal and stretch a dollar—valuable lessons that enabled her to save money from part-time jobs and put herself through community college before earning a scholarship to attend the local university. Even then, she'd commuted from home to save on the cost of campus housing and to continue helping out around the farm.

As a little girl, she'd never dreamed about sleeping in a frilly canopy bed or having a collection of beautiful dolls to play with. And she'd certainly never imagined that she would someday live in a place like this.

She paused, thinking about her parents and wondering what they would say if they could see her now. They'd always wanted her to have the best of everything, even if they couldn't give it to her themselves.

"But you gave me the most important thing of all," Solange whispered into the stillness of the room. "Your unconditional love."

Blinking back tears, she took a moment to send up a prayer of thanksgiving to God, then left to help Dane retrieve the rest of her belongings.

Chapter 8

Crandall Thorne reclined in the luxurious backseat of his Rolls Royce limousine with a glass of brandy in one hand, a copy of this week's *San Antonio Business Journal* in the other. Nothing about his relaxed demeanor and bland expression betrayed the way his nerves tightened and his pulse quickened as the back door opened and one long, curvaceous leg appeared, followed by another, as Tessa Philbin lowered herself into the limo.

Even after all these years and after all they'd been through, Crandall marveled that she could still have such an effect on him. As a man whose reputation as a shrewd, formidable businessman was as much a part of his legacy as his renowned charm and virility, it galled him to realize that one woman could have such a stranglehold on him. When it came to his feelings for Tessa Philbin, he was as powerless as a mom-and-pop store facing a hostile takeover by a major conglomerate.

That morning, Tessa was cool and effortlessly elegant in a silk wrap that subtly accentuated her trim figure and the shapeliness of her crossed legs. She wore one of those classic millinery-inspired hats that slanted over her eyes, but he didn't need to see her entire face to remember how beautiful she was, to note how smooth and supple her golden-brown skin remained, even at the age of sixty-six. Wearing a pair of Versace pumps and a diamond bracelet and earrings that had probably cost more than the salary of his highest-paid employee—which was substantial—she was the epitome of a pampered society wife.

Irrationally, Crandall felt a stir of resentment. There was a time he'd wanted to give this woman the world on a silver platter. It hurt like hell that someone else had beaten him to it. Especially someone as undeserving as Hoyt Philbin, the former mayor of San Antonio.

As the limo glided away from the curb, Crandall set aside his drink and the newspaper he'd been trying unsuccessfully to read since leaving the ranch an hour ago. "Hello, Tessa," he murmured, giving her a smile that didn't quite reach his eyes. "You're looking well."

She inclined her head coolly. "Same to you. And how's your health?"

"Never been better," he drawled. "Nothing like a case of acute renal failure to challenge a man's will to live."

Her ruby lips curved in the barest hint of a smile. "Yes, well, you have plenty to live for. I understand congratulations are in order. Caleb and his wife are expecting their first child?"

"That's right. Daniela's due at the end of February."

"Congratulations. You must be so thrilled. This will be your first grandchild."

"Perhaps." At the nonplussed look Tessa gave him, he settled more comfortably against the butter-soft leather seat, regarded her across the aisle that separated them and prepared to give a performance that would put Sidney Poitier to shame. "Thank you for agreeing to see me this morning."

She pursed her lips. "You told me it was important. Knowing what a tremendous risk we're taking by sneaking off together like this, I don't think you would have called me unless it was absolutely necessary."

Her cool voice held an undertone that warned him whatever he had to share with her had better be worth the trouble she'd gone to that morning to meet him. After telling her husband she would be attending a charity function and getting her chauffeur to drop her off at the venue, she'd then caught a cab to a shopping mall fifteen minutes away, where Crandall had picked her up. They'd figured that outside a crowded mall bustling with Christmas shoppers, no one would notice the wife of a former mayor climbing into the limousine of an unidentified man.

All the plotting and subterfuge had reminded Crandall of the days of their brief, ill-fated affair.

After years of not seeing or speaking to each other, they'd suddenly found themselves face-to-face at the same social function. It hadn't taken them long to realize the attraction they'd once shared as high school sweethearts had not diminished with time; if anything, it had grown stronger. Desperate to be together, they'd lied to their spouses and arranged clandestine meetings in restaurants, hotels and B and Bs, until the unthinkable happened—Tessa got pregnant.

Crandall would never forget the sheer agony of that day, a day that would alter the course of their lives forever, when Tessa came to him with the news that she was carrying his child—their love child.

Stricken, he'd demanded, "Are you sure it's mine?"

"Yes!" she'd cried, tears streaming down her beautiful face. "Hoyt and I haven't been together in weeks. He's been too busy studying for the bar exam!"

The birth of their daughter, Melanie, eight months later had confirmed that the child did, indeed, belong to Crandall. Even if he could have rationalized the baby's dark skin—when Tessa's husband was white—there was no denying the prominent features of a Thorne.

The agony Crandall had felt then was surpassed only by the anguish he would suffer nineteen years later when the girl showed up on his doorstep, demanding the truth about why she'd been given up for adoption.

Crandall would carry the terrible burden of what happened next to his grave.

Rousing himself from the painful reverie, he found Tessa

watching him warily. "What is it?" she asked in the strained voice of someone bracing herself to receive bad news. Lord knows they'd both had enough practice.

Crandall fixed her with a level gaze. "I think we may have a granddaughter."

Tessa's whole body jerked. Beneath the brim of her hat, her eyes widened with shock. "W-what did you just say?"

"I have reason to believe our daughter may have had a child before she died."

Tessa sputtered, "But she was only a child herself!"

"She was nineteen," Crandall tersely reminded her. "We both know she'd had a hard life, practically growing up on the streets. There's no telling how promiscuous she may have been by the time—"

"Stop!" Tessa cried, raising a trembling hand.

"Tess—"

"You're talking about that child as if she were a common prostitute you'd pass by on the street! She was a child, *our* child, and we abandoned her and left her to be raised by strangers!"

Crandall's temper flared. Leaning forward in the seat, he said scathingly, "I remember what happened. But I also recall, darling Tessa, that it was you and your *husband* who made the decision not to raise the child as your own. And it was *you* who begged me not to tell anyone the truth about us, even though our spouses eventually found out, anyway."

"You wouldn't have fought for Melanie, anyway!" Tessa cried, those dark, magnificent eyes flashing with fury and grief. "All you ever cared about was yourself and protecting your own hide! You knew damn well your *wife* wouldn't have welcomed your bastard child into her home, so you didn't even bother trying to seek custody of her!"

It was true, and Crandall knew it. Snapping his mouth shut, he sank back heavily against the seat cushions and closed his eyes, struggling to bring his blood pressure under control. He'd been warned by his doctors and his private nurse to avoid situations that would overly agitate him. If this situation didn't qualify as "agitating," he didn't know what did. But he'd summoned Tessa there for a purpose, and he wasn't letting her go until he'd fulfilled that purpose.

As he worked to regain his composure, he mentally reviewed his plan. Although it would have made more sense to tell Tessa the whole truth, he knew that was out of the question. If he told her the truth—that he'd learned about Solange twenty-four years ago and had kept the knowledge from Tessa all this time—she would never forgive him. Even if he told her he'd only recently made the discovery, she would still blame him for not coming to her sooner. Making her privy to his so-called suspicions early in the game absolved him of any wrongdoing.

There was another advantage to confiding in Tessa at this point. It would bring them closer together while they waited to learn whether or not they really had a grandchild. Tessa would want to be involved in the investigation every step of the way, which would give Crandall the perfect excuse to see her, a privilege heretofore denied him. The last time he'd been alone with her was following his wife's funeral twenty-four years ago. Tessa, who'd attended the service without her husband, had sought him out at the repast to offer her condolences. Crandall had been inconsolable, racked with grief and guilt for still desiring another woman hours after leaving the cemetery where his wife and the mother of the only child he claimed would be laid to rest.

As he and Tessa had stood on the terrace, where he'd retreated to escape the houseful of mourners, she'd reached up and placed a gentle hand upon his cheek. The gesture was meant to comfort, to let him know she was there for him in his time of sorrow, but he'd wanted so much more. He'd wanted to crush her in his arms and kiss her the way he'd longed to for years, pouring all his grief, loneliness, disillusionment and pent-up rage into the kiss. He'd wanted to drag her upstairs and make love to her in the bed he'd shared with his late wife, and when Tessa closed her eyes and leaned into him, he knew she wouldn't have stopped him. To this day, he was haunted by what would have happened if his fourteen-year-old son Caleb had not suddenly appeared on the terrace, staring at them with dark, wounded eyes.

Crandall had spent long, torturous years trying to atone for the fact that he'd never loved the boy's mother the way she'd loved him. To honor her memory, and to keep peace between himself and Caleb, he'd kept his distance from Tessa, throwing himself into work like never before, using his career to make him forget the one thing he truly wanted, but could never have.

Now that he and Caleb had reached an understanding about the past, and now that his son was happily married and on the verge of becoming a father himself, Crandall decided he'd done enough penance. He was sixty-six years old, alone and battling a failing kidney. Time was no longer on his side. The clock was ticking, and if he wanted to reclaim the only woman he'd ever loved, he had to act fast. But now that he'd devised a plan to lure her away from her no-good husband, Crandall realized he didn't want Tessa back in his life solely because they shared a grand-daughter. He wanted her back because she still loved him and regretted choosing another man over him all those years ago. And he was willing to do whatever it took to help bring her to that re-alization, even if it meant lying, cheating and stealing.

If he'd had even the slightest inkling that she really loved Hoyt Philbin, he would have given up on winning her back a long time ago. But he knew the truth, that she was trapped in a loveless sham of a marriage bound by the dictates of their elite social circle. As the wife of a mayor, Tessa had spent years making the right connections and cultivating the proper image. Leaving her husband for another man would not only shatter that image, it would force her to admit she'd made a terrible mistake in choosing Hoyt over Crandall, a decision she'd stubbornly defended for more than forty years, though anyone who knew her as well as Crandall could see that she was miserable.

Opening his eyes, he saw that she had turned her head to stare out the tinted window, giving him her proud, delicate profile. It was so strikingly similar to Solange Washington's that his breath snagged in his throat.

Beneath the silk wrap she wore, Tessa's chest rose and fell rapidly with the effort to control her ragged breathing. Her hands were clasped so tightly in her lap, the fine bones protruded.

Without turning her head to look at him, she said in a low voice, "What makes you think we have a granddaughter?"

Crandall hesitated an appropriate beat, then reached for a manila folder on the seat beside him. He opened it and removed several photos of Solange Washington taken over the past two days by a freelance photographer he'd hired. Wordlessly he passed the pictures to Tessa, who accepted them as reluctantly as if he were offering her a poisonous snake poised to strike.

The moment her eyes landed on the first image, she gasped and nearly dropped the stack of photos.

Crandall felt inordinately vindicated by her reaction. It was the same way he'd felt when Solange Washington had stepped through the door of his library on Monday afternoon, looking so much like a younger version of Tessa he half believed he'd stumbled upon a time warp that had sent him back thirty-five years. With her chestnut-brown hair, high cheekbones, slim nose, slanted dark eyes and full lips, Solange was a dead ringer for the woman who'd stolen Crandall's heart so long ago. Even her complexion—that unusual brown brushed with gold—was the same. Twenty-four years of knowing about her existence had not prepared him for the shock of actually coming face-to-face with her.

The photographer had captured her as she was running errands yesterday. In each photo, she wore a white peasant blouse with billowy sleeves and a long, red gypsy skirt, similar to an outfit Tessa had worn in an old photograph Crandall still had in his possession. Every once in a while—glutton for punishment that he was—he'd pull out the picture and stare at Tessa's brightly smiling face, wondering what had gone so terribly wrong between them.

As he watched, Tessa slowly lifted her hand and traced trembling fingertips over Solange Washington's hauntingly familiar image. "What's her name?" she whispered.

"Solange. Solange Washington. She applied for the position

of my personal assistant. I met her on Monday when she showed up for the interview."

When Tessa raised her head to look at him, Crandall was surprised to see tears glistening in her eyes. "Does she know…did she know who you were?"

"No." His mouth thinned to a grim line. "Or she pretended not to."

"What do you mean?"

"Solange Washington was adopted as a small child and grew up in a town called Haskell. According to her, she doesn't remember much about her past."

"I see." Tessa's gaze bored into his. "And you don't believe her."

Crandall brushed an invisible speck of lint off the knife-blade crease of his dark trousers. "What I find hard to believe," he said mildly, "is that after twenty-six years, Solange Washington decided one day to pack up and leave her hometown and make San Antonio, of all places, her new home. I also find it hard to believe that of all the jobs she could have applied for, she applied for one of mine."

"I'm not at all surprised that she applied for the position," Tessa said with a hint of impatience. "You know very well any number of people would kill to work for you. Why should this girl be any different?"

"She didn't grow up in San Antonio, for starters."

"That doesn't mean she's never heard of you before. Are you going to tell me you only received applications from people living in or near San Antonio?"

"Of course not," Crandall said gruffly.

"My point exactly. Besides, she was new in town and needed a job. I imagine your ad, offering free room and board, must have sounded quite attractive to her."

"There was no mention of free room and board in the ad. I did that on purpose." Crandall frowned. "The point is, one way or another, whether or not she got the job, she was going to find a way to get to me."

Tessa gave him a mocking look. "So you're convinced that

the girl is after something. What is it this time? Your money? Or your soul?"

"Possibly both," Crandall said, ignoring the biting sarcasm in her voice. "That's why I decided to hire her. If she's up to no good, I'd rather be able to keep a watchful eye on her." This part, at least, was the truth.

A shadow of cynicism twisted Tessa's mouth. "Keep your friends close and your enemies closer, Crandall?"

"Damn right," he snapped, unapologetic. Tessa could sit back in her ivory tower and judge him all she wanted, but if Solange ever learned the truth about who she was and decided to seek revenge, Tessa stood to lose just as much as he did. Her marriage had already suffered as a result of her infidelity and the birth of their illegitimate child. There was no telling how her husband, Hoyt, would react to the news that his wife's torrid love affair had not only produced a daughter, but a granddaughter as well. Talk about a gift that kept giving.

Tessa sifted through the photos, lingering over each one before shoving the pile back at Crandall. "So you're having her followed and investigated."

"I had these photos taken for you. I knew you wouldn't believe me unless you saw her with your own two eyes."

Tessa uncrossed and crossed her long, sleek legs. "We don't know for sure that she's Melanie's daughter."

"The hell we don't," Crandall growled. "We may be getting old, Tess, but we're not blind. That girl is the spitting image of you, and you know it. What *I* want to know is who sealed her birth records so tight my private investigator keeps running up against a brick wall."

Tessa frowned in confusion. "I don't under—" As comprehension dawned, her eyes narrowed to angry slits. "Wait a minute. Are you suggesting that *I* sealed her birth records?"

"You or that conniving bastard you married," Crandall bit off tersely, convincingly.

Tessa nearly leapt out of the seat. "How dare you! Do you even know what you're saying? If I had learned years ago that we had a granddaughter, do you honestly believe I would have kept something as important as that from you?"

"You might have done anything to keep the truth about Melanie from coming to light and jeopardizing your husband's political career," Crandall said with calm, implacable resolve, ignoring a prick of guilt. "If memory serves me correctly, he was preparing to run for mayor around the time Solange Washington would have been born."

"That's positively absurd!" Tessa exploded. "When Melanie came to my house that day, it was the first time since her birth I'd ever laid eyes on her or heard from her. If what you're suggesting was true, that would mean I'd secretly kept tabs on her all those years after she was adopted, and you know damn well I didn't!"

Crandall studied her lovely, outraged face, pretending to search for any signs of deceit. After all, this was the same woman who'd once declared her undying love to him just a week before announcing her engagement to another man.

When he made no reply, her expression turned to one of wounded disbelief. "My God," she whispered brokenly. "You don't believe me, do you?"

Crandall clenched his jaw. "Talk to your husband when you get home. Ask him how far he was willing to go to make sure none of the skeletons in your closet surfaced during his precious campaign."

"I'll do no such thing," Tessa fumed. "If you refuse to believe what I'm telling you, that's your problem, not mine." She glanced down at her diamond-encrusted wristwatch, then reached into her designer clutch purse and pulled out her cell phone. "I need to get back to the charity auction," she told him. "It was only supposed to last for two hours. Please ask your driver to take me back to the mall so that I can catch a cab to the hotel."

Crandall gave her a cold, narrow smile. "As you wish."

They returned to the shopping mall without exchanging another word. Crandall, fully expecting Tessa to launch herself out of the limousine before it came to a complete stop, was understandably surprised when she made no move to leave.

Gazing at him, she asked quietly, "What if you're wrong about Solange?"

He arched a dubious brow. "About her being our granddaughter?"

"No. About her motives for entering your life." Tessa smiled, a soft, wistful smile. "What if she genuinely has no idea who she is? Or what if she does know, but all she wants is to get to know you? Will you let her, Crandall? Will you let her into your heart?"

He hesitated. In all the years he had known of Solange's existence, he'd never allowed himself to contemplate the idea of having a relationship with her. Now that he'd met her in person, he understood why. She reminded him so much of Tessa, the woman who'd broken his heart and left him to pick up the shattered pieces, that it was easier for him to think of her as someone to keep at arm's length, someone who couldn't be trusted. Although he knew it was purely irrational, a part of him—a big part of him—feared that if he let down his guard with Solange, if he let her get too close to him, it was only a matter of time before she, too, broke his heart.

He couldn't let that happen.

He wouldn't.

As if she'd intercepted his thoughts, Tessa shook her head sadly at him. "I didn't think so." She reached for the door handle, then paused. "If you do learn that she's our granddaughter, I want to meet her, Crandall."

His eyes narrowed on her face. "I don't think that would go over too well with your husband," he said caustically.

"Let me worry about that." Her eyes turned softly imploring. "Will you keep me posted on the investigation?"

Crandall hesitated, then gave a short nod.

As he watched Tessa climb out of the limo and hurry to the waiting taxicab, a slow, triumphant smile crawled across his face.

And for the first time in over forty years, he allowed himself to anticipate the very real possibility that he would soon have Tessa back in his life—permanently.

Chapter 9

Later that night, Solange sat cross-legged on her bedroom floor surrounded by half-opened cardboard boxes. After Dane left, Rita had taken her on a tour of the house before Solange returned to her bedroom to begin unpacking. A sedate fire crackled in the fireplace, warding off the evening chill. Rita had warned her the nights could get downright cold in the mountains, and she'd been right. A foray onto the terrace to gaze up at the glittering night sky had sent Solange scurrying back inside after a few minutes, rubbing her arms and shivering. Laughing, Rita had left the room and returned bearing a mug of freshly brewed hot chocolate from the kitchen.

Alone now, Solange sipped the sweet, obscenely rich drink while she debated what to unpack and what to stash in the storage closet Rita had shown her earlier. With the exception of her clothes and a few personal items, nothing she'd brought with her really needed to be unpacked. The spectacularly furnished suite contained everything she would ever want or need, from extra linens, blankets and towels to a full range of fragrant soaps, lotions and toiletries. Someone had even been considerate enough to stock the bathroom with feminine products.

In the end, Solange unpacked her clothes and decided to stow the rest of her belongings, which seemed shabby and out of place in her new lavish digs. But as she reached for a box labeled FRAGILE in black Magic Marker, she paused, then grabbed her box cutter and went to work.

Inside, covered carefully with bubble wrap, were several wood-framed family portraits, along with an old leather-bound photo album and Solange's high-school yearbook. Had these items been kept in the farmhouse, instead of a storage shed in the backyard, they would have been destroyed in the fire. But, ironically enough, her mother had always insisted on storing important documents and other family memorabilia inside that musty old shed, contending that too much clutter in a house created fire hazards.

She couldn't have imagined that a leaky gasoline generator, not clutter, would cause the fire that would someday claim her life.

Solange's throat tightened as she reached inside the box for a photograph. Slowly she removed the plastic wrapping and gazed at a faded photo of herself at age nine, nestled between her parents against an artificial woodsy background. George and Eleanor Washington, a handsome couple in their late forties, had donned their Sunday best, which meant a simple tweed suit for him and a thrift-shop dress for her.

With a stab of nostalgia, Solange recalled tugging at the itchy lace collar of her yellow summer dress and whining because she was missing the Dallas Cowboys in their season opener against the despised Washington Redskins. The year before, while hanging out with the Somerset brothers, she had discovered the novelty of professional football, and had been addicted ever since. While Eleanor threatened bodily harm to her squirming daughter, George merely gave her an empathetic smile. He, as it later turned out, was a devout Redskins fan who'd been in the closet for years, because in Haskell, it was downright sacrilegious to root for any other team but the Cowboys.

Solange smiled softly, flooded with memories of watching Sunday-afternoon football games with her father, talking trash and teasing him about his dirty little secret when none of his friends were around.

A movement out of the corner of her eye interrupted her musings and made her glance up sharply. She was surprised to find Crandall Thorne framed in the doorway, his hands tucked deep into the pockets of his fine wool trousers as he watched her with an unreadable expression.

"Good evening, Miss Washington," he said quietly.

Scraping tears from her eyes with the heel of her hand, Solange scrambled to her feet, feeling as if she'd been caught loafing on the job by her drill sergeant. If she hadn't been clutching the photo to her chest, she might even have saluted him. Tall and broad-shouldered, Crandall Thorne struck such a commanding figure he made Solange feel clumsy and unsure of herself.

"Mr. Thorne—"

"I didn't mean to startle you," he said mildly. "I just got home and thought I'd come by to see how you were settling in. I trust you've found everything to your satisfaction?"

"Definitely," Solange said with a vigorous nod. "This room is amazing, and Ms. Rita has been the most gracious hostess. And your chef makes the best lasagna I've ever had in my life."

"I'm pleased to hear it."

Solange smiled. "You have a very beautiful home, Mr. Thorne."

He inclined his head. "I apologize for not being here to welcome you this afternoon, but I had some pressing matters to take care of in town. Rita tells me you had car trouble."

Solange grimaced. "Yes, unfortunately. The engine died on me. Dane Roarke was kind enough to give me a ride."

Crandall sent her a vaguely amused look. "I doubt kindness had much to do with Mr. Roarke's generosity," he said sardonically, "but I'll be sure to thank him, anyway."

Solange smiled. "And speaking of gratitude, Mr. Thorne, I wanted to thank you for giving me this job opportunity. I know you had misgivings about hiring an aspiring lawyer, so I appreciate your willingness to take a chance on me anyway."

Crandall passed a slow, appraising look over her face. "Do you believe you were the best person for the job, Miss Washington?"

Solange grinned. "Absolutely."

He stared at her a moment longer before nodding toward the framed photograph still clutched to her chest. "May I?"

She nodded.

When Crandall made no move to enter the room, she crossed the distance and handed the photo to him. He studied it for an impassive moment. "These are your parents?"

"Yes. George and Eleanor Washington."

Crandall arched a brow. "Your father was named after the first president?"

Solange chuckled. "I know. I used to get teased all the time, and as you can imagine, I've heard every joke under the sun."

"I can imagine." His heavy, dark brows furrowed together in a slight frown. "They looked too old to be running after a small child."

Solange bristled. Her chin went up a proud notch. "They were the best thing that ever happened to me."

Crandall lifted his head, giving her a swift, evaluative glance. "I never meant to imply otherwise, Miss Washington," he said in a tone that made it clear he still believed her parents had been too old to raise her.

Solange dug her fingernails into her palms, resisting the urge to snatch the photograph out of his hand. Who the hell was he to pass judgment on her parents? What gave him the right? And would he have made the same comment if she hadn't told him she was adopted?

He examined the picture a moment longer, then passed it back to her, his eyes tracing her features. "You haven't changed much. You look the same."

Solange forced a jaunty smile to her lips. "Considering I was nine years old at the time, I'll take that as a compliment."

"Fair enough." He dipped his hands back into his pockets. "Do you know how to ride a horse, Miss Washington?"

Solange chuckled dryly. "With all due respect, sir, that's like asking a fish if it knows how to swim. I grew up on a farm. Learning how to ride was a rite of passage."

"Of course. I should have known." A ghost of a smile played

around the edges of his mouth. "If you'd like, you can go riding tomorrow. I have one or two steeds that should meet with your approval."

This time, when Solange smiled, there was nothing forced about it. "I'd like that very much."

He nodded shortly. "I'll let you finish unpacking. Have a good night, Miss Washington."

"Thanks. You, too."

As he turned to leave, he said, "Oh, and one more thing, Miss Washington."

"Yes?"

"The next time someone asks you to participate in something unethical or illegal, such as, say, taking a lie-detector test, stick to your principles and refuse." He paused, a hint of censure beneath the cool smile he gave her. "That's what any good lawyer would do."

Solange swallowed, then nodded. "Yes, sir."

After he left, she released a long, deep breath and returned to the box she'd been unpacking. As she unwrapped the remaining photographs, she reflected upon Crandall Thorne's parting words. She may have failed his first test, but her presence in his home that evening was proof that he, like Solange, believed she could do the job she'd been hired for. If he'd had any serious misgivings about her, he wouldn't have offered her the position. Contrary to what she'd told him, she wasn't arrogant enough to believe she was the most qualified applicant he'd come across during his search, especially if he'd received hundreds of résumés, as she suspected. Although she'd admitted to being an aspiring attorney and had ruined his nice shirt on her way out of the house, he'd still chosen her.

In that moment, Solange vowed to do everything in her power to make sure he never regretted his decision.

She finished unpacking, then went to take a shower in the large, luxurious bathroom adorned with custom ceramic tile, cultured marble counters and gleaming brass fixtures.

Feeling like a pampered guest at an exclusive resort, she dried off with a thick terry-cloth towel, smoothed scented lotion all over her body and slipped into a clean, oversize T-shirt. Grabbing the paperback mystery novel she'd bought while running errands that week, Solange padded barefoot into the separate seating area and stretched out on the chaise longue before the flickering fire. The logs made a soft hissing noise as they burned, sending up an occasional spray of bright embers.

Lulled by the sound, she soon found herself drifting off to sleep.

When her cell phone rang, it was as if she'd been doused with a bucket of ice water. She jerked upright, feeling disoriented, then scrambled off the chaise and hurried over to the bed, where she'd left her purse earlier.

She dug out her cell phone and answered without glancing at the caller ID, assuming it could only be one person. "Hey, girl."

There was a startled pause on the other end. "Solange?" ventured a deep, all-too-familiar voice. A voice she'd never expected to hear again. "Solange, this is Lamar."

The air stalled in her lungs. She lowered herself slowly onto the bed, holding the phone in a sudden death grip.

"Are you there?"

She swallowed hard, closing her eyes for a moment. "I'm here," she murmured, striving for a calm she didn't feel. "What do you want, Lamar?"

"I, uh, wanted to see how you were doing. It's been a while."

"Yes, it has."

Lamar cleared his throat nervously. "I've been meaning to call you ever since I heard that you'd moved to San Antonio. I was going to call you earlier, but then I got sent to Washington, D.C., to take some classes. I just returned last week."

Solange said nothing, letting the silence hang between them. *Let him squirm,* she thought peevishly. God knows he had that, and a helluva lot worse, coming to him.

After another moment, Lamar said brightly, "Did Jill tell you I saw her at the bank the other day?"

"She may have mentioned something about that."

"She told me you'd landed a nice job with Crandall Thorne,

that big-time defense attorney. I've heard he travels in the same social circles as judges, politicians, philanthropists and celebrities. Congratulations."

"Thank you," Solange murmured.

"I was really surprised to hear that you'd left home."

"Why? Because all you've ever seen me as is a small-town girl with even smaller aspirations?"

"No! You know that's not what I meant. In fact, nothing could be further from the truth. I've been all over the world, and you're still the most ambitious woman I've ever met, Solange."

Something in his voice made Solange wonder whether she'd just been complimented or insulted. The fact that it mattered at all sent a stab of frustration slicing through her. Impatiently, she glanced up at the antique clock on the wall. "Look, it's getting late. I really need to—"

Without warning, Lamar let out a sharp, ragged breath. "How long are you going to blame me for what happened between us?"

Solange nearly dropped the phone. *"Excuse me?"*

"You heard me. How long will you treat me like a leper for the way things ended between us?"

"In case you've forgotten," Solange said, coolly succinct, *"you're* the one who broke up with me. At a New Year's Eve party, mind you, where you knew I wouldn't make a scene in front of all those people."

"I know the timing was bad," Lamar agreed grimly, "but believe me when I tell you I didn't plan it that way. It just—"

"Happened?" She gave a brittle, mirthless laugh. "How original. Do you realize that's the exact same thing Wyatt told Jill when she caught him in bed with another woman?"

"Damn it, Solange," Lamar snapped. "I'm not Wyatt! I never cheated on you, and you know it!"

"Sometimes I wish you had!" she cried. "God knows that would have been a whole lot easier to explain than the vague reason you gave me! You told me you needed space in the same breath you assured me I wasn't smothering you. What was I supposed to think, Lamar?"

"Solange—"

She drew a deep, steadying breath. "It doesn't matter anymore. That was nearly a year ago. So much has happened since then. So much has changed."

"Not my feelings for you," Lamar said fervently. "I still love you, Solange. I never stopped, and I probably never will."

Solange grew very still, her heart hammering inside her chest. Jill's voice echoed through her mind, clear as a church bell. *When I saw him at the bank today, I realized he still loves you. He never stopped.*

Could her best friend have been right? Did she dare believe what Lamar was telling her?

In a carefully measured voice, Solange said, "If that's true, if you still have feelings for me, then why did you break up with me?"

Lamar sighed harshly. "Because I was a damn fool," he said, full of self-deprecation. "When I told you I needed space, it was because I lacked the courage to tell you what I really wanted, what I *really* needed."

She frowned. "I don't understand."

"When I broke up with you, Solange, I never imagined you'd let me go so easily."

Solange arched a brow. "You expected me to *beg* you to come back?"

Lamar gave a dry, humorless chuckle. "Of course not. I know what a proud, stubborn woman you've always been. I had no illusions about you *begging* for anything. What I expected—what I hoped—was that you'd realize how much you missed me, how much you needed me, how right we were for each other." He paused for a moment. "I was hoping you would finally decide you wanted to marry me."

Solange made a soft, strangled sound. "W-what did you say?"

Lamar heaved a deep, resigned breath. "I'm not getting any younger, Solange. I'll be forty next year. I'm tired of being a bachelor. I haven't enjoyed that status since the day I laid eyes on you at that county fair, looking like an African princess banished to the life of a dairy maid in your checkered red-and-white shirt and cutoff shorts. I think I was a goner even before I tasted your canned strawberry preserves."

An errant chuckle escaped before Solange could stop herself. "Lamar—"

"It was love at first sight for me, and I thought you felt the same way, but every time I even *hinted* at marriage, you clammed up on me or changed the subject."

"That's not true." Even as the vehement denial left her mouth, Solange remembered her response to Dane Roarke's question about her marital status. *God, no,* she'd said without hesitation, as if she were appalled by the mere idea. Had she always reacted that way—or had her response been tainted by bitterness over her breakup with Lamar?

"I don't remember any discussions of marriage," she hedged.

"We never actually progressed to the 'discussion' phase," Lamar said wryly. "Like I said, every time I broached the subject, you got that deer-in-the-headlights look and carefully steered the conversation in another direction. After a while, I realized that as good as our relationship was, we wanted different things out of life. You wanted to attend law school and become a family-law attorney. I simply wanted to settle down *with* a family."

"Oh, Lamar." Solange closed her eyes, stretching out on the queen-size bed. "I wish you'd shared these things with me before."

"I probably should have. In fact, I *know* I should have. But would it have made a difference?"

"What do you mean?"

Lamar fell silent for so long she wondered if he'd been dropped from the call. But a quick glance at her cell phone confirmed they were still connected.

Finally he spoke. "If I'd asked you that night to marry me," he said quietly, "would you have agreed?"

Solange's heart thudded. Sweat dampened her palms. "I—I don't know," she croaked out. "That was almost a year ago. Like I said, so much has changed."

"Including your heart?"

"Lamar—"

"Do you still love me?"

Fresh anger and resentment swept through her. She sat up quickly. "Wait a minute! Let's not get ahead of ourselves. *You* broke up with me, remember? For several weeks you did your level best to alienate me, ignoring my phone calls and making up excuses not to see me. And whenever you *did* give me the time of day, you were cold and distant, practically a stranger. You let me think you'd grown tired of me! You have *no* right to come barging back into my life, after all this time, demanding to know how I feel about you!"

"You're right," Lamar said solemnly. "I'm sorry for hurting you, and for not being there for you after your parents died. Staying away from you was the hardest thing I've ever done in my life. I thought you hated me and wanted nothing to do with me."

"I *did* hate you," Solange growled, "and I *didn't* want anything to do with you."

"What about now? Now that you know what was going through my head at the time, does it change anything?"

He sounded so hopeful she almost felt sorry for him. Almost.

Pinching the bridge of her nose between her thumb and forefinger, she said wearily, "I don't know what you want from me, Lamar."

"I want a second chance," he said urgently. "I want to be with you again. Come home, Solange. You don't belong in San Antonio—"

"Where I belong," she interrupted through gritted teeth, "is no longer your concern."

"Damn it, Solange! Don't be like that. I love you, and unless my instincts are wrong, you still love me, too."

Solange said nothing, neither denying nor confirming his assertion. She knew a part of her would always love him. But was that enough to justify taking him back after the way he'd hurt her? Could she trust him with her heart again?

Was it too late for them?

Sensing her indecision, Lamar persisted. "I've tried dating other women, but it's no use. You're the only woman I want, the only woman I'll *ever* want. If you agree to marry me, I promise to devote the rest of my life to making you happy." His voice lowered to a soft, beseeching caress. "You know I could take good care of you. I earn more than enough for both of us, and next year I'm up for another promotion. You wouldn't even have to work. You could stay home or go to law school—whatever you want. All I'm asking is to be part of the equation."

Solange frowned, staring up at the ceiling. It was tempting, so damned tempting, to accept what he was offering—love, stability, an escape from the loneliness she'd felt ever since her parents had died. If she married Lamar, she wouldn't be alone in the world anymore. She'd belong to a family again; she'd belong to him, and he to her. And her parents would have approved. They'd adored Lamar, and had hinted more than once that they wouldn't mind having him as a son-in-law.

"Solange?" Lamar gently prodded. "I love you. Please say yes. Please say you'll marry me."

"I—I need time, Lamar. This…this is a lot to digest at once."

"I know."

"I'm not ready to move back home. To be perfectly honest, I'm not sure I ever will be. I came here to start over. I need to be able to do that."

"I understand. I don't want to push you. But before you hang up the phone, Solange, I think you should know that I'm very determined to get you back in my life. I'm fully prepared to put in a request to be reassigned to Fort Sam Houston, one of the military bases there in San Antonio."

Solange couldn't suppress an impatient groan. "Lamar—"

"Don't bother trying to talk me out of it," he said firmly. "I let you go once before, and it was the biggest mistake I've ever made in my life. Don't expect me to let you go a second time, not without putting up a fight."

Solange closed her eyes, too mentally drained to argue. "Good night, Lamar."

"Good night, princess. Sleep well."

Sleep well? Solange thought sarcastically as she returned the cell phone to her purse and switched off the bedside lamp, leaving only the soft glow of firelight to illuminate the room.

She'd be lucky if she slept a wink that night. Thanks to Lamar Rogers, it was going to be one of the longest nights of her life, second only to the night her parents died.

Chapter 10

Dane knew the moment he arrived at the ranch the next morning and took one look at Solange's face that something had changed.

Seated alone at the round oak table in the sunny breakfast nook, Solange looked up as Rita escorted Dane into the room. When their eyes met, the smile she gave him was brief, almost perfunctory, before she quickly glanced away.

What was *that* about?

"You're just in time for breakfast," Rita cheerfully informed Dane as she set a large, steaming bowl of grits on the table, which was already covered with mounds of food—blueberry pancakes, thick, crispy slices of bacon, home fries, scrambled eggs, assorted fruit. Even as he surveyed the appetizing spread, his stomach growled, reminding him that the last time he'd eaten was around 3 p.m. yesterday, during his previous trip to the ranch.

"Don't just stand there gawking," Rita laughingly admonished him. She pointed to an empty chair at the table across from Solange. "Have a seat, baby."

Remembering his promise not to argue with the woman, Dane slid into the proffered chair and accepted a plate laden with food. But his gaze was on Solange, who looked fresh and exquisitely wholesome in a yellow peasant blouse and snug-fitting jeans. Her hair was pulled back in a loose ponytail with the long bangs swept to one side, emphasizing her dark, exotic eyes. Upon closer examination, Dane noticed faint dark circles beneath her eyes, which told him she hadn't slept very well. He wondered what, or who, was to blame.

"Morning," he murmured.

She met his eyes over the rim of her coffee cup. "Good morning, Dane."

No other woman had ever made his plain, monosyllabic name sound so special, so unique. He could only imagine the way it would sound on her lips as he made love to her, as her slick, beautiful body shuddered in the throes of an orgasm.

He watched, with wicked amusement, as her eyes widened a fraction, as if she'd read his mind. Her hand trembled a little as she replaced her cup in the saucer.

"How did you enjoy your first night at Casa Thorne?" Dane asked lazily, determined to engage her in conversation, no matter how reluctant she seemed.

Before she could respond, however, Crandall chose that moment to enter the room. He took one look at Dane and scowled. "What the hell are you doing at my breakfast table, Roarke?" he demanded.

Rita, returning from the kitchen with a pitcher of orange juice, sputtered with indignation. "Crandall Thorne! Is that any way to treat a guest? I swear you wake up on the wrong side of the bed every morning! Just sit yourself down so I can fix you a plate. Ornery as the devil, that's what you are. Lord have mercy. And for your information, I invited Dane over this morning. Gloria baked one of her raspberry truffle cakes for him to take to his aunt's house this afternoon for Sunday brunch."

Crandall claimed a chair at the table, grumbling, "I'm sure you didn't tell him to be here *this* early."

Dane shrugged, unperturbed by the old man's rancor. "What can I say? It's Sunday. There was no traffic."

"And you didn't anticipate this?"

Dane's expression was one of wide-eyed innocence. "I'm from Houston, sir. There's *always* traffic in Houston."

A muffled sound across the table drew his attention to Solange, who looked like she was trying very hard not to laugh, though the twinkling mirth in her dark eyes gave her away. Dane winked at her, and was rewarded by the flush that spread high across her cheekbones.

Crandall, watching the exchange over the rim of his glasses, grunted and reached for the folded newspaper Rita had placed on the table beside him.

"It's such a glorious day outside," Rita remarked once the meal was under way. While she, Solange and Dane enjoyed a lavish country breakfast, Crandall, for health reasons, had to content himself with a bowl of oatmeal, a serving of fresh fruit and a slice of dry wheat toast.

In retaliation for the old man's earlier rudeness, Dane asked Rita to pass him the plate of fragrant buttermilk biscuits, then took perverse pleasure in watching as Crandall's hungry gaze followed the plate across the table. When Dane made an exaggerated show of biting into a hot, flaky roll, Crandall's eyes narrowed on his face in a manner that promised swift retribution.

Very deliberately, Crandall picked up his glass of orange juice, then paused, his head tipped thoughtfully to one side. "Speaking of beauty, how's that young lady you've been seeing for the past month, Roarke? The dental hygienist?"

Dane nearly choked on his food.

"What was her name again?" Crandall pondered aloud. "Allison, Cynthia, Rachel—"

"Renee," Dane supplied hoarsely. "Her name is Renee. And, uh, we're not dating anymore."

"Aw, that's too bad. She seemed like such a nice girl, much classier than that exotic dancer you were seeing last month. As if there's anything remotely 'exotic' about what those girls do for a living." With a lamentable shake of his head, Crandall smiled wryly at Solange. "Dane here is quite the ladies' man. If you're not careful, my dear, you might be next on his Rolodex. He seems to be working in alphabetical order these days. Renee, Solange—"

"Oh, hush!" Rita scolded. "Can't you see you're embarrassing the poor boy?"

Crandall chuckled good-naturedly. "Nonsense, woman. It takes a lot more than that to embarrass Dane Roarke, isn't that right, son?"

Dane inclined his head, conceding the match point to Thorne, whose answering smile whispered of triumph. Dane made a mental note to remind his cousin Daniela not to discuss his love life with others—least of all a ruthless old man who had the keen memory of an elephant.

When Dane finally chanced a look at Solange, she was frowning slightly, studying him through cool, narrowed eyes. If he could've strangled Thorne and gotten away with it, he would have.

Rita reached over and gave his hand a gentle, conciliatory pat. "I meant to ask you yesterday, Dane. How are your parents doing?"

Reluctantly pulling his gaze away from Solange, Dane answered, "They're doing well, Ms. Rita. Dad's finally scaling back at the shop and letting my brother Derrick take more of an active role in running the business."

"Well, it's about time," Rita said approvingly. "Your mother must be thrilled. I know she's been pleading with him for years to cut back on his workload and spend more time at home with her."

"Yes, ma'am, she has been." Dane grinned. "Last week she even convinced him to take pottery classes with her."

Rita whooped with delight. "Good for her! I don't know how she managed that feat, but I'm glad she did."

"Me, too. Taking a class together will be good for both of them."

"Mmm, hmm. I know what *else* will be good for them. That cruise they're going on next month." Smiling broadly, Rita turned to Solange. "Dane is sending his parents on a Caribbean cruise for their fortieth wedding anniversary. Isn't that awfully sweet of him?"

Solange looked at Dane, a faint smile flitting around the corners of her mouth. "Yes, it is."

Dane shrugged dispassionately. "It's no big deal. They've never been on a cruise before—they were long overdue."

Rita guffawed. "Pay him no mind," she told Solange. "He's being far too modest. His mama tells me he's always done thoughtful things for her, ever since he was a little boy. Whenever she had to work nights cleaning office buildings, and she would drag her tired self home in the mornings after his father had already left for the shop, she said Dane would always be waiting for her with a hot bowl of lumpy oatmeal or a plate of runny eggs and burnt bacon." Rita laughed. "She told me those were some of the best meals she'd ever eaten."

Dane couldn't help but chuckle at Rita's not-so-subtle attempt to undo the damage caused by Crandall's underhanded revelation that Dane had an active love life. He was a little embarrassed by all the attention—until he glanced over at Solange and saw a new softness in her eyes as she looked at him.

He wasn't the only one who noticed. Scowling at Rita, Crandall grumbled, "For someone who plans to make a trip to the market before noon, you sure aren't moving very fast, woman."

"Don't you worry about me," Rita said sweetly. "I still have plenty of time to get there before it closes." When Crandall grunted and returned his attention to the newspaper he'd been reading, she winked conspiratorially at Dane. He grinned and forked up a bite of pancake.

Rita turned to Solange with a mildly inquisitive smile. "What do your parents do for a living, Solange?"

Dane glanced up from his plate in time to see a shadow cross Solange's face. "My parents passed away in January," she said quietly.

"Oh, no," Rita said sympathetically. "I'm so sorry, baby. I had no idea."

"That's all right. You had no way of knowing." Solange offered a tremulous smile. "To answer your question, they were farmers."

"You grew up on a farm?"

"Yes, ma'am."

"So you know what it's like to wake up at the crack of dawn to milk a cow, feed a coop full of noisy chickens, bale hay and muck out horse stalls—*before* going to school?"

Solange grinned. "That about sums it up. Did you grow up on a farm, too, Ms. Rita?"

"You bet I did," Rita said proudly. "I was raised on a small farm right outside San Antonio. Lived there until I was thirty, when my folks sold the property to some land developers. Saddest day of my life, having to walk away from the only home I'd ever known."

"I would have felt the same way," Solange ruefully admitted. "I once threatened to run away from home if my parents even *thought* about selling the farm."

Laughing, Rita reached over and squeezed Solange's hand. "I knew there was a reason I liked you, child. I told Crandall he was doing the right thing by hiring you. No one understands the meaning of hard work better than a girl who was raised on a farm."

"Not that I've ever needed to consult you on my hiring decisions," Crandall intoned dryly from behind the newspaper he was reading. "But if it makes you feel more important, then by all means, take credit for my decision to hire Miss Washington."

Rita rolled her eyes, drawing low chuckles from Solange and Dane. Their gazes met and held across the table before Solange quickly glanced away, busying herself with pouring syrup over the remainder of her pancakes.

Rita divided a speculative look between them. After another moment, she smiled and clapped her hands together. "I have a wonderful idea! Dane, why don't you join Solange when she goes horseback riding this morning?"

Solange's head snapped up so fast it was a wonder she didn't give herself whiplash. "Wha—?"

"Dane has been to the ranch several times but has never gone riding," Rita told her. "Today is a perfect opportunity to rectify that, since you're already going. You two can keep each other company."

Solange's eyes darted wildly from Rita to Dane. She looked like she'd rather be trapped in a very dark room with Jeffrey Dahmer than be forced to endure another minute of Dane's company. He didn't know whether to be amused or offended.

Crandall was glaring balefully at Rita over the top of his newspaper. "Mr. Roarke isn't here to go horseback riding," he snapped.

"I don't see why not," Rita said pragmatically, as if the matter were as simple as flipping on a light switch. "He has to wait until Gloria arrives with the cake, anyway, which won't be until she gets out of church. What better way to pass the time than to go horseback riding with Solange? I'm sure she wouldn't mind his company, would you, baby?"

Solange looked like she minded very much, but was too polite to say so. "Um…no, not at all," she mumbled.

Rita gave a satisfied nod. "Good. Then it's all settled," she said briskly, confirming Dane's long-held suspicion that it was she, not Crandall, who ran things at Casa Thorne.

Lifting the porcelain carafe, Rita glanced innocently around the table. "More coffee anyone?"

Chapter 11

Half an hour later, perched astride a chestnut-colored sorrel named Aurora—handpicked for her by the stable boy because the color of her hair reminded him of the horse's—Solange tried her best to concentrate on enjoying the scenic jaunt through the lush, rolling acres of Crandall Thorne's property. A procession of large Spanish oaks flanked the dirt trail she was following, and patches of pale blue sky shone through the canopy of dry branches like slivers of stained glass. A cool, invigorating breeze, ripe with the scent of pine and earth, caressed her face and sifted through the strands of her hair, loosening her ponytail. It was a glorious day, perfect for being outdoors.

All she could think about was the man riding alongside her.

Seated astride a black, sleekly muscled Arabian, Dane looked relaxed and completely in control of his mount. Dressed in a ribbed black turtleneck, black jeans and black boots, he seemed an innate extension of the horse, as dark and powerful as a rebel warrior leading an army into battle. For someone who'd only been on horseback "once or twice" before, he sure could have fooled her.

"I think that's the longest you've looked at me all morning," came his deep, amused drawl.

Solange jerked her gaze away, heat suffusing her cheeks. "Sorry. I didn't mean to stare at you."

Dane chuckled softly. "You won't hear me complaining. I'll take being stared at over being ignored any day of the week."

Solange felt a traitorous stab of guilt. "I haven't been ignoring you," she lied.

"No? You've hardly said three words to me all morning."

Solange shifted slightly in the leather saddle, keeping her eyes carefully averted. "I've had a lot on my mind."

"Hmm. Boyfriend trouble?"

She bristled, whipping her head around to glare at him. "I really don't think that's any of your business."

His crooked grin was a slash of white in his dark, handsome face. "I figured as much. So where is he? You left him behind in Haskell?"

Solange said nothing, staring resolutely ahead at the rugged mountain range that loomed in the distance.

"Do you want to talk about it?" Dane invited, undaunted by her silence. "I'm a very good listener."

Solange snorted derisively. "I bet you say that to all the girls."

"Not at all," he said silkily. "Truth is, I don't do much talking—or listening—with other women."

At the unmistakable implication, Solange's mind was filled with an image of him, naked and glistening, clamped between some woman's legs. Inexplicably, a knot of anger tightened in her chest. Without a word, she dug her heel into the horse's side and spurred the animal into a full gallop.

Dane thundered after her, pulling up beside her before she could get very far. Aurora, either yielding to the sudden proximity of the larger horse or the leashed power of its rider, slowed to a docile gait.

Dane's expression was grim. "Don't pass judgment on my personal life," he said curtly, "and I won't subject *you* to crass innuendo about it. Agreed?"

Solange swallowed, her heart hammering against her ribs. "Fine," she bit off. "And the next time I tell you to mind your own business, please do so."

"Fine." Dane regarded her in stony silence, a muscle working in his tightly clenched jaw. After another moment, he nudged his horse forward, choosing to lead the way instead of riding alongside her.

Solange watched him sullenly, feeling like a chastened child. Truth be told, she *felt* small and petty. Dane had been nothing but kind to her, and she'd repaid his kindness by treating him like an unwelcome houseguest. It wasn't *his* fault she found herself torn between a fierce attraction to him and her unresolved feelings for her ex-boyfriend. And it certainly wasn't his fault that Lamar's unexpected marriage proposal had sent her world tilting on its axis, shaking the very foundation she'd spent the past year trying to rebuild. She hated that she'd spent half the night tossing and turning, her mind churning with a thousand what-ifs and visions of the safe, happy future she could have with Lamar; yet the moment Dane had sauntered into the room that morning, she'd had trouble remembering her own name, much less her newfound resolve to keep her distance from him until she made a decision about Lamar.

Her eyes traced the strong lines of his broad back, which tapered down to a trim waist and that firm, magnificent butt that actually made her envy the horse he sat upon.

She could *not* get involved with him. Crandall Thorne's tactless slip of tongue—if it could be called that—had confirmed her belief that having a relationship with Dane Roarke was out of the question. Although Crandall might have exaggerated about Dane dating women according to the alphabetized entries in his Rolodex, Solange had no doubt that Dane ran through enough females to fill several address books. He probably didn't know the first thing about monogamy and commitment.

Don't pass judgment on my personal life, he'd told her. And he was right. What he did in private—or public, for that matter—was none of her business.

Especially if she decided to marry Lamar.

Solange was so absorbed in her thoughts that she lost track of her surroundings until Aurora came to a sudden stop. The sight that greeted Solange brought a soft gasp to her lips.

They had reached a clearing that led them to the top of a ridge, and below them lay the ranch and surrounding valley, lush and green like a rumpled velvet curtain. And beyond the valley, the mountains rose toward the heavens—proud, majestic sentinels framed against an endless expanse of brilliant blue sky. The view was so stunning, so utterly spectacular, that Solange feared it would disappear, like a mirage, if she blinked.

"Oh my God," she breathed.

"I know," Dane murmured quietly beside her. "Pretty amazing, isn't it?"

"Breathtaking. I've never seen anything like it. Talk about God's country."

"Yeah. In the hands of a devil."

Solange let out a choked laugh. Shaking her head, she shot Dane a look of mild reproach. "I thought I told you to stop bad-mouthing my boss."

His mouth curved in an unabashedly irreverent grin. "You did. I never actually agreed to comply, though."

"No, I guess you didn't. What is it with you two, anyway? You bicker worse than George and Florence on *The Jeffersons*."

Dane chuckled, leaning forward in the saddle. "I'm almost afraid to ask which one of us you think is Florence."

Solange laughed again, the tension between them all but forgotten. Gazing out across the valley and to the mountains beyond, she felt her breathing slow to an almost meditative state. She gave a long, dreamy sigh. "Crandall Thorne is very lucky to own this property. To have access to this incredible view anytime he wants. I hope he truly appreciates it."

"I'm sure he does," Dane murmured. "According to his son, Caleb, the old man has learned to appreciate a lot of things he didn't four years ago."

"What happened four years ago?" Solange asked curiously.

"He was diagnosed with acute renal failure. It nearly killed him. He had to undergo a complete lifestyle change, which included cutting back on his workload and retreating to a quieter, more peaceful environment."

"Well, it certainly doesn't get any more peaceful than this," said Solange, gesturing to encompass their scenic surroundings. "Only a fool would question the healing powers of this place."

"You said it, not me."

She arched a brow. "Wait, let me guess. Crandall didn't want to live here?"

"Not at first," Dane drawled. "He likened it to being banished to the wilderness. Once his health began to improve, however, he came to his senses and realized life was too damn short to waste it on looking gift horses in the mouth."

Hearing the trace of grudging respect in his voice, Solange hid a knowing smile. Something told her Dane would rather be tortured by an army of terrorists than admit to respecting anything about Crandall Thorne.

"I'm definitely glad he decided to stay here," she said. "Not only for his own benefit, but for mine, as well." As Dane watched her, she lifted her face to the pale morning sun and exhaled on a deep, contented sigh. "I could just sit here forever and daydream."

"I know what you mean." After another moment, Dane swung down nimbly from his horse and came around to her side. Without thinking, Solange accepted his proffered hand and allowed him to help her dismount, though she'd done it without assistance a thousand times before.

Too late, she realized what a colossal mistake she'd made, as she found her body being dragged along the warm, solid length of Dane's before he set her down. Although the contact lasted no more than a few seconds, her body reacted as if he'd pinned her, naked, to the ground. Heat sizzled through her veins, stinging her nipples and turning her knees to gelatin.

Startled, her eyes flew to his face, only to find his dark, heavy-lidded gaze on her mouth. Her breath snagged sharply in her throat. The air between them quivered with sexual awareness. She couldn't move, couldn't speak, could only lean weakly against him with her hands braced upon the hard, muscled pad of his biceps. And then he shifted ever so slightly, bending a little so that her hands slowly slid up his chest and came to rest on the broad expanse of his shoulders. A tiny shiver of pleasure worked its way down her spine. Her lashes lowered, her eyes riveting on the lush, sensuous curve of his bottom lip.

"Solange—"

The ragged need in his deep, husky voice finally snapped her out of her trance. Hastily she dropped her arms and took a step backward, trembling from a heady combination of fear and arousal.

"Thanks for, uh, helping me down," she managed hoarsely.

Dane hesitated, staring at her a moment longer before nodding once. "You're welcome," he said gruffly.

Solange wiped her damp palms on the thighs of her jeans and walked away on unsteady legs, needing to put as much distance between them as possible. She didn't even want to think about what had just happened—or *not* happened—a moment ago. It was too unsettling to contemplate.

Lowering herself onto the thick blanket of grass, she drew her knees up to her chin and watched out of the corner of her eye as Dane murmured quietly to the horses and rubbed their silky necks. His preoccupation with the animals bought her time to bring her galloping pulse under control, so that by the time he sauntered over and dropped to the ground beside her, she felt immeasurably calmer. So they were attracted to each other. That didn't mean they had to sleep together, she reasoned, nor did they have to tiptoe around each other like a couple of skittish mares. They were both mature, sensible adults. Surely they could enjoy the simple pleasure of a morning horseback ride without ripping each other's clothes off.

Dane stretched out along the grass, clasped his hands behind his head and closed his eyes, his black lashes sweeping down to rest upon his cheekbones. He looked like a dark warrior taking a break from battle to catch a power nap.

Swallowing hard, Solange said softly, "You're good with them. The horses, I mean. And you ride like a natural."

Dane lifted one shoulder in a dismissive shrug. "I'm a fast learner."

"Maybe. Or maybe you've gone riding more often than you let on."

One dark eye cocked open to look at her. "Are you calling me a liar, woman?"

Solange laughed, shaking her head. "I wouldn't dare! Not only do you outweigh me by at least a hundred pounds, but any man who puts his body on the line to help raise money for breast-cancer research must be the epitome of goodness and honesty."

A slow, lazy grin curved his mouth as he looked up at her from beneath his lashes. "Just trying to do my part."

She smiled back at him. "Well, I guess I'll do *my* part and support the cause by buying a calendar."

"Don't do that."

"Why not?" she asked in surprise.

"You don't want a calendar filled with half-naked men on your wall."

She sputtered, "How do you know what I want?"

"Because I do. Besides," he added, subtle challenge glinting in his eyes, "I don't think your boyfriend would appreciate it too much. I know I wouldn't, if you were mine."

The teasing smile on Solange's lips died like a flame that had been suddenly doused. The words *if you were mine* echoed through her mind, filling her with an emotion she didn't want to identify.

Looking away, she cleared her throat. "I'll buy the calendar and mail it to my best friend in Haskell."

"Atta, girl," Dane said softly.

As silence lapsed between them, Solange let her gaze wander to where the horses stood contentedly side by side, their heads hanging down as they nipped at each other in idle play. If only human relationships could be so simple, so pure and unspoiled, she thought with an inward sigh.

She glanced away from the horses to find Dane watching her with a quiet, thoughtful expression. "So you left behind a boy-friend and best friend," he murmured. "Got any other family members living in Haskell?"

Solange shook her head, plucking at a long blade of grass. "My grandparents on both sides passed away a long time ago, and my parents were never very close to any of their remaining relatives, most of whom are scattered around the country. Only a few showed up for the funeral. Once it was over, they hopped back on the next plane and left town without so much as a backward glance." Her lips curved ruefully. "Sorry. I didn't mean to sound bitter."

"You didn't," Dane said gently. "And even if you did, no one could blame you."

She gave him a grateful smile. "In their defense, it's not as if they left behind an underage child to fend for herself. I'm a grown woman, perfectly capable of taking care of myself. If I had been a minor, I'm sure one of my relatives would have offered to take me in." She paused, adding with a touch of cynicism, "Especially if I came with a large inheritance."

"But you didn't," Dane surmised.

She shook her head sadly. "My parents worked their butts off to hold on to the farm, but one bad crop season could set them back financially several years. When they died and the farm burned down, I had to sell the land back to the county and use most of the proceeds to settle their debts. I can assure you," she said with a wry grin, "a wealthy heiress I am *not.*"

Dane chuckled softly. "That's all right. I've always gotten along better with poor people, anyway."

Solange laughed, punching him playfully on the arm. "Wise guy."

Grinning, he crossed his big, booted feet at the ankles, the movement drawing her attention as she leaned back on her elbows. "Just what shoe size do you wear, anyway?" she teasingly inquired.

He glanced down. "Sixteen."

"Hmm. I suspected as much." *And you know what they say about men with big feet.*

When she heard the low, sexy rumble of his laughter, she realized she'd voiced the naughty thought aloud. An embarrassed flush stole across her cheeks as Dane drawled, "Why, Miss Washington, if I didn't know better, I would think you were sexually harassing me."

She rolled her eyes in exasperation, fighting the tug of a grin. "In your dreams, Roarke."

"Mmm. Or maybe in *yours*."

Unfortunately, he wasn't too far off the mark. For the past ten minutes, she'd been struggling not to stare at the way the stretchy fabric of his turtleneck clung to the hard, sinewy muscles of his torso. More than once, she'd found herself willing his shirt to inch up so she could catch another glimpse of his beautifully sculpted bare chest, the sight of which was permanently branded on her memory.

"Do you have any plans for the holidays?" she blurted, eager to change the subject before her imagination began to wander into dangerous territory. "Will you be spending Christmas in San Antonio or Houston?"

"Houston, probably. With my parents and my brother and his family. My mom always prepares a big, lavish meal and buys everyone a ton of gifts. She loves to play Santa."

"That sounds nice," Solange murmured with a soft, poignant smile. "My mother used to do the same thing. No matter how tough things were, she always went out of her way to make Christmas extra special."

Dane turned his head to look at her with an expression of gentle sympathy. "I'm sorry about what happened to your folks," he said in a low voice.

"Me, too." She gazed up at the soft white clouds drifting lazily across the sky. "But I know they're watching over me, protecting me in their own way."

"I bet they are," Dane quietly agreed, and Solange could tell he wasn't merely offering an empty platitude, as people often did when consoling the grief-stricken; he really meant what he said. Her heart swelled with gratitude.

A companionable silence fell between them, broken only by the piercing cry of an eagle that soared high above them. For the second time in two days, Solange felt an incredible sense of peace and contentment wash over her. The sun was warm on her face, the thick grass a soft bed beneath her. Dane lay close to her, so close she could smell him—soap and an intoxicating scent that was uniquely male, uniquely him. She could feel his heat and vitality, as potent as a physical touch. If she could have lain there forever, with him beside her, she would have.

Shaken by the thought, she sat up abruptly. "I guess we'd better start heading back before they think we've been eaten by a mountain lion."

Dane chuckled, a deep, rumbling sound that made her belly quiver. "I think you're the only one Crandall would mourn."

Solange laughed. "I wouldn't be too sure about that. Something tells me he'd hire a new personal assistant within the week."

Dane grinned as they rose together. "Don't sell yourself so short, Angel Eyes. I'd give him at least two weeks to replace you."

Solange smiled distractedly, her insides warming at the endearment that had slipped so naturally from his mouth. *Angel Eyes.* He thought she had the eyes of an angel. God help her.

As they started back toward the waiting horses, she suddenly stopped. "Wait a minute. This view reminds me of something I've always wanted to do."

As Dane eyed her curiously, she ran toward the edge of the cliff, but not too close, and proceeded to spin around in circles while belting out the lyrics to *"The Sound of Music."*

Dane threw back his head and roared with laughter.

As Solange completed her last twirl, her ponytail came loose, sending her hair flying about her face and shoulders. Laughing, she bent to retrieve her scrunchie from the ground as Dane approached, smiling and clapping softly.

"Bravo. That was quite a performance," he drawled. "I think Julie Andrews would have been impressed."

Solange blew her long bangs out of her eyes and grinned up at him, breathless with exhilaration. "Really? You think so?"

"Most definitely. I know I was." His dark, heavy-lidded eyes roamed across her face, glittering with frank male appreciation and something else, something that made her heart skip several precious beats.

He shook his head slowly. "God, you are so beautiful," he whispered huskily.

Instantly the air around them grew hotter, thicker. Gazing up at him, Solange felt as if she were teetering precariously at the mouth of the cliff, poised to be pushed over the edge in a dizzying free fall from which she would never return.

Her lips parted, trembling, but no sound came forth.

Then, before she could react, Dane captured the nape of her neck with his fingers and slanted his head over hers. His mouth descended and seized hers with a raw urgency that ignited her blood.

Even as her mind shouted in protest, she gave herself up to the kiss, feeling the sweet, hard pressure of his lips upon hers, opening her mouth at the insistence of his hot, probing tongue as it slipped between her teeth to touch her, taste her. She shivered, a soft moan escaping as she curved her arms around his neck. His hand slid up to cradle the back of her head as he deepened the kiss, his other hand banding around her waist to draw her against the hard length of his body. She was drowning, drowning in sensation and a fierce need that was unlike anything she'd ever imagined.

Without breaking the kiss they sank to their knees. Desperate for the feel of hot male flesh, Solange tugged his shirt from his waistband and reached beneath the turtleneck to splay her hands across his bare, muscular chest. He shuddered, tightening his hold on the back of her head as he ravaged her mouth like a starving man.

With his free hand, he cupped her left breast, and she gasped. Through the cotton fabric of her peasant blouse and lace bra, he sensuously traced the outline of her nipple with his thumb. Her breast swelled, her nipple beading like a pearl beneath his touch. His erection pressed against her belly, thick and impossibly hard. Mindlessly she ground herself against him, the sensitive flesh between her legs throbbing with need, aching for fulfillment only he could provide.

He eased one side of her blouse off her shoulder and kissed the soft, sensitive spot where her neck and shoulder met. Solange trembled hard, her head falling back on a soundless cry. Dane took full advantage of the exposed arch of her throat, his mouth homing in to suckle her hungrily. She locked her arms around his broad back and clung to him for dear life.

"I want you so damn bad," he uttered raggedly, sinking both hands into her hair as he rained hot kisses along her throat. "I want to feel you wrapped around me."

Through the fog bank of desire clouding her brain, his words—and the stunning reality of that moment—registered. Solange stiffened against him, her eyes flying open as sanity returned, along with a healthy dose of alarm.

Oh, God, what had she done?

Or, better yet, what had she *almost* done?

Shaken to the core, she quickly pulled away from Dane, making him groan softly in protest. Struggling to catch her breath, she watched as his lashes slowly lifted to reveal the smoldering heat in his midnight eyes. His nostrils were slightly flared, his sensuous bottom lip slick and shining. He looked a little wild and dangerous, and so damn sexy it took every ounce of self-control she possessed not to launch herself back into his arms.

"Th-that was a mistake," she whispered shakily.

"Right," Dane murmured, a trace of mockery in the curve of his mouth. "Because you have a boyfriend. What was his name again?"

"Lamar," Solange supplied without thinking.

Dane inclined his head in the barest hint of a nod, his eyes narrowed on hers. "Lamar's a very lucky man."

Solange made no reply to that. Instead she climbed to her feet and busied herself with brushing dirt and grass from her knees. "It's late," she said without looking at him. "I'm ready to go back."

"Of course," Dane said softly.

But as they mounted their horses and started down the mountain trail, one unsettling thought kept echoing through her mind.

There is no going back.

Chapter 12

It took the entire ride back to the ranch house to cool Dane's raging libido.

Every time he relived kissing Solange, touching her and having her warm, lush body pressed against his own, he grew hard—painfully hard. He had to force himself to think about other, less stimulating things, like the remaining Christmas gifts he needed to buy, or how he was going to handle a particular surveillance assignment that week.

When they reached the barn, Solange swung down quickly from her horse, refusing the assistance of the young stable hand who had emerged from cleaning out a stall to meet them. The dark-haired Hispanic boy smiled at Solange, his teeth flashing white in his ruddy face.

"Did you enjoy your ride, *señorita?*" he eagerly inquired, wiping his soiled hands on a cloth rag.

"Yes, thank you, Tomas," Solange said with a quiet smile. She passed him the reins, then stroked a hand down the sorrel's silky neck and leaned close to murmur something that made the animal's long ear twitch in response. Solange winked at Tomas, who blushed like an infatuated puppy. Then, barely sparing a glance at Dane as he dismounted from his horse, she turned and started up the hill toward the main house.

Dane and Tomas watched her departing form in shared admiration—the long, shapely legs covered in snug denim; the way her thick, shoulder-length hair swung from side to side as she walked, her hips rolling in an easy swagger that was purely feminine and maddeningly sexy.

After another moment, Tomas turned to him with a worried frown. "What did you do to Señorita Washington?"

"Not as much as I wanted to," Dane muttered under his breath. At the confused look the boy gave him, he chuckled softly and clapped him on the shoulder. "Don't worry about her, my friend. Women can be unpredictable creatures at times, as you'll see for yourself someday."

Tomas grinned, looking even younger than fifteen. "You sound like my father. He says the same thing."

"You should listen to him. He knows what he's talking about." Dane reached over and ruffled the boy's hair playfully. "By the way, Tomas, how do you like working on the ranch?"

Tomas beamed. "I love it! It's the best job I've ever had." He paused for a moment, his dark brows furrowing together thoughtfully. "Well…I guess it's the *only* job I've ever had. But you know what I mean."

"Yes, I do. And I'm glad to hear it. But you look like you could use some help down here," Dane observed, leading his horse into the large stable. Inside the old building, the pungent odors of leather and oil, manure and dry straw, horses and cobwebs permeated the air. As he passed the first stall, a bay mare whinnied softly in greeting. Dane smiled and tipped his head in response.

"I'm usually the only one here on Sunday mornings," Tomas said, following him into the barn with the chestnut sorrel Solange had ridden in tow. "But now that Señor Thorne has decided to open the ranch to visitors for hourly horseback rides on the weekends, I guess we'll need more help."

"Good, because I have a friend who might be interested. He's about your—"

"Roarke! Where the hell are you?"

Halfway down the straw-covered aisle flanked by dark stalls,

Dane glanced over his shoulder and met Tomas's wide-eyed, anxious stare. "It's Señor Thorne!" the boy whispered. "You'd better go. I'll take care of the horses," he rushed on when Dane hesitated, frowning.

"He can wait another—"

Tomas's expression turned beseeching. "If he sees you helping me with the horses, he'll think I'm not doing my job. *Por favor, señor.* You *have* to go."

After wavering another moment, Dane reluctantly handed over the reins, then turned and started toward the entrance to the stable as Crandall appeared, his nostrils flaring with displeasure—from the stench of the animals or from having to search for Dane, he couldn't be sure.

Either way, it gave Dane a surge of perverse satisfaction. As far as he was concerned, any man who was tyrannical enough to cause a fifteen-year-old kid to quake in his boots deserved to have his nose rubbed in a little horse dung.

"There you are," Crandall growled as Dane approached. "We've been waiting for you back at the house. We didn't expect Miss Washington to return without you."

"Yeah, well, she was in a bit of a hurry," Dane drawled.

The old man's eyes narrowed suspiciously on his face. "What did you do to her?"

Dane let out a choked laugh. "That's the second time in ten minutes someone has asked me that question. If I didn't know better, I would think y'all didn't trust me."

Crandall scowled. "I *don't* trust you, Roarke. Not where beautiful young women are concerned."

"Touché," Dane quipped, brushing past him on his way out of the stable. "Then I suppose I should thank you for letting me go riding alone with Miss Washington."

"I didn't *let* you," Crandall sourly reminded him. "I got suckered into it by that matchmaking busybody housekeeper of mine. Damn meddlin' woman."

"Hey, that's no way to talk about Ms. Rita. Besides, it's not *her* fault you can't say no to her."

"I say no plenty of times," Crandall grumbled, but without much conviction. "Anyway, Gloria's here with your cake. So I guess that means you can hit the road."

Dane arched an amused eyebrow. "In a hurry to get rid of me?"

Crandall looked him square in the eye. "Let's get something straight, Roarke. I like you well enough—"

Dane snorted rudely. "Coulda fooled me."

Crandall pinned him with a look that had undoubtedly made jurors quake in their chairs. "Solange Washington left her home and everything she knew to come work for me. That means I have a vested interest in her welfare. If you think I'm going to stand by and watch you amuse yourself with her until something prettier and shinier comes along, think again."

Dane held his hostile stare for a prolonged moment, then chuckled softly. "Relax, Thorne. Even if I had less-than-honorable intentions toward Miss Washington, she made it perfectly clear she's not interested."

Crandall gave a brisk, satisfied nod. "Good. Then she's even smarter than I thought."

"Yeah, she is." Reliving the explosive kiss he and Solange had shared, Dane muttered under his breath, "One of us had to be."

Long after Dane left the ranch and returned to the single-story bungalow he'd been renting from his cousin for the past year, his mind kept replaying the conversation with Thorne. He supposed he couldn't really blame the old man for behaving like a pushy, overprotective father. If he had even an inkling of just how badly Dane wanted Solange, he'd probably ban him from his property or get a restraining order.

As much as it killed him to admit it, Dane knew Thorne was right about him. Although he wanted nothing more than to make love to Solange, to possess her body in a way neither of them would ever forget, he had no intention of getting serious about her. Not because there was anything wrong with her. On the contrary. She was smart, beautiful, funny and sexy as hell, the kind of woman that could, without even trying, make a man lose his damn mind. God knows he'd already lost more than a few precious hours of sleep thinking about her, fantasizing about her, imagining their naked, sweaty limbs entwined in his bed. Kissing her had only fueled his craving, making him want her the way an alcoholic craved his next drink.

But he couldn't have her, because even if he'd wanted more than a sexual relationship with her, and even if there was the slightest chance of her dumping her boyfriend in favor of him, he wasn't sure he could let go of his personal demons in order to let her inside, to trust her completely. He knew what it was like to trust the wrong woman, to let down his guard only to be betrayed in the worst imaginable way.

It wasn't an experience he cared to repeat.

Dane frowned, peeling off his turtleneck and kicking off his jeans as he headed into the bathroom to take a shower. It was the third time in less than a week he'd found himself reliving the devastating circumstances that had led to his abrupt departure from the FBI.

And this time, as he twisted on the shower faucet and stepped into the glass-encased stall, he let the old, painful memories flow as freely as the hot water that sluiced down his body.

He'd joined the Bureau right out of college and spent the next fourteen years working hard to ensure no one ever questioned his right to be there. He'd served on various task forces and had been instrumental in the capture of several Wanted fugitives. Although he'd resented the bureaucratic wrangling that often made it difficult for agents to do their jobs, and had been told by more than one supervisory special agent that he had problems with authority, Dane had enjoyed his work and looked forward to a long, fulfilling career with the Bureau.

When he was asked to serve on a task force investigating a local crime syndicate suspected of committing sports bribery, Dane never imagined that he, along with his partner, Stan Rupert, would become the targets of the investigation.

The task force was headed by Rosalind McCray, a senior agent who'd recently been transferred to the Philadelphia field office from Chicago. Tough, beautiful, intelligent, with a sharp-witted sense of humor that had helped her to survive in the male-dominated agency, Rosalind was a breath of fresh air. She and Dane, as the only African-Americans assigned to the investigation, had hit it off immediately.

Late one night, long after the other members of the task force had packed it up and gone home, Dane and Rosalind had found themselves alone in the old warehouse that served as the group's base of operations. Over greasy slices of takeout pizza and stale beer, they'd talked about everything from their families to career aspirations. Rosalind told him in no uncertain terms that her top priority, next to catching bad guys, was climbing the ranks in the Bureau, for which she made no apologies. Dane had raised his bottle in a mock toast to her, and she'd laughed. The next thing he knew, they were kissing and groping each other. His staunch rule against dating colleagues had crumbled like a cracker the moment her blouse came off. They'd made love that night, and although they both regretted crossing the line afterward, it wasn't long before they wound up in bed again.

Over the next several months, Dane had wined and dined her, and because she claimed to share his love for sports, he'd surprised her with courtside tickets to NBA basketball games, courtesy of the home team's star player, who happened to be an old college buddy of Dane's.

He had no way of knowing that such an innocent gesture on his part would someday come back to haunt him.

When the sports-bribery indictments came down on several bookies and members of a notorious crime syndicate who had conspired with two basketball players to shave points in a series of playoff games, Dane was stunned to learn of his partner's involvement in the illegal scheme. He was even more shocked to find himself being interrogated by Rosalind, who claimed to have incontrovertible proof of his guilt. The so-called evidence, as it turned out, had been planted by his partner in an effort to cover his own tracks. Doctored phone and audio recordings, manipulated computer data, falsified eyewitness statements—you name it, Stan Rupert had thought of it.

It had taken an intense series of Justice Department hearings, and months of having to endure the scrutiny and suspicion of his colleagues and the media, before Dane's name was finally cleared.

But by then it was too late. The damage had already been done. Not just to his career and reputation, but to his personal life as well, namely his relationship with Rosalind. Even if he could have forgiven her for her complete lack of faith in him, the fact that she'd suspected him of criminal conduct for months and had continued sleeping with him while secretly building a case against him was more than he could stomach. As far as he was concerned, any woman capable of that level of deception was nothing but poison. Although Rosalind had apologized profusely, wept and begged his forgiveness, Dane had not relented. Even the sight of her on her hands and knees—an astonishing act from such a proud, fiercely independent woman—had failed to keep him from walking out the door and never looking back.

While in federal custody, Stan Rupert, overcome with guilt for trying to frame his former partner, had taken his own life. His rambling letter of apology to Dane arrived on the day of his funeral.

Dane was too numb to curse, or mourn, the man he'd once considered a close friend.

But Rupert's death was the straw that finally broke his back.

One day he was receiving job-promotion offers from the contrite management, the next day he strolled into his supervisor's office and handed in his letter of resignation, then simply walked away from his life as an FBI agent.

In the two years since, whenever he allowed himself to reflect upon all that had happened, Dane realized that what bothered him the most—even more than his partner's treachery or the loss of his job—was Rosalind's betrayal. Not because he'd loved her or hoped to have a future with her, but because he'd trusted her, and in his book, once trust was violated, it could never be restored.

Frowning darkly at the thought, Dane shut off the water and stepped from the shower. As he reached for a large bath towel, the phone in his bedroom rang. Grabbing the towel and wrapping it around his waist, he left the bathroom and crossed to the night-stand as the phone trilled a third time.

He couldn't help but smile at the number displayed on the caller-ID screen. Lifting the receiver, he said, "Hey, Aunt Pam."

There was a startled pause on the other end, followed by Pamela Hubbard's warm, familiar laughter. "No matter how many times you do that to me, boy, I'm always caught off guard."

Dane chuckled. "How're you doing, Aunt Pam?"

"I'm doing just fine. Of course, I'll be even better if you tell me you're on your way over for brunch."

He smiled. "I'm on my way over for brunch," he said, though he couldn't fathom eating another large meal after stuffing himself on Rita's big country breakfast that morning. But no way was he telling his aunt, who'd always been like a second mother to him, that he'd cheated on her with another woman's cooking.

"Wonderful!" she exclaimed. "The gang's already here. Daniela, Riley, Janie and Lourdes are helping me put the finishing touches on the meal, and Caleb, Noah, Kenneth and Kenny Junior are waiting on you to play basketball. Everyone would have been so disappointed if you couldn't make it again."

Dane held the phone away from his ear and grinned at it. No one did emotional blackmail better than Aunt Pam. Well, except maybe his own mother. And his cousin Daniela. Not to mention Veronica, his passive-aggressive sister-in-law. Hell, it seemed every woman in his life had it down to an art form.

His grin widened at the thought. "Don't worry, Aunt Pam," he said, returning the receiver to his ear. "I'll definitely be there. And I'll even bring dessert."

Chapter 13

At seven o'clock the next morning, Solange was summoned to Crandall's library, where he'd apparently been up for hours poring over a stack of legal briefs, a half-empty mug of black coffee cooling on a corner of the cluttered desk.

She'd barely uttered a word of greeting before he told her she would be attending an Alamo City Chamber of Commerce meeting that morning, where a state senator named Richard Allen Vance would be speaking.

"He's running for reelection next year," Crandall informed her without lifting his head from his paperwork. "He's been criticized for not doing more for poor blacks in his district. I want you to attend the meeting on my behalf and report back to me on what he has to say."

Solange nodded. "What time does the meeting begin?"

"Eight-thirty. Which gives you an hour and a half to get ready and make the drive into town. Here's the address and directions to the convention center." As she approached the desk, he peered at her over the wireless rim of his glasses, openly dissecting her beige V-neck sweater and gray wool slacks. "Is that what you plan to wear?"

The way he said it made it clear he expected her to change

into more appropriate attire. "I, uh…I'll find something else," Solange said before backing quickly out of the room.

She dressed in ten minutes flat, donning one of the best business suits she owned, a navy blue number with a fitted high-cut jacket and a pencil skirt with a modest slit up the back. She shoved her feet into a pair of matching pumps and hurried from the house before she could be subjected to another inspection.

The Alamo City Chamber of Commerce was an African-American organization that had been founded to provide, encourage and promote programs that contributed to the economic growth and development of minority and small businesses throughout San Antonio. In addition to a monthly meeting, they sponsored an annual leadership institute and were planning to launch a youth entrepreneurship program in the near future.

Their meetings were held at the Henry B. Gonzalez Convention Center in downtown San Antonio. Even with the detailed directions Crandall had provided, Solange still managed to get lost. The downtown *she* was used to consisted of one main street that boasted a sprinkling of tiny shops and eateries, while downtown San Antonio was much larger—a labyrinth of meandering streets lined with historic buildings and Spanish colonial missions, old whitewashed structures that sat empty, Mexican restaurants on every corner and lushly manicured parks. It was a colorful maze that bustled with morning commuters and early-bird tourists aboard red-and-green streetcars.

By the time she found the convention center, located on the famed Riverwalk, and pulled into the parking garage, she had seven minutes remaining before she'd be late. Bypassing the old elevator, she sprinted up the stairs and hurried through the large building in search of the right conference room.

When she reached her destination, she was relieved to find people talking and milling about, while others helped themselves to coffee, fruit and breakfast pastries arranged on a table in the back of the room.

With a small sigh of relief, Solange made her way over to the table and poured herself a cup of pulpy orange juice. While she munched on a raspberry Danish, she surveyed the roomful of strangers. Although most were dressed in business attire, she noticed that a few attendees wore jeans, T-shirts and sneakers.

No one's looking down their nose at them, she thought, still somewhat irked that Crandall had made her change before she left the house. If he intended to hassle her about her clothes every time he asked her to go somewhere, she'd have to splurge on a brand-new wardrobe with her first paycheck, which hadn't been in her plans.

Something told her when it came to dealing with her new employer, she'd have to get used to doing *a lot* of things that weren't in her plans.

At that moment, her gaze was drawn to the door, where a handsome man in his midforties, with skin the color of almonds and neatly cropped hair dusted with gray at the temples, had entered. She knew by the expensive cut of his dark suit and the small entourage that accompanied him as he strode purposefully into the room that he must be Senator Richard Allen Vance, the guest speaker.

A hushed silence swept through the room as conversations came to an abrupt halt and people headed quickly to their seats. Balancing her cup of orange juice and a notepad, Solange made her way toward the front and claimed an empty chair in the fourth row.

"Is this seat taken?" inquired a deep, masculine voice. A voice that had echoed through her dreams all night long, joined by images so carnal she'd awakened more than once drenched in perspiration and panting for breath.

Solange glanced up sharply. Her heart thudded at the sight of Dane Roarke standing there in a double-breasted navy blue suit with a crisp ivory shirt and a blue-and-burgundy-striped silk tie. He looked so incredible, so powerfully male, that Solange could only stare at him in awestruck silence.

That sensuous mouth twitched. "I'll take that as a no," he murmured, and before she could react, he lowered himself into the chair beside her. As he did, his warm, hard-muscled thigh brushed hers, sending a rush of tingling heat through her entire body. She jerked away as if she'd accidentally touched a hot burner.

"W-what are you doing here?" she demanded in a tone that inadvertently accused him of following her.

Dane chuckled, low and soft. "Same thing you're doing. I came to hear the senator speak."

Of course. It was a free country. He had just as much right to be there as she did. She'd have to be a paranoid idiot to imply otherwise. "Are you a member of the Alamo City Chamber of Commerce?"

"Roarke Investigations is. My cousins and I take turns attending the monthly meetings. Guess I drew the lucky straw this time." He smiled at her, slow and sexy, and her pulse accelerated. "What about you?"

"I'm here on Mr. Thorne's behalf."

Dane nodded. His lazy gaze ran the length of her, lingering for a moment on her tightly crossed legs sheathed in sheer nylon, before returning to her face. "Look at that," he said huskily. "We're wearing the same color. We must have read each other's minds this morning."

When her nipples puckered against her lace bra, Solange blamed it on the air-conditioning, and not on the way his dark, heavy-lidded eyes and hypnotic voice were wreaking havoc on her nerve endings.

"Maybe you should sit somewhere else," she lightly suggested. "That's what women usually do when they show up at a party wearing the same dress—they stay as far away from each other as possible."

Humor tugged at the corners of his mouth. "Nice try," he drawled, leaning back in his chair and stretching out his legs. "But I think I'll take my chances and stay put. Besides, the place appears to be filling up pretty fast."

A quick glance around the room showed Solange there were still several empty seats left. She considered pointing this out to him, but before she could open her mouth, a man approached the podium at the front to introduce the guest speaker.

Over the next two hours, Senator Richard Allen Vance eloquently discussed his views on the state of the black community in San Antonio and shared his vision for urban revitalization, education reform and economic development in low-income areas of his district. Although Solange diligently took notes, she found it difficult to concentrate on anything beyond Dane's nearness. His clean-scented male warmth surrounded her, teasing and tantalizing her senses. His long, muscular legs were stretched out before him, and every so often he'd shift in his chair, adjusting his position. Once, when his knee accidentally brushed hers, Solange stiffened as her nipples hardened and liquid heat erupted in her belly, trailing a searing path through her veins.

Dane's eyes met hers. *Sorry,* he mouthed.

Solange nodded wordlessly, not trusting her voice. Their eyes held for a prolonged moment before she forced herself to return her attention to the podium.

After the senator finished speaking, he fielded questions from members of the audience, many of whom were downright confrontational.

"When you first ran for the Texas Senate seven years ago, you made some of the same promises we just heard," said one middle-aged black woman. "Why should we believe you'll keep any of those promises once reelected, when you've failed to do so for the past seven years?"

Over half of the room began clapping and murmuring in hearty agreement.

Dane leaned close to Solange and whispered, "Tough crowd."

She grinned at him, though she couldn't help feeling a twinge of sympathy for the senator, who wore a brave smile on his face as he waited for the noise to die down.

Clearing his throat, he said quietly but firmly, "Thank you for your honesty, ma'am. As you might imagine, it distresses me to hear that so many of you believe I haven't fulfilled my duties to the constituents of my district. If you look at my legislative record, however, you will see that many of the issues I have voted in favor of have greatly benefited the small-business community, Texas schoolchildren, senior citizens, those in the health-care industry and many others. Let me assure you that my work in the Senate isn't finished. There's still much work to be done, and with your continued patience and support, I truly believe we can make our district one of the best in the state."

This time it was Solange who leaned over to whisper in Dane's ear. "Spoken like a true politician."

He chuckled softly and winked at her, and they shared a con-spiratorial smile.

Senator Vance announced that he had another speaking engage-ment, for which he apologized profusely, and encouraged everyone to contact his office with additional questions or concerns. A few attendees weren't to be put off so easily, detaining him even as he tried to edge out the door with his staffers in tow.

Solange, who'd returned to the refreshment table to snag another raspberry Danish, watched in amusement as the senator tried, as discreetly as possible, to extricate himself from the growing crowd without offending anyone. His senior aide, whoever he or she was, deserved to be fired, Solange mused.

A moment later, the smile froze on her lips when she glanced across the room and saw Dane talking to a beautiful brown-skinned woman in a tailored forest-green skirt suit that accentu-ated her curvy build and long, shapely legs.

Solange frowned. One minute Dane had been laughing and conversing with a group of older businessmen—not that she'd been tracking his movements or anything—and the next minute he was flirting shamelessly with a woman who would, in all like-lihood, become his newest conquest.

Not that the so-called victim seemed to mind.

As Solange watched, the woman laid a familiar hand upon his arm and smiled up at him as if he were the last man on earth. Solange supposed she couldn't really blame her. Dane cut quite a dashing figure in his double-breasted Italian suit. Who was she kidding? He was wearing the *hell* out of that suit. But then again, Dane Roarke could wear the hell out of a burlap sack.

As Solange stood there watching him and the woman engage

in their little mating dance, the Danish and a half she'd eaten turned to a wad of dough in her stomach. She carefully wrapped the remainder in a napkin, tossed it in the trash along with her empty cup and started quickly from the room. Several men gave her interested smiles as she passed, but all she cared about was making her escape.

As she neared the exit, she heard Dane call out, "Solange, wait up!"

She kept walking, pretending not to hear him above the noisy drone of conversations. She hurried through the door and down the long, carpeted corridor toward the escalator, but it was no use. In no time at all he'd caught up to her with those determined, ground-eating strides of his.

"I didn't hear a fire alarm go off," he said, sounding vaguely amused and not in the least out of breath, which only increased her annoyance. He could at least have the courtesy to *sound* winded after chasing her down the hallway.

She shot him an impatient look. "I'm kind of in a hur—"

Dane reached out, gently grasping her elbow and halting her steps. A pair of dark, penetrating eyes searched hers. "So you were going to leave without saying goodbye?" he asked softly.

Solange bristled, her chin lifting in haughty defiance. "What difference does it make? You seemed to have your hands full." The moment the caustic words left her mouth, she knew she'd made a big mistake. She'd come off sounding like a scorned lover, jealous because he'd been paying more attention to another woman. Which was ridiculous. She had no right to be jealous when she'd made it perfectly clear to him yesterday that she had no interest in dating him.

Judging by the knowing gleam that filled Dane's eyes, he thought the same thing. Solange waited in silent dread for him to point out her own hypocrisy, but to her immense relief, he merely smiled—a soft, relaxed smile that hinted at something wicked.

"Have lunch with me," he murmured.

Her traitorous heart gave an involuntary leap. Swallowing hard, she shook her head quickly. "I—I can't. I need to get back to the ranch before noon." Not that she'd been given such a directive, but surely Crandall would expect her back from the meeting within a reasonable time frame.

"And besides," she added for good measure, "it's too early for lunch. It's barely eleven o'clock."

Dane chuckled softly. "By the time we settle on a place to eat and get a table, it'll be eleven-thirty. Does that work better for you?"

Again she shook her head, though not as quickly as before. "I really can't, Dane."

"Why not? Not even Thorne is tyrannical enough to prevent his employees from taking a lunch break. And don't tell me you're not hungry," he added, his eyes twinkling with mirth. "I saw you go back for a second Danish back there."

Solange couldn't help but chuckle self-consciously. "I didn't have much of an appetite at dinner last night. And didn't your mother ever teach you that it's impolite to make fun of a woman pigging out on pastries?"

Dane grinned. "Let me take you to lunch. I bet you haven't even had a chance to visit the Riverwalk yet."

"Well, no—" she hedged.

"Good. No better time than the present."

Without giving her another chance to refuse, Dane took her hand and led her down the escalator. Solange was so busy trying not to think about how perfectly their palms fit together, or how good his warm, calloused skin felt against hers, that it didn't occur to her to pull away.

They left the building through a side door that led them directly to the Riverwalk, a beautifully landscaped waterside promenade that ran below street level.

Lapsing into companionable silence, they joined a flow of tourists and locals as they strolled past lush vegetation and towering palms that lined the banks, along with sidewalk cafés, galleries, clubs, luxury high-rise hotels, restaurants, shops and boutiques that featured a colorful array of Mexican-made imports, art and clothing. Holiday lights dangled from building rooftops and a canopy of cypress, oak and willow trees.

As they followed the meandering path along the river, the sounds of an acoustic guitar and companion cello could be heard from the open doorway of a restaurant. And then, just a few steps later, the dueling guitars of native mariachis filled the warm afternoon air with the festive culture for which the city was celebrated.

Dane glanced over at her. "What do you think?"

"It's beautiful," Solange breathed, taking in her surroundings with a rapt expression. None of the glossy travel brochures she'd been given when she checked into the Alamo City Inn did the place justice. Standing there, soaking up its lush, scenic beauty, she could see why the Riverwalk was the number one tourist destination in the state of Texas.

Solange slowed to watch as a brightly colored water taxi filled with tourists drifted lazily down the canal of the San Antonio River. Several people waved and called friendly greetings; smiling, she lifted her hand and waved back.

That was when she realized Dane had never released her other hand.

Oddly enough, she was in no hurry to get it back.

"You ready to eat?" he asked, looking at her.

She nodded, still smiling. "Lead the way."

He took her to an upscale restaurant named Boudro's. At his request, they were seated outdoors at a cozy table nestled along the river. As Solange picked up a menu, she tried not to think about how incredibly romantic the setting was, how perfect for a first date.

We are not *on a date,* she told herself emphatically. *We're just two casual acquaintances having lunch on a nice winter afternoon.*

"What do you recommend?" she asked Dane when the waiter materialized to take their orders.

"Everything's good," he said. "But since this is your first visit, I highly recommend the *empanada langosta.* You won't be disappointed."

Solange had to admit that the pan-seared lobster tail on a spinach and pepper jack cheese empanada *did* sound delicious. "Then that's what I'll have," she said decisively, closing her menu and passing it to the smiling waiter.

"Make that two," Dane told him, adding a guacamole appetizer and two prickly-pear margaritas to the order.

When the waiter left, Dane grinned across the table at her. "So you *do* trust me. I'm touched."

She smiled. "Don't get carried away. Only when it comes to recommending good food." *But certainly not when it comes to my heart.* She narrowed her eyes at him. "Are you trying to get me drunk already?"

"Maybe," he said with a teasing wink. "Seriously though, you can't eat at Boudro's without having one of their margaritas, or the guacamole appetizer. Wait till you try it."

Solange's stomach rumbled in anticipation. Digging her cell phone out of her purse, she said, "I think I'll call Mr. Thorne just to let him know I'm having lunch before heading back to the ranch."

A sardonic smile tilted the corners of Dane's mouth. "Isn't he lucky to have such a conscientious employee," he drawled, leaning back in his chair.

Solange poked her tongue out at him, to which he responded by throwing back his head and laughing.

At that moment, the phone was answered on the other end. "Hi, Ms. Rita," Solange said quickly. "I'm sorry—I thought I was calling Mr. Thorne's business line."

"You did, baby, but most of his calls are automatically routed to the main line. Did you need something?"

"No, not really. I just wanted to let him know that I decided to have lunch after the meeting, and I should be back by one-thirty."

"Oh, baby, you didn't have to check in!" Rita said with a laugh. "You take as much time as you need. Shoot, Crandall's not even home. He said he had several appointments in town and wouldn't be back until late afternoon."

"Really?" Solange couldn't help feeling a twinge of relief. She'd definitely make it back to the ranch long before he returned. "Did he leave any special instructions for me?"

"Not that I know of. He did tell me that the meeting you attended this morning was at the convention center. Are you having lunch on the Riverwalk?"

"Yes, ma'am. It's absolutely gorgeous here."

"It sure is. I'm glad you had a chance to see it for yourself."

"Me, too."

"Well, don't let me keep you from your lunch, baby. See you in a little while."

"Thank you, Ms. Rita."

"Of course. Oh, and before I forget." There was an amused, knowing smile in Rita's voice. "Tell Dane I said hello."

Heat suffused Solange's cheeks. Her eyes flew to Dane, who was already watching her—specifically her mouth—with a hot, heavy-lidded gaze that made her loins ache. *Good Lord.* There should be laws prohibiting a man from looking at a woman like that, she thought, especially when the man in question was as fine as Dane Roarke.

"Uh, y-yes, ma'am, I'll tell him," Solange stammered into the phone before flipping it shut and stuffing it back inside her purse.

"Ms. Rita says hello," she mumbled, crossing her legs tightly under the table.

Slowly those long-lashed eyes lifted to hers. "She must have heard me laughing. Hope I didn't get you in trouble."

"Not at all." The only kind of trouble Solange was in had nothing whatsoever to do with Rita Owens.

Fortunately, at that precise moment, the waiter returned with their drinks and guacamole appetizer, which he proceeded to prepare right at the table.

Welcoming the distraction, Solange watched in mild fascination as he deftly sliced and combined avocado, onions, cilantro, lime, tomatoes and seasonings in a large bowl. He'd barely left the table before she was reaching for a hot, crispy tortilla chip to sample the dip.

As the zesty, delicious flavor exploded in her mouth, she closed her eyes in languorous pleasure. "Mmmm," she moaned. "Ohhh, that *is* good, Dane. You were so right."

"Glad to hear it." His deep voice sounded rough, tight.

Opening her eyes, Solange saw him staring at her with a look of such raw hunger her cheeks felt scalded. Averting her gaze, she reached for another chip, keeping her pleasure to herself the second time around.

Dane took a long sip of his margarita, then removed his suit jacket and draped it across the back of his chair before helping himself to the guacamole.

Solange watched him beneath her lashes, remembering how his magnificently sculpted bare chest looked underneath the white broadcloth shirt, reliving the feel of granite-smooth flesh beneath her exploring hands. Since yesterday, she'd been trying her damnedest to forget about the hot, mind-blowing kiss they'd shared on the mountain ridge, but it was no use. The kiss had remained lodged in her memory, haunting her throughout the evening so that she'd scarcely touched her dinner, and later, fueling the most vividly erotic dreams she'd ever had in her life.

Almost as shocking as the kiss itself was the realization that if Dane kissed her again, she wouldn't be able to stop him.

Which was what made her decision to have lunch with him the epitome of insanity. The more time she spent with him, the harder it became to resist her attraction to him. She'd had enough trouble keeping her eyes and hands to herself during the meeting earlier. Every time his knee accidentally brushed hers, her body had reacted as if he'd reached beneath her skirt with one hand and sensuously stroked and caressed her inner thighs. Heaven knows she'd wanted him to touch her that way—and a whole lot of other ways.

"I wouldn't recommend that."

The low, dangerous timbre of Dane's voice snapped her to attention. Confused, she blinked at him. "What?"

He sat forward slowly, his dark, piercing eyes intent upon her face. "I wouldn't recommend that you continue staring at me the way you've been doing for the last three minutes," he said huskily. "I'm a gentleman, Solange, but every gentleman has his breaking point. If you knew how close I am to reaching mine, you'd probably get up and run from this table."

Oh, God. Beneath the table, Solange's knees trembled hard. Ducking her head, she drew in a long, deep breath and willed her heart rate to slow down.

This is crazy. What on earth am I doing here?

Thankfully, the arrival of their meals spared her from answering her own question. As the waiter set their plates on the table with an elaborate flourish, she assiduously avoided eye contact with Dane, afraid he'd see not only desire reflected in her eyes, but honest-to-goodness fear. She was playing with fire, and if she didn't tread cautiously, she was going to get seriously burned.

As they began eating, she cast about for safe conversational territory. "Do you come here often?"

"To Boudro's or the Riverwalk?"

"Both."

"I've only been to the restaurant a few times," Dane replied, "but I can't count the number of times I've been to the Riverwalk. Like I mentioned to you before, my family visited San Antonio every summer and every other Christmas when I was growing up."

Solange nodded, swallowing a succulent bite of lobster tail. "Are either of your parents originally from San Antonio?"

"My dad. He moved to Houston to attend college and decided to stay after he met my mother. As much as she loved him, she couldn't bear the thought of parting with her family, and he couldn't bear the thought of parting with her."

Solange smiled. "How romantic. And how did *his* family feel about his decision to stay in Houston?"

Dane chuckled softly. "They weren't too thrilled about it, but they came around eventually. Guess they realized it wasn't worth starting a family feud over, when he'd only be living two and a half hours away."

"Wise people."

"That, and they knew he'd do whatever he wanted, anyway. My father has always marched to the beat of his own drum."

"Something tells me the apple doesn't fall too far from the tree," Solange said teasingly.

Dane's lips curved in a slow grin. "Let's keep that our little secret. How's your food?"

"Excellent." She picked up her drink and took a long, appreciative sip. As she set down the glass, she smiled at him. "You're batting three for three. The margarita's just as good as you said it would be. I'm beginning to think I can trust you with other things. What do you know about stocks and bonds?"

Dane laughed, forking up a bite of lobster. "If you really want to know about investments, you should talk to my cousin Daniela. She used to be an accountant and the bookkeeper for Roarke Investigations, and at one time or another she also did some freelancing as a financial advisor. She really knows her stuff."

Solange nodded, smiling. "A woman of many talents. Isn't she also the one who redecorated the guest wing at the ranch?"

"Yep. That's her."

"Does she still work at the detective agency?"

Dane shook his head. "She graduated from law school in May and, up until a week ago when she went on maternity leave, she'd been working as a junior associate at Crandall's law firm, trying to gain some litigation experience. She and her husband, Caleb, plan to open a family-law practice within the next three years, when the baby's a little older."

"Really?" Solange brightened. "Maybe when I finish law school, they'd consider hiring me."

Dane eyed her speculatively over the rim of his glass. "You interested in practicing law?"

She nodded vigorously. "I've always wanted to, but there never seemed to be a right time to apply for law school, and before my parents passed away, I'd never seriously considered leaving Haskell. Money was also a factor. As you know, law school can be pretty expensive."

He frowned. "You worked for a law firm. Didn't they offer tuition reimbursement?"

"Unfortunately, no. And, again, I would've had to leave home to attend law school, which wasn't really an option for me. Not with my parents getting on in years and needing my help more and more around the farm." She paused to watch as a river taxi full of passengers floated by, leaving gentle ripples in the murky water. "You know, three months before they died, my mother made me promise her that I wouldn't get stuck in Haskell for the rest of my life, that I'd travel and see the world and follow my dreams wherever they took me. It was so unexpected—she'd never said anything like that to me before. And yet I didn't remember it until after I'd arrived in San Antonio, when I was having serious doubts about my decision to leave home, and her voice came back to me with those words." Turning her head, she smiled faintly at Dane. "Isn't it funny how the mind works, suppressing certain memories until just the right time?"

He was watching her with a quiet smile of understanding. "I think it's a gift from God."

"Oh, it was. Most definitely." With a long, deep sigh, she swept an appreciative glance around. "And speaking of gifts, the Riverwalk is a dream. I love it here."

"It's pretty at night, too. Especially during the holiday season when they put up the big tree at the Alamo. You should come back one of these nights to see the whole place lit up with all the Christmas lights."

"It sounds pretty amazing," Solange said, adding ruefully, "I don't know when I'll have another chance to get back down here, though. I think Mr. Thorne is going to keep me too busy for sightseeing."

"In that case," Dane drawled, his eyes glinting with amusement and something else—something that should have set off a warning bell in her head, "we'd better make the most of your time here today."

Chapter 14

Over the next hour, they laughed and talked about anything and everything, surprised to discover how much they had in common—from favorite mystery novels to their least favorite movies, to their views on religion, war and politics. Dane regaled Solange with hilarious anecdotes of hanging out at the Riverwalk with his older brother and cousins as they tried unsuccessfully to pick up girls; she, in turn, shared stories about growing up in a rural community where the highlight of many teenagers' lives was going cow-tipping in the dead of night, which, to her everlasting shame, was *not* just an urban legend perpetuated by city slickers. Dane laughed so hard tears rolled from the corners of his eyes.

Even after their lunch plates and empty glasses had been cleared away, they lingered, polishing off the chips and guacamole as a way of prolonging not only the meal, but their time together.

When they finally left the restaurant, they strolled along the bank, walking so close together the sides of their legs brushed. Instead of heading straight to the garage where they were both parked, they made a detour, slipping inside a tiny candy shop filled with the delicious aromas of chocolate-covered confections. Ignoring her protests, Dane bought Solange half a pound of Belgian fudge, which she laughingly promised to share with Rita, a fellow chocoholic.

As they left the shop, Solange was already unwrapping and sampling the decadently rich fudge. "Oh my God," she breathed, slowing to a stop.

Dane chuckled softly. "That good, huh?"

She nodded, turning to him. "You *have* to try this."

He leaned down to accept the sweet offering from her hand. As his warm, silken mouth closed around her fingertips, heat pooled between her legs. A soft, startled gasp escaped her lips.

Her heart thundered at the very male look that filled his eyes as their gazes locked. Slowly he ran his tongue over her fingers, gently, deliberately sucking the chocolate into his mouth. She shivered uncontrollably, her breasts swelling against the lace confines of her bra.

All too soon he pulled away. "You're right," he murmured silkily. "That is good."

Ensnared by the smoldering heat of his gaze, Solange drew her fingers into her own mouth and tasted him, watching his nostrils flare and his eyes turn molten with desire.

"Solange." Her name emerged as a low, husky growl.

She felt flushed and wanton, unbearably tempted to surrender to him, to give him anything he asked of her.

Her breath caught sharply as he lowered his head, slanting his sensuous mouth over hers. Her lips parted on a soundless moan. But instead of kissing her, he let their breath mingle warmly, provocatively. Heightening her arousal.

What happened next was a heady blur.

One minute they were standing in the middle of the busy sidewalk outside the candy shop; the next thing she knew, they were checking into a room at the nearest hotel along the river. Dane didn't so much as bat an eye at the steep one-night room rate he was quoted, handing the desk clerk a credit card without averting his hungry, possessive gaze from Solange.

The elevator doors had barely slid closed behind them before he pulled her into his arms and seized her mouth in a fierce, ravenous kiss that made her moan and cling to him as if her very life depended upon it. She was beyond the point of no return. She didn't care that what they were doing was pure insanity, and something she would probably regret later. All that mattered was that she needed him, wanted him like nothing and no one she'd ever wanted before. And she intended to have him.

When they reached the seventh-floor room, Dane kicked the door shut and hauled her against him with rough urgency. Their voracious mouths fused together, tongues frantically mating. They tore at each other's clothing with desperate hands, ripping off suit jackets and yanking at shirt buttons with reckless disregard. Solange quickly stepped out of her pumps and reached beneath her skirt, grasping her panties and the waistband of her panty hose and dragging both down the length of her legs. Dane paused in the middle of unbuckling his belt to watch her with hot, glittering eyes. She could see the thick bulge of his erection outlined against his pants, and it made her grow even wetter than she already was. When she reached out to touch him, however, he captured her wrist and shook his head once.

"Later," he growled, low and savage. "I'm too hungry right now."

Her belly quivered with arousal. Her heart beat a wild tattoo in her chest.

Too impatient to bother removing her snug skirt, Dane wrenched it up over her thighs, then lifted her into his arms and carried her over to the antique cherry dresser. He deposited her on the edge of the cool, smooth surface, which was the perfect height—not too high and not too low.

She leaned back on her elbows and watched in breathless anticipation as he unzipped his pants and quickly sheathed his long, thick erection with a condom he'd removed from his wallet. He shoved her thighs wide apart and stepped between them, lifting and wrapping her quivering legs around his hips. He positioned the blunt tip of his shaft at the sensitized entrance to her body, nudging it against the slick, swollen folds until she had to bite down on her lip to hold back a scream of pleasure.

His dark, searing gaze locked with hers as he gripped her buttocks and drove himself inside her, hard and deep. She cried out sharply and arched her back, clutching his big, muscled shoulders for balance.

He withdrew and thrust again with a harsh, tortured groan. "I knew you'd feel this way," he whispered raggedly. "Like honey and silk."

They rocked and glided together, sighing and moaning with the consuming pleasure of each deep, penetrating thrust. Dane wound his hand through the heavy strands of her hair, tilting her face back and staring into her eyes with an expression of such fierce possession tears stung her eyelids. As she watched, he lowered his head and claimed her mouth in a rough, devouring kiss that left her head spinning.

Closing her eyes, she skated her open mouth along his jaw and tightened her legs around his hips and buttocks, urging him deeper inside. He shouted hoarsely as he lifted her from the dresser and drove into her. His slamming thrusts made her cry out in ecstasy. Every part of her welcomed the erotic invasion of his body. She loved the wet, slapping sounds of contact and the marvelous friction of their coupling.

As an exquisite pressure built inside her, she opened her eyes and stared into his dark, sensual face. She dug her nails into his back and sobbed his name as her body convulsed in the grip of the most powerful orgasm she'd ever experienced. The spasms were so intense she thought she would pass out.

A moment later Dane stiffened and exploded inside her with a loud, exultant groan.

They remained joined for several minutes, his face buried against the curve of her neck, her legs locked around his waist as his thick penis throbbed inside her. She could have stayed like that forever.

At length he set her back onto the dresser and kissed her closed eyelids before raising his head and gazing down at her.

"That definitely took the edge off," he murmured huskily. "What do you say we move to the bed and take this to the next level?"

* * *

Solange clung to Dane as he carried her over to the king-size bed, which was draped in satin, and set her down on her feet. She stared down at him, her dark eyes at half-mast, her luscious lips parted and trembling. Her tousled chestnut-brown hair was backlit by a beam of afternoon sunlight that slanted through an opening in the drawn curtains. She looked like an angel. A seductive, exotically beautiful angel.

Without releasing her gaze, Dane finished undressing himself, removing his pants, underwear, socks and shoes. Her breath quickened audibly as he stood before her, naked and fully aroused. The way her eyes devoured him made him so hard he ached to lay her down and bury himself deep inside her. But he had to go slow this time, pace himself, savor every moment of their lovemaking like it would be their last—because it probably would.

Stepping to the bed again, he reached around her waist and slowly unzipped her skirt, sliding the fabric over the gentle swell of her hips and down her long, curvy legs. His erection throbbed painfully as he stared at the neat triangle of soft dark curls that hid her sex. He eased her legs gently apart and slid his hand upward, his fingertips skimming the sensitive flesh of her inner thighs. Her whole body shook.

"Dane…" she whimpered helplessly.

"Shhh. Let me look at you. You are so damn beautiful."

He could see every detail of her, the way a few golden strands of hair blended with the darker brown, the shadowy cleft of her labia. As she watched, he reached between her silky thighs and cupped her mound. She let out a startled cry. He brushed the pad of his thumb against the slick nub of her clitoris, tracing lazy, sensual circles that made her groan and writhe against him. Her intoxicating scent filled his nostrils, soap and a trace of the exotic perfume she wore mingled with the heady musk of their lovemaking.

With his other hand, he grasped her buttocks and tilted her pelvis closer. His gaze locked with hers as he parted her tender folds and pressed his mouth to her hot, moist sex. She moaned at the erotically intimate kiss, clinging to his shoulders for

support. A jolt of pure, driving need swept through his body.
Cupping her bottom with both hands, he stroked his tongue back
and forth across her plump feminine lips. She was salty-sweet,
slippery and delicious, and he couldn't get enough of her.

He feasted on her until her cries grew more frenzied, her
breath coming in rapid, shallow gasps. When her thighs began
to quake uncontrollably against his hands, he thrust his tongue
inside her one last time, making her scream his name as she came
in a violent rush. As her knees buckled, he banded his arms
around her waist and held her upright, his heart slamming against
his ribcage, his penis throbbing for release. He pressed his face
against her soft belly and closed his eyes, fighting for control.

When her body had stopped trembling and her breathing
quieted, he drew away and looked up at her. "Lie down," he
huskily commanded.

As she moved to comply, he turned away, removing the used
condom and replacing it with a fresh one.

When he turned back to the bed, he found Solange lying on
her side with her head propped in her hand, her lustrous hair
spilling over one shoulder as she watched him with a look of
sultry invitation. It was enough to make him salivate.

"There's just one more thing between us," she said coyly.
And then she reached down and unclasped the front hook of her
bra.

Dane stared, transfixed, as the most beautiful pair of breasts
he had ever seen spilled from the scrap of black lace—firm, perfectly round, with nipples the color of melted chocolate.

With a rough, inarticulate sound, he practically dove into the
bed and stretched out alongside her. She gave a breathless little
laugh as he ran his hands greedily over the deep indentation of
her waist and her ribs, before cupping her breasts in his hands.
He pressed them together and rubbed his face against them in
masculine appreciation. They spilled from his palms—warm,
soft and luscious. Heat sizzled through his veins.

With his eyes trained on hers, he bent to draw one erect nipple
into his mouth. Her breath hitched sharply, and she closed her

eyes on a soft cry. His tongue circled her nipple while he played with the other one, teasing and stroking it into a tight little point. Switching his mouth to her other breast, he pressed the burning length of his shaft against her soft belly. She reached down and wrapped her warm fingers around him, making him groan hoarsely in pleasure.

In a blur of movement, she sat up quickly and knelt at his side. Holding his gaze, she took him deep into her mouth, latex and all, and he sucked in a sharp, ragged breath. She wasn't shy or hesitant, rolling off the condom so she could lick and tease his bare flesh. Lust clawed through him. He rocked his hips and thrust upward into the hot, silken cave of her mouth until he thought he'd explode.

Deciding he'd exercised more than enough restraint for one afternoon, Dane pulled away and rolled her over, onto her stomach. With unsteady hands, he retrieved the condom and smoothed it back into place. As Solange rose on all fours, he cupped the lush roundness of her buttocks, his fingertips probing the hot, moist crevice between her thighs. Her legs parted eagerly as he positioned himself behind her. With one long, penetrating stroke he filled her.

Solange moaned loudly and arched against him, clutching fistfuls of the satin bed linens. Grasping the sides of her waist, Dane thrust high and deep inside her, and her moans grew louder as she gyrated her hips to the beat of his strokes. He plunged harder and faster, the tight, slick clasp of her body sweeping away the last vestiges of his self-control. He wound a fistful of her hair around his hand and pulled back her head, slanting his mouth over hers in a hard, plundering kiss.

A moment later, she cried out as her body clenched around his penis in pulsing contractions, wrenching an orgasm from him that tore through his body with brutal force.

Shuddering and breathing hard, he kissed the sweat-dampened hair at the nape of her neck, then gathered her into his arms and drew them both down onto the bed. With a deep, languorous sigh, Solange snuggled against him for a few moments, then suddenly froze.

Dane groaned in protest as she bolted upright, then launched herself from the bed. "I have to go! Mr. Thorne will be expecting me there when he gets back!"

Dane sat up slowly, propped his weight on his elbows and watched in amusement as she scrambled around the room, gathering her discarded articles of clothing.

"We've got this incredible room for one whole night," he reminded her. "We could have an early dinner, take a romantic stroll along the Riverwalk, then come back here and have each other for dessert. What do you say, Angel Eyes?"

Solange whirled around so fast her breasts bounced enticingly. The look she leveled at him would have shamed a lesser man. "This isn't funny, Dane. I really have to go."

Scowling, he fell back against the pillows and heaved a deep, resigned sigh. "All right."

After another prolonged moment, he swung his long legs over the side of the bed and stood. "I'll walk you back to your car. But don't blame me when you're tucking your sweet little grandchildren into bed one day, and they look up at you with wide, innocent eyes and ask you why you never took the time to see the Riverwalk lit up at Christmastime like a Norman Rockwell painting."

In the middle of tugging on her rumpled skirt, Solange stopped and burst out laughing.

Chapter 15

It was three o'clock by the time Solange returned to the ranch—nearly eight hours after she'd left that morning for the meeting. As she crept into the silent house, she felt like a wayward teenager sneaking in past her curfew, something she'd done often enough while growing up.

"Oh, you're back. How was lunch?"

Solange whirled around, heart in throat, to find Rita standing in the wide entryway leading from the kitchen. Her smile was warm and inquisitive.

Solange swallowed hard. "Um, hi, Ms. Rita. Lunch was good."

"Where did you eat?"

"Boudro's."

"Really? I've never been there before, but I've heard it's a wonderful restaurant."

"It is. You should definitely go sometime." Solange fidgeted nervously. "Is… Has Mr. Thorne returned yet?"

"No, dear." Rita gave her a small, knowing smile. "You beat him back."

Solange tried not to let her relief show. "I, ah, didn't mean to be gone so long."

"That's all right, baby," Rita said with a dismissive wave of her hand. "All you would've been doing around here is hanging out with me and watching soaps. I'm sure you had a much better time with Dane."

You can't even begin to imagine. "H-he's a very nice man," Solange stammered, her face heating at the memory of his fierce, possessive lovemaking. Her nipples still stung from his hungry mouth, and her thighs still ached and burned from the force of his deep, powerful strokes. Just thinking about the way he'd taken her in that hotel room made her feel hot and flushed all over.

"What happened to your shirt, baby?"

Solange glanced down quickly and remembered, too late, that Dane had popped three of her buttons in his haste to undress her. Afterward, she'd been in such a hurry to leave that she'd completely forgotten to fasten her jacket to hide the missing buttons on the silk blouse.

Lifting her head, she stared in stricken silence at Rita, whose dark eyes twinkled with suppressed mirth.

"I brought you something," Solange blurted, thrusting the bag of gourmet fudge at the older woman.

Rita looked pleasantly surprised. "You brought something for me? What is it?"

"Belgian fudge. I remembered you saying how much you like chocolate."

"Oh, that was awfully kind of you, baby," Rita said, stepping forward to accept the gift. "But you really shouldn't have. I'm too old to be indulging in sweets. Besides, you don't have to bribe me." She winked conspiratorially. "Your secret's safe with me."

And while Solange stood there blushing to the roots of her scalp, Rita turned and shuffled back into the kitchen, chuckling as she went.

Thirty minutes later, Solange had just emerged from the shower when her cell phone rang. Wrapping a thick terry-cloth towel around her body and wringing out her wet, freshly shampooed hair, she padded to the counter where she'd plunked down her purse earlier, and dug around for her phone.

She hoped it wasn't Lamar again. He had already called her twice since their last conversation, but she hadn't gotten around to returning his messages. Not because she wanted to spite or punish him; she simply wasn't ready to deal with another marriage proposal. Especially in light of what had just happened between her and Dane.

Locating her phone, she glanced at the unfamiliar number displayed on the screen before pressing the talk button. "Hello?"

"Hey, you," Dane greeted her, the low, husky timbre of his voice pouring heat into her ear.

She felt an answering tingle in the pit of her stomach. "Hi," she said shyly.

"Hi, yourself. I just wanted to make sure you got back safely."

"I did. Thank you for leading me out to I-35. I probably would have gotten lost if you hadn't shown me the way."

"No problem. Was the old man there when you arrived?"

"No, thank goodness."

"Mmm. So that means I could have enjoyed you a little longer."

Oh, God. Solange sank weakly onto the stool in front of the vanity mirror. A fine sheen of perspiration broke out across her skin. She didn't know whether it was caused by the steam from the shower or her elevated body temperature.

"When can I see you again?" Dane asked huskily.

"I don't know." She caught her lower lip between her teeth. "Dane—"

"Don't say it was a mistake," he growled in soft warning. "You know damned well what we shared this afternoon was anything but a mistake."

She closed her eyes, her heart drumming wildly. He was wrong. Of course they'd made a mistake. But, God help her, she couldn't remember another time in her life when making a mistake had felt so good...so perfect.

Eve probably told herself the same thing as she bit into the forbidden fruit.

"You don't belong with him," Dane said in a low voice.

Snapping back to attention, Solange said, "With who?" and immediately wanted to kick herself when Dane chuckled softly.

"My point exactly. You've already forgotten his name."

"I have not! I just… I mean… You and me—" She broke off helplessly. He had her so flustered she didn't know her up from down.

"You and me," Dane murmured. "Mmm. I like the sound of that."

The velvety purr of his deep voice had erotic images stealing through her mind. "I have to go," she said weakly.

"You haven't answered my question."

"Which one?"

"When can I see you again?"

She groaned. "I don't know. Really, I don't. It could be a while. Like I said before, I'm going to be pretty busy."

"All work and no play…"

She laughed. "I know, I know."

"Seriously, though." Dane's voice softened. "I had a great time this afternoon, and I'm not just talking about what happened in the hotel room. I really enjoyed spending time with you, Solange. I can't remember the last time I laughed so much."

She warmed with pleasure, cradling the phone to her ear. "I feel the same way," she admitted. And she did, which scared the hell out of her. Developing feelings for Dane Roarke was not only foolish; it was downright dangerous.

Yet there she was, dancing closer and closer to the seductive flames.

"It's so quiet there," Dane murmured. "Where are you, and what are you doing?"

"I'm in the bathroom," she said, rubbing droplets of water from her arm. "I just got out of the shower."

He made a low, rumbling sound that bordered on a groan. "Don't tease me, woman."

"You asked."

"I know. Next time we're taking a shower together."

Instantly her body grew hot and weak, so sensitive that the mere brush of the towel across her skin aroused her. She didn't even bother challenging his assumption that there would be a next time.

She already knew there would.

"I—I should go," she said abruptly. "Mr. Thorne will probably want to be debriefed on the senator's speech when he gets home."

"All right," Dane said grudgingly. After another moment, he said, "Are you sure I can't talk you into meeting me back at the hotel tonight? You could sneak out when everyone's asleep—"

Solange gave a shaky little laugh. "Nice try. Goodbye, Dane."

No sooner had she hung up the phone than a firm knock sounded on her bedroom door. She quickly rewrapped the towel around her body and hurried out of the bathroom.

"Yes?" she called through the closed door.

"It's me, Solange," Rita answered. "Crandall has returned and would like to see you in his study."

Uh-oh. Solange swallowed as a knot of apprehension fisted in her stomach. Did he know how long she'd been gone that day? Would he take one look at her and figure out what she'd spent the afternoon doing, and with whom?

Would he decide he'd made a mistake by hiring her?

There's only one way to find out. "Please tell Mr. Thorne I'll be there in a few minutes," she said weakly.

Crandall didn't like to be kept waiting.

Others attributed his impatience to an entitlement complex he'd developed because he was a multimillionaire, but Crandall knew better. He'd been this way for as long as he could recall. He remembered being angry as a child when he had to wait too long for dinner, because his mother was off tending to the uppity white family whose house she cleaned and maintained six days a week. And he remembered the seething irritation he'd felt in college when one of his professors had been habitually late to class.

When Crandall began practicing law, he'd made a point of always being on time, whether it was to a meeting with a client or to a court hearing. And when he became successful and wealthy enough to call the shots, he'd vowed never to accept tardiness from any of his employees.

It had been fifteen minutes since he'd sent Rita to fetch Solange.

Where the hell was she?

Just as he rose from his chair to go in search of his wayward granddaughter, the phone on his desk rang. He snatched it up and barked impatiently, "Thorne speaking."

"Well, hello to you too, Crandall," said a coolly amused voice.

His pulse quickened. His hand tightened on the receiver, gripping it as if it were a lifeline. "Good afternoon, Tessa," he said, striving for a calm, measured voice. "To what do I owe the pleasure of this call?"

She hesitated. "I wanted to know if you've learned any more about Solange Washington."

"Not since the last time we spoke," Crandall lied, without an ounce of guilt. "I told you I would keep you informed of any new developments in the investigation."

"I know. I…I just thought I'd call and make sure." There was another pregnant pause, then Tessa blurted, "I want to meet her, Crandall."

He fell silent for a prolonged moment, then said, "I don't think that's such a good idea," though inwardly he was rejoicing. His plan was working!

"Maybe it's not a good idea," Tessa agreed, "but it's what I want."

"It's too risky. What if she takes one look at you and realizes she's seeing a future version of herself? And besides, I thought we decided to wait until my private investigator confirmed her identity before you'd be introduced to her."

"We did, but I've changed my mind. Are you going to allow me to meet her or not, Crandall?"

Instead of answering, he paced to the French doors that overlooked a small courtyard. The stucco walls were covered with a network of brown vines and the black wrought-iron table and chairs were covered with a light film of dust. During the warmer months, he and his son liked to sit outside and play chess, but since getting married, Caleb hadn't had time to visit the ranch as often as he used to.

"Crandall?" Tessa gently prompted.

He heaved a sigh. "What about your husband? If I arrange a meeting between you and Solange, how would you keep it from Hoyt?"

"He's not here. He left this morning for a political convention in Boston. He won't be back until Wednesday."

"How convenient for you," Crandall drawled sardonically. "So while the cat is away, the mouse intends to play. *Tsk, tsk,* Tessa."

She made an impatient sound. "I don't need *you* to berate me for sneaking around behind my husband's back. God knows I feel guilty enough."

"Yet you're willing to do it, anyway."

"Yes." Her tone softened, turned almost imploring. "I want to see my granddaughter, Crandall. You of all people should understand how important this is to me."

He did. For as long as he'd known Tessa, she'd always wanted children. As high-school sweethearts they'd talked about getting married one day and having a brood of their own. The oldest of seven siblings, Tessa couldn't imagine a home that was devoid of the laughter, joy, bickering and running feet of children. When she married Hoyt Philbin, it was with the assumption that he shared her desire for a large family. But Hoyt had other plans. His promising political future took precedence over Tessa's need to become a mother. When she gave birth to Melanie, who was a little too dark-skinned for Hoyt's liking, he'd forced Tessa to give the baby up for adoption, promising her that they'd have other children when his political career was more established. But as the years wore on and he kept putting her off, Tessa began to realize he'd never wanted children in the first place. He'd used his career aspirations—and her own infidelity—as excuses for not keeping his promise to her. By the time some of his closest political advisors convinced him that having a large family would bolster his public image, it was too late. He and Tessa were unable to conceive, and adoption, as far as Hoyt was concerned, was out of the question.

It wouldn't have surprised Crandall in the least to discover that Hoyt had gone behind Tessa's back and gotten a vasectomy. That was the kind of man he was, the kind of scheming, vindictive coward who'd spent years and a small fortune having Crandall investigated for everything from bribery and witness tampering to economic espionage and public corruption. The fact that he'd never been able to substantiate any of these outrageous claims had only fueled his hatred of Crandall and made the two men the bitterest of enemies.

Crandall dreamed of the day Tessa would finally leave the worthless bastard and go where she belonged—with him.

"Tomorrow evening," he pronounced. "You can meet Solange tomorrow evening."

"Where?" Tessa asked.

"Here at the ranch. I'll throw an impromptu dinner party, invite other people so she won't suspect anything."

"All right." A note of apprehension crept into Tessa's voice. "Who are you thinking about inviting?"

His mouth curved cynically. "No one who will report back to your husband that you were here, I assure you." He glanced over his shoulder as a gentle knock sounded on the door. "If you'll excuse me, Tessa, I have another appointment."

"Of course." She paused, then added quietly, "Thank you, Crandall."

He clenched his jaw, his heart constricting painfully. "See you tomorrow night at seven."

As he crossed to the desk and hung up the phone, there was another knock on the door. "Come in," he called.

He stood behind his chair as Solange slowly entered the room. She'd changed into a pistachio-colored velour sweater and crisp khaki slacks over a pair of suede brown loafers. Her hair had been pulled back into a tight bun, but he could still see that it was wet, making it appear darker than usual.

She offered him a tentative smile. "Ms. Rita says you wanted to see me."

"Yes. Have a seat, Miss Washington," he said, gesturing her into one of the visitor chairs. As she sat and crossed her long legs, he deliberately remained standing.

"You washed your hair?" he inquired, arching a brow at her. "In the middle of the afternoon?"

"Um, yeah," she replied, looking slightly self-conscious as she reached up with a slender hand to touch her hair. "I didn't have enough time before I left this morning."

"I see." Lips pursed, Crandall studied her a moment longer, sensing there was more to the story than she'd have him believe. "I wanted to find out how the meeting went this morning. What did Senator Vance discuss?"

He listened as she gave him a brief rundown of the presentation, although the senator's people had already furnished him with a copy of the speech days ago.

"What did you think of him?" he asked when Solange had finished speaking.

A thoughtful frown creased the smooth line of her brow. "I haven't really decided, to be honest with you. At times he seemed sincere enough, but then he'd say something that reminded me why I generally distrust politicians. And I don't think he answered questions from the audience as well, or effectively, as he could have."

Crandall smiled wryly. "You don't think he'll get reelected?"

"Hard to say. More than half the people in the room seemed less than pleased with him, but there were plenty who detained him afterward not only to ask more issue-related questions, but also to inquire about his family and to make small talk. Which leads me to believe he still has a strong, loyal constituent base."

Crandall nodded, pleased by the astute observation. "You're probably right. Did you get a chance to meet him?"

She shook her head. "The line was too long, and he was on his way to another speaking engagement."

"I see."

Hearing the note of disapproval in his voice, Solange gave him a worried look. "Did you want me to meet Senator Vance?"

"It certainly wouldn't have hurt." Choosing his words carefully, he said, "Please keep in mind that when I send you to these functions, Miss Washington, you're representing me and my firm, which means I expect you to behave like a professional at all times and network as much as possible."

She nodded. "Yes, sir. I understand."

"Good. Which brings me to another matter. Your clothing."

"My clothing?"

"Yes." He pulled out his chair and sat, calmly regarding her across the desk. "I realize you had a modest upbringing—"

She bristled, her chin lifting a notch. She was as beautiful as Tessa had ever been, and just as proud.

"—and your previous employer Ted Crumley told me himself he wasn't able to pay you as much as he would've liked. So I understand that you've had to be frugal with your earnings. However, now that you work for me and will be representing me at various functions, it's absolutely imperative that you dress the part, so to speak. That's why I've arranged for my daughter-in-law to accompany you on a little shopping excursion tomorrow."

Solange frowned. "With all due respect, sir, I really can't afford—"

"The clothing allowance is on me." He smiled blandly. "Consider it part of your signing bonus."

"That's awfully kind of you, Mr. Thorne, but I really couldn't—"

Crandall didn't know too many young women who would have balked at being treated to an all-expenses-paid shopping trip. "You really don't have a choice, Miss Washington," he snapped impatiently. "I've already contacted Daniela to make the arrangements, and it's all settled."

Solange opened her mouth, looking like she wanted to offer another protest. After one look at his stern face, however, she wisely reconsidered. "Well, if you insist—"

"I do."

"All right." Those bow-shaped lips curved in a slight smile. "Thank you, Mr. Thorne. Your generosity is appreciated."

He gave a short nod. "You're welcome."

"Will that be all, sir?"

"Not quite. I'm throwing a small dinner party tomorrow

evening. Just a few close friends and family members will be invited. Do you own a decent cocktail dress?"

She hesitated, then shook her head.

"Get one tomorrow," he instructed.

"All right. I will."

As she rose to leave, he said, "Oh, by the way, Miss Washington?"

"Yes?"

Crandall leaned back in his chair, his head tipped thoughtfully to one side as he regarded her. "This may be nothing, but after you left the house this morning, I overheard Rita on the phone telling Dane Roarke that you'd be attending the meeting at the convention center."

Solange grew very still. "Oh?"

Crandall nodded, watching her closely. "Just in case he happened to show up at the meeting, I thought you should know it wasn't a coincidence—as he may have led you to believe."

"I see." Although her expression remained impassive, Crandall knew he'd struck a nerve. Good. If the girl had any silly, romantic notions about Dane Roarke, Crandall was only too willing to strip her of them. A man like Roarke would only bring her heartache and disillusionment. The sooner she realized this, the better.

"Thank you for sharing that news with me," she said evenly. "If you need me for anything else, I'll be in my room."

Crandall inclined his head, then watched as she turned and left the room with an air of quiet dignity.

And for the first time ever, he wondered if, perhaps, he was making a terrible mistake by not telling her the truth about who she really was.

Soon enough, he told himself, thinking ahead to tomorrow night when they would all be together—him, Tessa and their long-lost granddaughter.

Soon enough.

Chapter 16

After leaving the Riverwalk hotel, where he'd spent one of the most memorable afternoons of his life making love to Solange, Dane went home to shower and change before heading to the office.

When he arrived, his cousins Kenneth, Noah and Daniela were seated in the reception area, laughing and talking as if they hadn't spent most of the previous day together at their mother's house for Sunday brunch.

The receptionist had left early, and Christmas tunes drifted merrily from hidden speakers.

"So you finally decided to show up," Kenneth Roarke remarked as Dane stepped through the door. "We were beginning to wonder."

Dane chuckled. "What is this? You guys taking an extended lunch break or something?"

They all laughed. "You know business slows down around this time of year," Noah reminded him.

"Yeah, people don't believe in spying on their cheating spouses during the holidays," Kenneth added drolly.

Grinning, Dane sauntered over to Daniela and planted a kiss on her smooth, upturned forehead. "What're you doing here, baby girl? You ready to come back to work for the family business?"

"Not quite," Daniela Thorne said with a rueful grin. "I had a doctor's appointment today, so I decided to swing by afterward and check up on you fellas."

"How'd everything go?" Dane asked. "You and the baby doing okay?"

"We're doing just fine. Caleb Junior weighs almost three pounds, which is what he's supposed to weigh at twenty-eight weeks, and the doctor says he's probably going to be tall like his daddy, his uncles and his favorite cousin, Dane."

Kenneth snorted. "Who says Dane's going to be his favorite cousin?"

Dane laughed. "I hate to break it to you, my friend, but the kid has already spoken. Watch and weep." He dropped to his haunches in front of Daniela and laid the flat of his palm upon her gently rounded belly. Almost at once, he felt a hearty kick against his hand, which made Daniela giggle.

Dane threw a smug grin over his shoulder. "See, what'd I tell you?" he bragged. "The kid loves me. He only does that when *I* touch Daniela's stomach."

"You *and* Caleb," she said.

Dane's grin widened with triumph. "See?"

Kenneth scowled. "Well, if you ask me, he's not kicking you because he likes you. That's his way of telling you to get lost."

Dane chuckled. "Aw, don't be jealous just because your nephew's gonna want to hang out with me more than you."

"You're *both* wrong," Noah, seated nearby, chimed in. "*I'm* going to be Caleb Junior's favorite, just like I'm the twins' favorite."

Kenneth looked affronted. "What? *I'm* their father—"

"Boys, boys!" Daniela laughingly intervened, reminiscent of the way she'd refereed their childhood skirmishes. "Are you trying to send me into preterm labor? You know all this bickering isn't good for me or the baby."

"Sorry, El," the three men muttered sheepishly.

"That's all right." Daniela smiled, idly rubbing her swollen belly. "Between Caleb, the three of you and Daddy Thorne, it's good to know that my son will be surrounded by such strong male role models." While her older brothers basked in the praise, she leaned forward and whispered conspiratorially in Dane's ear, "Pay them no mind. You're *my* favorite cousin, so why wouldn't you be my child's?"

Dane grinned at her.

Daniela, who'd once been a gangly teenager with a mouthful of braces and wild hair, had blossomed into an extraordinarily beautiful woman. The skinny arms and legs that had once been fodder for merciless teasing had been replaced by an hourglass figure that turned male heads wherever she went, and her unruly mane had been tamed into soft, lustrous black curls that now tumbled past her shoulders. Her long-lashed dark eyes sparkled, and her face had the pregnancy glow often referred to by other women.

"Marriage and pregnancy really agree with you," Dane told her with an affectionate smile.

Daniela grimaced. "*Marriage* agrees with me. The jury's still out on the whole harvesting another human being thing. I spent the first three months with my head stuck in a toilet, I couldn't sleep through an entire night without having to get up and pee every hour and now my ankles swell up like water balloons if I'm on my feet for more than a few hours."

Dane chuckled sympathetically. "Hang in there, kiddo. You only have three more months to go."

She shot him a withering look. "Easy for *you* to say, He Who Hath No Womb. And don't even get me started on that husband of mine."

"What has Caleb done?" Noah asked, sounding distinctly amused. "Other than give you unlimited back rubs, make runs to the store at ungodly hours of the night to satisfy your weird cravings, tell you on a daily basis how beautiful you are and force you to take an early maternity leave from the law firm so you could rest during your final trimester?"

Daniela glared at her brother, fighting the tug of a smile. "As I was about to say before I was so rudely interrupted," she said, directing her words at Dane, "Caleb has been nothing but good to me, which only makes me feel guilty for any whining and complaining I do."

"Yeah, well, there's a solution to that," Kenneth muttered under his breath.

Dane and Noah snickered, which earned them dirty looks from Daniela.

Dane reached up and chucked her lightly on the chin. "Seriously though, El. We all think you're going to make a wonderful mother, even if we don't tell you often enough."

Her expression softened with gratitude. "Thank you, Dane," she said tenderly. "You're a sweetheart."

He flashed a wolfish grin. "Don't tell anyone else, though. I've got a rep to maintain."

"Yeah, we know," Kenneth said drolly. "I was speaking to one of our clients this afternoon, and he could have sworn he saw you at the Riverwalk earlier today, having lunch with a young woman he described as 'very fetching.'"

Noah chuckled, shaking his head at Dane. "No wonder you were so eager to trade places with me at this month's chamber of commerce meeting. I should have known something was up when you called early this morning to let me know you'd be going to the meeting instead."

Dane grinned. "Maybe I really wanted to hear the senator speak."

"Like hell." Kenneth and Noah guffawed.

Daniela smiled, arching an inquisitive eyebrow at Dane. "Come on, fess up. Who's the mystery lady?"

"No one you know," he said evasively, rising and walking over to the reception desk to retrieve his mail, all too aware of the three pairs of eyes that followed him.

"Where'd you meet her?" Daniela persisted.

Dane snorted. "Like I'm really going to tell you. And by the way," he added, turning from the desk, "thanks for telling old man Thorne about me and Renee."

"Which one is Renee?" Kenneth asked.

Noah laughed. "The dental hygienist. Keep up, man."

Daniela frowned in confusion. "I didn't tell Daddy Thorne

about… Oh, wait a minute. Yes, I did," she admitted with a sheepish grin. "He said he was looking for a new dentist, because the one he'd been seeing for years had retired. So I told him about Renee and the office where she works. Why? Did he say something to you?"

Dane scowled. "Let's just say he brought her up—and a few others—at an inopportune moment." The instant the words left his mouth, he realized his mistake.

Daniela traded amused, knowing looks with her brothers. "You mean he put your business out there to a woman you were trying to impress," she translated.

With a grunt, Dane turned and started down the hall toward his office. He wasn't surprised when his cousins followed him.

"When did Daddy Thorne bring up Renee?" Daniela started firing questions at him. "Were you at the ranch? Did he have company? Who was there at the…" She trailed off as comprehension dawned. "Wait a minute. You're not talking about his new personal assistant, Solange Washington, are you?"

Dane plopped down in the leather chair behind his desk, tossed his mail on a growing pile of paperwork and met Daniela's incredulous stare. "I don't know what you're talking about," he said, straight-faced.

This set off a chorus of disbelieving groans. "Please don't tell us the woman you were having lunch with today was Crandall's personal assistant," Kenneth demanded.

Dane's mouth twitched. "Okay. I won't tell you."

"*What?* Damn it, Dane." Kenneth barged into the tiny office, hot on the heels of his sister, who claimed one of the visitor chairs while Noah lounged in the doorway, arms folded loosely across his broad chest. Noah—ever the calm, cool, collected one. There was a reason Dane had always gotten along better with him than Kenneth, who had a tendency to make mountains out of molehills.

"Crandall Thorne is our biggest client," Kenneth said, jabbing an accusing finger at Dane from the opposite side of the desk. "You can't go messing around with his personal assistant!"

Dane cocked an eyebrow. "Since when does he get to dictate what his employees do in their private lives?"

"Since he became one of the richest, most powerful men in Texas! Since his law firm consistently makes *Fortune*'s list of the one hundred best companies to work for!"

Dane scowled. "What the hell does that have to do with anything?"

"I think what my brother is trying to say," Noah interjected dryly, "is that it might not be good for business if you get on Crandall's bad side by breaking his poor assistant's heart."

Dane took umbrage. "Who says I'm gonna break her heart?"

Kenneth snorted rudely. "Come on, man. This is us you're talking to, remember? We all know how you operate. You're the proverbial love 'em and leave 'em guy."

"Maybe this time is different," Dane countered, a note of subtle challenge in his voice as he glared at his older cousin. "Maybe this *woman* is different."

The hushed silence that swept across the room was deafening. Three pairs of dark eyes stared at him with identical expressions of stunned disbelief. Dane would have found his cousins' reactions rather comical—if he wasn't reeling from shock himself.

Maybe this woman is different.

Had he actually spoken those words out loud? And what had possessed him to say such a thing in the first place?

Kenneth was the first to break the silence. "Nice try," he said, grinning and shaking his head. "You almost had us going there for a minute."

Dane smiled, but only briefly. Noah and Daniela were studying him with a look of quiet speculation that made him decidedly uncomfortable. He shifted in his chair, then sat forward and busied himself straightening a sheaf of papers on his desk.

Kenneth glanced at his watch. "I have to go. I promised Janie I'd be home early to attend the twins' Christmas recital at school." He pointed sternly at Dane. "Stay away from Crandall Thorne's personal assistant."

Dane met his gaze unflinchingly. "I can't do that," he said in a voice edged in steel. And it was true, he realized with some surprise. He could no more stay away from Solange than he could deny that he was a Roarke, born and bred.

Kenneth threw up his hands in surrender. "Talk some sense into him, please," he told Noah and Daniela before stalking out the door.

When he'd left, Dane divided a warning look between the two remaining siblings. "Save your breath."

Noah laughed, holding up his hands in mock surrender. "Hey, I'm the guy who spent five years secretly pining away for my best friend's fiancée. I'm the *last* person to be telling anyone who they should, or shouldn't, date."

Daniela grinned. "And you know I wouldn't dare, considering how hard I fell for Caleb when all I was supposed to be doing was 'investigating' his father. However, at the risk of appearing to side with Kenny—God forbid—he may be right in this case. In the four years since I've been married to Caleb, I've had an opportunity to really get to know Daddy Thorne. He has a big, soft heart and can be incredibly generous when he wants to be, but he also doesn't forgive or forget easily. When it comes to members of his family or his employees—many of whom he considers family—he can be very protective. Territorial, even. So if you're not interested in having a serious relationship with Solange, it may not be worth making Crandall angry or losing his valuable business."

Dane grabbed a letter opener and went to work opening his mail. "Everyone needs to calm down," he muttered irately. "Just because a client saw me having lunch with Solange doesn't mean I plan to run off and elope with her."

Noah and Daniela exchanged glances. "Then I guess we have nothing to worry about," Noah murmured.

"Exactly."

"I see." Daniela made an exaggerated show of studying her manicured fingernails. "So you probably wouldn't care if I told you that I'll be spending most of the day tomorrow with her."

Dane glanced up from his task. "Doing what?"

"Daddy Thorne asked me to accompany her on a shopping

trip. He says she needs a new wardrobe, but he gets the impression she wouldn't really know where to start."

Dane chuckled. Not that he would know, either. He'd spent more time trying to get Solange out of her clothing than *into* it. "Well, knowing what a clotheshorse you've always been, El, the old man made the right choice in asking you to go shopping with her. I'm sure you'll help Solange pick out some really nice outfits." *And skimpy lingerie would certainly be appreciated,* he thought wickedly.

"Yeah, we're going to have a lot of fun hanging out together," said Daniela. "I can hardly wait to meet her. And then tomorrow evening, Caleb and I are attending a dinner party at the ranch. Crandall called to invite us just as I was leaving the doctor's office. He apologized for the short notice, but said this would be a great way to introduce Solange to a few more people."

Dane stared at his cousin, the mail he'd been opening all but forgotten. Since parting with Solange that afternoon, he'd been thinking of ways to see her again. A dinner party at Thorne's ranch gave him a perfect excuse.

There was just one problem.

"Think you could, ah, wrangle an invitation for me, as well?" he said, giving Daniela his most disarming smile.

She sent him a blank look, all wide-eyed innocence. "Now why would I want to do something like that?"

Noah, still leaning in the doorway, threw back his head and roared with laughter.

Dane scowled without any real rancor. "Come on, Daniela. Don't make me beg."

"Why would you do that? You don't even like Daddy Thorne all that much. Why would you beg for an invitation to one of his dinner parties?" At his aggrieved look, Daniela grinned smugly. "I knew it! You *do* have a thing for Solange Washington. Now I *really* can't wait to meet her."

"You and me both," Noah drawled with an amused expression. "Maybe I ought to show up at this dinner party as well.

Should be rather entertaining to watch our little Dane follow his crush around like a lovesick puppy."

Dane leveled him with a look that would have cut through granite. Noah merely laughed.

Returning his attention to Daniela, Dane said, "So what do you say, El? Can you hook me up with an invite, or what?"

Daniela smiled, rising from her chair belly-first. "I'll see what I can do. It'll take some creativity—Daddy Thorne wanted to keep the gathering small, and he might not be too thrilled about having you there, especially if he knows what you're after."

No kidding, Dane thought as his cousins left the office. He already knew that Thorne would not welcome his presence at the dinner party. On Sunday, he'd practically run Dane off his property, and all but warned him to stay away.

Dane had no intention of complying. He had to see Solange again, even if it meant incurring the old man's wrath and having to endure his insults throughout the evening. He hoped his involvement with Solange wouldn't cost the agency its biggest client, but—selfish as it might sound—it was a risk he was willing to take.

He didn't dare examine too closely the reason he was willing to risk so much for a woman he'd met less than a week ago. There was nothing to examine, he told himself. He and Solange were two mature, consenting adults enjoying a mutually satisfying physical relationship. And when it was over, when they'd gotten enough of each other—as was inevitable—they'd say goodbye and go their separate ways. No drama, no hard feelings. No regrets.

Dane paused, frowning to himself.

If all that were true, why did he have a hard time believing he'd ever get enough of Solange?

And, even scarier, why was he suddenly fighting mental images of her, radiantly beautiful and swollen with their child?

I'm such a fool.

The denunciation reverberated through Solange's mind as she blow-dried her hair after leaving Crandall's office, where he'd dropped his bombshell on her.

The more she thought about the way Dane had played her, the madder she became. She couldn't believe the underhanded tactic he'd resorted to in order to see her again! As if it weren't bad enough that he'd somehow manipulated Rita into telling him where Solange would be that morning, he'd shown up at the convention center with that cockamamie story about him and his partners taking turns attending the monthly meetings, and Solange had fallen for it. What a naive little fool he must think she was. She'd played right into his hands, first agreeing to have lunch with him, then allowing herself to be whisked away to the nearest hotel for a session of raw, uninhibited, mind-blowing sex.

That's what it had been. *Sex.* She refused to assign any other term to what she and Dane had done. They'd been like two wild animals in heat, tearing at each other's clothes and bypassing the bed in order to consummate their passion. And oh, how they'd consummated it.

Solange grimaced at the memory, even as her traitorous body quivered in response. What on earth had she been thinking, sleeping with a man she'd known less than a week? True, she was no prude or wide-eyed innocent, despite the strict upbringing she'd had. She'd snuck out of the house to attend parties and school dances; she'd made out with boys; and at the age of eighteen, she'd lost her virginity to a guy she'd known since childhood, whose family owned a farm right down the road from hers. It was the summer before she was to begin attending the local community college, and he'd convinced her that she needed a hands-on lesson in human sexuality before she set foot in any college classroom. While the experience had been anything but earth-shattering, she'd had no regrets afterward. In fact, she'd learned a lot about herself and her body that day, discovering what she liked and what she *didn't* like.

Amazing that in one encounter, Dane Roarke had not only known just how to pleasure her, but had introduced her to new delights and more erogenous zones than she'd ever known existed.

Blushing furiously, Solange yanked her comb through a stubborn tangle in her thick hair. She had never, *ever,* been as reckless or stupid as she'd been that afternoon. She'd always prided herself on being cautious and responsible and exercising impeccable judgment when it came to the opposite sex. Just to be sure he was really into her, she'd made Lamar wait three whole months before they slept together—which was practically unheard of nowadays. Yet Dane, who she'd already determined was no good for her, had needed less than a week to get her naked and between the sheets. Five days, to be exact. How embarrassingly sad.

The worst part of it was that she had no one to blame but herself. She couldn't blame her reckless actions on the one margarita she'd consumed with lunch, nor could she blame the incredibly romantic setting of the Riverwalk.

She alone was responsible for the terrible lapse in judgment she'd made that afternoon. She had been seduced by a master—a gorgeous, virile man who was accustomed to going after what he wanted and meeting with no resistance. She'd been a willing—no, *eager*—participant, enjoying every last minute of the wicked seduction.

And now, as she stood before the bathroom mirror contemplating her flushed cheeks, smoky eyes and painfully erect nipples protruding from her sweater, Solange was faced with yet another dilemma.

Now that she'd experienced lovemaking with Dane, she knew she'd been ruined for all other men.

Including Lamar.

Chapter 17

At 8 a.m. sharp the next morning, the Rolls Royce limousine carrying a drowsy, bleary-eyed Solange glided to a stop at the curb in front of the high-rise apartment building where Caleb and Daniela Thorne resided.

Solange, who'd dozed off and on during the fifty-minute drive from the ranch to compensate for a restless night, gave a small start as the back door was opened by Crandall's longtime chauffeur—a stoic, distinguished-looking gentleman who was known only as Mr. Bailey.

Solange climbed out of the luxurious limo and murmured her thanks to the driver before crossing to the entrance of the building. A uniformed security guard stationed at the reception desk in the marble-tiled lobby called Daniela to let her know her guest had arrived, then escorted Solange to a gleaming bank of elevators and tipped his cap to her.

She was inexplicably nervous as she rode the elevator to the sixteenth floor. She felt as if she were meeting her boyfriend's family for the first time, which was utterly ridiculous since Dane was not her boyfriend—and never would be.

The moment Daniela Thorne flung open the door, Solange realized she'd had no reason to be nervous.

Daniela beamed a wide, welcoming smile at her. "Why, hello, Solange! It's so good to finally meet you! Come in, come in," she urged, gently clasping both of Solange's hands and tugging her inside the penthouse.

"It's good to meet you, too," Solange said with an answering smile. "I've heard such wonderful things about you."

"That goes both ways." Daniela grinned, and Solange wondered what, if anything, Dane had told his cousin about her. "May I offer you a cup of coffee or juice?"

"No, thank you. I had breakfast before I left this morning—Ms. Rita insisted."

Daniela laughed. "I'm not surprised. She loves to mother and fuss over all of us like we're her children. Every time Caleb and I visit the ranch, she makes me eat and eat until I'm positively stuffed. Especially ever since I became pregnant. 'You're eating for two now,' she's always reminding me. As if I could forget this bowling ball I've been carrying around for months."

Solange smiled. Daniela Thorne was a strikingly beautiful woman with glowing brown skin, curly black hair that was swept off her slender neck into a neat twist, exotic features and glittering dark eyes that reminded Solange of Dane's, even down to the enviably long lashes. Although she was casually dressed in jeans and a red cashmere sweater that gently hugged the swollen mound of her belly, she still managed to look effortlessly sleek and stylish. Standing beside her, Solange felt rather gauche in her own jeans and faded Dallas Cowboys sweatshirt.

"When are you due?" she asked.

"End of February," Daniela replied.

"Really?" Solange couldn't hide her surprise. "You barely look four months pregnant!"

Daniela made a pained face. "Girl, I know. It's the bane of my existence. For all this boy has put me through, you would think he'd at least have the courtesy to make me *appear* seven months pregnant. It's hard to moan and gripe about swollen ankles and a sore back when you're not as huge as a beached whale, know what I mean?"

Solange chuckled. "Well, I really appreciate you taking the time to go shopping with me today. Apparently Mr. Thorne doesn't approve of my, uh, modest wardrobe," she added with a small, self-deprecating smile.

"Oh, don't you worry about that," Daniela said dismissively. "If you ask me, this whole shopping excursion is a way for him to spoil you without letting you know that's exactly what he's doing. He told me not to worry about a spending limit, so, girl, we are gonna shop till we drop!"

Solange grinned, her spirits buoyed by Daniela's infectious warmth and humor.

As her hostess headed from the room to put on her shoes, Solange swept an appreciative glance around the spacious penthouse. There was a gleaming expanse of hardwood floor, and colorful, contemporary furnishings were tastefully arranged around a large living room that boasted twenty-foot ceilings, a wood-burning fireplace and a pair of tall French doors that opened onto enclosed side porches. Fifteen-foot windows with wrought-iron bars commanded a panoramic view of the sunny downtown skyline.

"You have a very beautiful home," Solange remarked, wandering over to the windows and peering outside.

"Thanks, Solange," Daniela called from the back. "It was my husband's bachelor pad for years. Ever since we got pregnant, he's been asking me if I want to move to a house in the suburbs so the baby will have a backyard to play in as he grows up. But I'm not ready to leave downtown. I absolutely love it here! There's so much to do and see—the historic Majestic Theatre, museums, art galleries and parks that are within easy walking distance, and the Riverwalk is only a block away. Have you been to the Riverwalk, Solange?"

"Um, yes. It's lovely." Solange was glad Daniela could not see the hot blush that flooded her cheeks.

"I adore the Riverwalk. I've had so many wonderful experiences there, including my first date with Caleb. It was the most romantic night of my life, a night I'll never forget."

Solange knew the feeling, unfortunately.

Carefully composing her features, she turned as Daniela re-appeared, wearing a pair of low-heeled designer leather boots and applying a slick coat of raisin-colored gloss to her full lips. "If Caleb really insists on moving," Daniela said, "I suppose I could readjust to living in the suburbs. Before we got married, I lived in the King William District—a quaint, historic part of town—in an adorable little bungalow. I couldn't bear to sell it when I moved in with Caleb, so we decided to keep it and rent it out. My cousin Dane is living there now. You've met him, haven't you?"

Solange swallowed convulsively. "A few times," she answered vaguely.

Daniela nodded. "He's renting out my house until he decides whether or not to return to Philadelphia."

Solange's heart gave an involuntary little thump. Her gaze sharpened on Daniela's face. "He's moving back East?"

"Oh, I hope not. I've been doing my best to convince him to stay in San Antonio. Next to my brother Noah, Dane is the second best friend I've ever had. He's five years older than me and grew up in Houston, but we've always been very close. Whenever he visited us during the summers, we always had so much fun together, and between him and Noah, I never had to worry about bullies. Dane likes to tease me about being named after him, even though we all know I was named after my great-great-grand-mother." She rolled her eyes playfully. "Anyway, he's turned my cozy little bungalow into quite the bachelor pad. I figure if he likes living there enough, he'll decide to stay. And, hey, if he finds another reason to make San Antonio his permanent home, that's even better."

When Solange said nothing, Daniela smiled brightly at her. "Ready to shop?"

They were driven to The Shops at La Cantera, a beautiful, upscale retail village that drew affluent shoppers from across the state and from as far south as Mexico, according to Daniela.

Even without that knowledge, Solange would have been a little dazzled as she stepped from the limousine. In Haskell, her shopping choices had been woefully limited to a few strip malls that housed a JCPenney or Sears—and sometimes both, if she was lucky. She'd certainly never been to anyplace as impressive as this sprawling open-air marketplace, which boasted high-end department stores and restaurants, and was surrounded by luxury hotels and golf courses.

"You need at least three black skirts of slightly varying lengths, three pairs of black slacks and two matching jackets." Daniela ticked off the items as she tugged Solange along to Neiman Marcus. "And those are just the basics. You'll also need several well-cut suits that are stylish and trendy, but still very professional. You're young, so you want to be taken seriously, but you don't have to look matronly in the process."

Solange wondered just what Crandall had told his daughter-in-law about Solange's attire. She didn't dress *that* badly, did she?

Before Solange could answer her own silent query, Daniela shoved a red skirt suit at her from the DKNY collection. "Bold colors really make a statement, and I think you'd look great in this suit. No, don't look at the price! Crandall said we shouldn't worry about a spending limit, remember?"

Solange, gaping at the price tag, opened her mouth to protest, but no sound would come forth; she imagined she must look like a guppy out of water, gasping for air.

Daniela chuckled. "Don't worry, we're not going to bankrupt your boss before you've even received your first paycheck. You may find this hard to believe, especially considering that we're standing in the middle of Neiman Marcus, but I can be a very frugal shopper when I want to be. I love a good bargain, so I'm going to make sure we get the most bang for our buck. Now come on, let's find the dressing room and see how stunning you look in this suit."

Over the next two and a half hours, Solange submitted to being inspected, poked and prodded, and ordered back and forth to dressing rooms in three different department stores while overly solicitous salespeople hovered nearby, eager to do

Daniela's bidding simply because she'd casually mentioned being related to Crandall Thorne.

As the two women were leaving Macy's, their arms laden with shopping bags, a long, deep sigh escaped Solange, drawing a sympathetic chuckle from Daniela.

"I'm sorry," she said sheepishly. "I've worn you out, haven't I?"

Solange let out a choked laugh. "*Me?* What about you? You're the expectant mother here. Aren't *you* exhausted? I mean, like, aren't your ankles swollen by now?"

Daniela shook her head, amused. "Girl, there are three things I *always* have energy for. Shopping for clothes, going antiques hunting with my mother and, well, let's just say the third is what got me in this condition in the first place," she said, grinning and rubbing her gently rounded belly.

Solange laughed.

"I'm starving," Daniela announced. "Wanna grab lunch before we finish shopping?"

Solange's laughter quickly turned into a groan. "You mean we're not finished yet? What else is there to get? I think we bought every pant and skirt suit made by Donna Karan and Diane von Frankenberg."

"Furstenberg," Daniela smilingly corrected. "And, no, we're not finished yet. We still have to find you the perfect little black dress, a new handbag or two and other must-have accessories. Do you like Chinese?"

"Food or clothing?"

Daniela grinned. "Girl, you are crazy. You know very well I'm talking about food."

"I love Chinese food."

"Great! Let's dump these bags in the limo, then head over to P.F. Chang's. I've been craving their lettuce wraps for weeks."

Over lunch at the sleek, trendy restaurant filled with early holiday shoppers, Solange and Daniela laughed and conversed as if they'd been acquainted for years instead of a few hours. Daniela asked Solange a lot of questions about her family and life in Haskell, and shared stories about her own upbringing.

"It sounds like you and your family are very close," Solange remarked as the waiter refilled her water glass, which she'd drained after a few bites of the delicious, but very spicy kung pao shrimp.

"We are close," Daniela agreed. "We had to be after my father died. I was barely a year old, so I have no memories of him. My mother was fairly young herself. She went back to school to get a degree in nursing so she could take care of me and my brothers. We all had to grow up very quickly, and even though it took my rebellious brother Kenneth a bit longer to get that message through his thick skull, I think we turned out pretty well."

"I'd say. You're all well-educated, happily married and the proud owners of a very successful private-investigation agency."

Daniela grinned. "Yeah, but these days I'm more of a silent partner. I left the business three years ago to attend law school and become an attorney."

Solange nodded. "Dane mentioned to me that you're currently on maternity leave. What was it like working at Crandall's law firm?"

"Well, I can tell you that in the six months I worked there as a junior associate, I learned a great deal about criminal law and litigation. Crandall has some of the best attorneys in town working for him, and I'm not just saying that because he's my husband's father and he was kind enough to offer me a job fresh out of law school. Instead of shunning me or giving me a hard time just because I'm the boss's daughter-in-law, a few of the senior partners really took it upon themselves to mentor me and show me the ropes, and although I know I'm not interested in practicing criminal law, the knowledge and experience I've already gained will prove invaluable when Caleb and I eventually launch our own firm. Have you ever thought about going to law school, Solange?"

"Definitely. That's part of the reason I accepted the position with Crandall. Of course," she added grimly, "during my interview he informed me in no uncertain terms that he has no interest in being a mentor to anyone."

Daniela laughed. "Oh, pay him no mind. One thing you'll

learn about your new boss is that his bark is much worse than his bite. Don't worry, you're going to learn a lot from him. He won't be able to stop himself from teaching you, whether he calls it 'mentoring' or not. Making everyone around him smarter, better—that's just what he does. Caleb is the same way, which makes him a natural in the classroom."

Solange smiled a little. "Why doesn't he work at his father's law firm?" she asked curiously. At the look of mild discomfiture that crossed Daniela's face, Solange said quickly, "I'm sorry. Was that too personal? I shouldn't have—"

Daniela waved a dismissive hand. "Don't worry about it. I get that question all the time, so I should be used to it. Caleb did work at the firm for five years and was hugely successful as a defense attorney. His reasons for leaving make for a long, complicated story, the details of which I won't bore you with at this time. Suffice it to say that he loves being at the university and plans to continue teaching one or two classes even after we open our practice. What field of law are you interested in studying, Solange?"

"Family law."

"Really? That's what Caleb and I are going to specialize in!"

"I know. Dane mentioned that, too." Solange smiled hopefully. "Think I could come work for you when I graduate from law school?"

Daniela gave her one of those warm, irrepressible grins. "Consider yourself hired." She picked up her water and took a long sip, her eyes calculating above the rim of the glass. "Tell me, Solange. What about family law appeals to you?"

"Well, the firm I worked for back home was a family-law practice, and I really enjoyed interacting with our clients and helping the attorneys prepare for trial. Many of the cases we handled were difficult—child custody cases could be downright heartrending. We always wished we could do more, especially whenever we felt a judge's ruling wasn't in the child's best interests. Having to stand by and watch in helpless frustration as a child is returned to an abusive home is one of the worst feelings I've ever experienced." She paused for a moment, slowly shaking her head. "Another reason I think family law appeals to me is that I was adopted, and every time I meet a particularly dysfunctional family, it makes me think about how lucky I was to have such kind, loving adoptive parents. At the risk of sounding like a cliché, I want to help make a difference in the lives of others who haven't been as fortunate." When Daniela remained silent, she ducked her head over her food and mumbled self-consciously, "Sorry. I'll get off my soapbox now."

Daniela chuckled. "Don't be silly. You have no reason to apologize. That's the kind of passion and conviction Caleb and I will be looking for in any associate we hire. So hurry up and get your law degree so we can hire you!"

Solange smiled. "I'm working on it, believe me." She picked up and absently toyed with a pair of chopsticks that had been resting untouched by her plate. "One of the other things I'd really like to do is become a court-appointed special advocate for children. I always wanted to just show up at the local CASA office and volunteer, but between attending college, working full-time and helping my parents around the farm, there just never seemed to be enough hours in the day. And I didn't want to give anything less than my all to those children, who would come to depend on me."

Daniela nodded. "That's perfectly understandable. Maybe you and Crandall can work out some type of arrangement that allows you to volunteer and still work for him."

"Oh, that would be wonderful. But I figured I'd wait a few more months, prove myself first, before I approach him with the idea."

"Good thinking. You know," Daniela said thoughtfully, "hearing you talk reminds me of the way Dane feels about his involvement in the Big Brothers Big Sisters program. He takes his responsibility very seriously, and let me tell you, the kids positively adore him. And not just the ones that are assigned to him, either. He's chauffeured vanloads of them to the zoo, museums, SeaWorld and to Spurs basketball games, and he really takes a genuine interest in how they're doing at school and at home. Everyone—the children, parents, teachers and program coordinators—loves him."

Solange listened with a combination of fascination and incredulity. The man Daniela was describing didn't sound like a scheming, heartless womanizer. He sounded like an honest, caring and sensitive man, a man who gave freely of himself and asked for little in return. He sounded… Well, he sounded too good to be true. Which meant he probably was.

Solange had stopped believing in the existence of Mr. Perfect a long time ago, but if everything Daniela was telling her about Dane was true—in addition to the things Solange had experienced for herself—then that's what he was: Mr. Perfect.

A magnificent lover, a hard worker, a man cherished by his family and friends and a veritable hero to neglected children.

Definitely too good to be true.

"Maybe you should talk to Dane about participating in the Big Brothers Big Sisters program," Daniela cheerfully suggested. "That's something you could do on the weekends that Crandall wouldn't object to. May I?" she asked, pointing her fork at Solange's plate.

"Of course. Help yourself." Smiling, Solange watched as Daniela speared a shrimp and popped it into her mouth, chewing in blissful silence for a moment.

"Absolutely delicious," she pronounced. "I could eat here every day. Well, at least on the days when I'm not eating at my mother's. There's nothing like my mama's home cooking. I'll have to invite you over sometime for Sunday brunch so you can experience what I'm talking about. Crandall's personal chef Ms. Gloria ain't no slouch, either. I can't wait to see what's on the menu for dinner tonight." She chuckled ruefully. "Girl, listen to me, carrying on and on about food. Can you tell I'm eating for two?"

Solange grinned. "The way you cleaned your plate seconds after the waiter set it down on the table tipped me off."

Daniela laughed. "You and I are going to get along just fine, Solange Washington."

"Yeah," Solange agreed, her lips curving into a lopsided smile.

"We'll get along even better if you promise me this is the last time I'll ever have to go shopping with you."

This time Daniela laughed so hard Solange was half afraid she'd go into premature labor.

It was three o'clock by the time they left The Shops at La Cantera. Instead of returning to her downtown penthouse, Daniela asked the driver to drop her off at St. Mary's University so she could catch a ride home with her husband.

As the limo pulled up in front of the law center, a tall, broad-shouldered man wearing a black turtleneck and dark jeans that rode low on his lean hips emerged from the main building and started purposefully down the steps. As he drew nearer to the Rolls Royce, Solange slowly lifted her head from the back of the seat and stared. With skin the color of toasted walnut, strong, masculine features and dark, piercing eyes, Caleb Thorne was stunningly handsome.

Solange's jaw dropped.

Noticing her reaction, Daniela chuckled softly. "I know. I felt the same way the very first time I met him. And even after being married to him for the past four years, I still catch myself ogling him every now and again."

Solange grinned sheepishly. "Sorry. Didn't mean to ogle your husband."

Daniela laughed. Not waiting for Mr. Bailey to come around and let her out of the limo, she reached for the handle just as Caleb pulled open the door. He reached down for her, and she launched herself into his arms with a speed and agility that belied her protruding belly.

"Hey, sweetheart," Caleb murmured, gazing down at her with an intimate little smile. "How was your day?"

"Wonderful," Daniela replied, her arms curved around his neck as she returned his smile. "Solange and I had a great time. Although if you ask her, she might beg to differ, poor baby."

Caleb chuckled dryly. "My father should have warned her she'd need the stamina of three Olympic gold medalists to go shopping with you."

"That would have been nice," Solange agreed, sliding across the backseat and stepping out of the limo.

When Caleb Thorne glanced over at her, Solange wondered if she'd only imagined the flash of startled recognition that filled his eyes, eyes that reminded her of his father's. And, come to think of it, hadn't Crandall given her that same odd, startled look when she'd first arrived for the interview?

As Daniela performed the introductions, Solange said politely, "It's nice to meet you, Mr. Thorne."

He inclined his head. "The pleasure's all mine. And please, call me Caleb."

Solange smiled. "All right. Thank you for loaning Daniela to me for the day."

"You're welcome, though I'm probably the one who should be thanking you for being brave enough to put up with my father. How's everything going so far?"

"Can't complain. He's been nothing but kind to me. I've been wondering when he's going to give me some real work so I can actually earn my keep."

Caleb smiled, albeit distractedly. "Give him time. He'll crack the whip eventually." Those dark, appraising eyes narrowed on her face. "Do you have any family living in San Antonio, Solange?"

"Not that I know of. Why do you ask?"

"No particular reason. You just…look familiar. Anyway, welcome to San Antonio. I hope my father won't drive you too crazy. Ain't that right, Mr. Bailey?"

Solange watched in astonishment as the old chauffeur, wearing the same stoic expression he'd worn all morning as he stood ramrod straight by the limo, suddenly broke into a wide, toothy grin. "Now, son, don't you be putting no ideas about your father in the young lady's head. You know he's always been very good to me. Wouldn't be right for me to imply otherwise."

Daniela laughed. "That's right, Mr. Bailey. Don't let this one—" she poked Caleb in the ribs "—get you into trouble."

Caleb grinned, pulling his wife closer and kissing her forehead. Solange smiled at the mischievous wink he sent her, but she was remembering Dane's own warnings to her about Crandall. He, too, had called her brave for wanting to work for Thorne. Not for the first time since accepting the job, Solange wondered what was *really* in store for her as Crandall's personal assistant.

"And speaking of trouble," Daniela said, addressing Solange, "you'd better get back to the ranch and start getting ready for tonight. The dinner party begins at seven, and we all know how Crandall feels about promptness." She frowned. "Which reminds me, I haven't even decided what to wear yet."

"You're going home to take a nap," Caleb told her in a firm tone that brooked no argument.

Daniela tried, anyway. "But I need to pick out something—"

"Nap," Caleb growled. "No way are you going to be on your feet all day, only to turn around and stay out all night at my father's dinner party. Either you take a nap, or we're not going."

"Oh, all right." Daniela heaved the dramatic sigh of a martyr and shook her head at Solange. "You see what I have to put up with?"

Solange grinned. She could think of far worse things to contend with than a strong, loving, slightly overprotective husband.

Caleb Thorne could be a lot worse.

He could be Mr. Perfect. Too good to be true.

Chapter 18

The first of the guests began arriving at the ranch at six-thirty. Although the invitations had been issued just the day before, everyone had eagerly accepted. No one was crazy enough to turn down an invitation to one of Crandall Thorne's lavish affairs, which had become increasingly scarce over the years. And no one was audacious enough to risk his displeasure by showing up a minute late.

At Crandall's request, Solange served as hostess for the evening, which afforded her the privilege of standing beside him to greet guests and direct them to the living room for champagne and hors d'oeuvres before dinner.

Although Crandall had billed the evening as a small, intimate gathering, the number of guests that arrived suggested otherwise. Solange counted at least twenty people in attendance, among them some of Crandall's closest friends, employees, business associates and, of course, Caleb and Daniela, who showed up looking as fabulous as if they'd just stepped from the cover of a glossy magazine in which they were featured as the couple of the year.

Crandall, beaming with pride, grabbed his son in a quick bear hug and bragged about his beautiful, expectant daughter-in-law to everyone within earshot.

When Daniela's gaze landed on Solange, her eyes widened as if she were seeing her in the dress for the first time. "Wow, you look stunning! I knew that dress had your name written all over it the moment I saw it. Work it, girl!"

Solange smiled. "I'm definitely trying." She had never worn anything as glamorous—or expensive—as the little black cocktail dress with spaghetti straps, a ruched bodice and a soft bubble hem that flared slightly above her knees, courtesy of Chanel. Heeding Daniela's instructions, she'd arranged her hair into an elegant chignon that exposed the graceful column of her throat and drew attention to the scooped neckline of her dress, where a simple diamond pendant dangled low enough to accentuate the modest glimpse of cleavage. Completing the overall effect was a sexy pair of black stiletto sling-backs.

She'd hardly recognized herself in the mirror when she'd finished dressing. She looked and felt like a million bucks. Even Crandall had smiled and given her a nod of approval as she'd descended the staircase to join him before the guests began arriving.

Just as she was about to compliment Daniela on the gorgeous silk sheath she wore, she was distracted by the arrival of an unexpected guest.

Dane Roarke.

He stepped through the front door in an impeccably tailored dark suit worn with a crisp white shirt open at the collar—the living, breathing embodiment of raw sex appeal.

Solange's breath snagged in her throat. She glanced away quickly, but not before Daniela caught her eye. Her expression was openly speculative.

Dane greeted Crandall, who managed not to snarl at him—most likely out of respect for Daniela. Solange wagered that Daniela alone was responsible for her cousin's presence at the dinner party that evening.

She pasted a smile on her face as Dane came to a stop in front of her. "Good evening," she said politely, as if she were greeting any other guest instead of the man who'd taken her mind, body and soul to unparalleled heights of ecstasy the day before.

"Good evening," he said in a low, husky drawl that did dangerous things to her heart rate. As his lazy gaze ran the length of her, she fought to ignore a thrill of pleasure that swept through her at the frank male appreciation that filled his dark eyes. "You look beautiful."

"Thank you. You look nice, too." It was the understatement of the year, which had been her intention. After calling him every name in the book for the way he'd deceived and manipulated her at the meeting yesterday, Solange had decided that the next time she laid eyes on him, she wouldn't give him the satisfaction of knowing how hurt or angry she was. Instead she'd play it cool and collected, let him see just how little he mattered to her in the grand scheme of things.

"They're serving champagne and hors d'oeuvres in the living room, if you want to help yourself," she told him.

Dane inclined his head, those fathomless eyes probing hers. If he found her behavior strange or unsettling, he refrained from commenting.

Daniela, who'd been conversing with Caleb along with the ranch foreman and his wife, returned at that moment. "Dane, will you go with me to get some hors d'oeuvres in the other room? I'm starving, and dinner won't be served for another twenty minutes."

"Of course." With one last lingering look at Solange, Dane started away with his cousin, who slipped her arm companionably through his, then threw back her head and laughed at something he leaned down to murmur in her ear.

Solange watched their departure, wondering if Dane had made a joke about her, then telling herself she shouldn't care.

Crandall's voice interrupted her musings. "Solange, I'd like you to meet an old friend of mine."

Solange turned to offer a perfunctory smile to their newest arrival. This time it was an elegantly coiffed woman of ageless beauty with supple, golden-brown skin and eyes the color of sable. She was stylish grace in a beaded, deep plum top and black satin pants worn with pearl teardrop earrings and a matching choker clasped around her sleek throat.

"Solange, this is Mrs. Tessa Philbin," Crandall said with a congenial smile. "Tess, this is my new personal assistant, Solange Washington."

Solange automatically thrust her hand forward. "A pleasure to make your acquaintance, Mrs. Philbin."

The woman hesitated a fraction of a second before taking her hand. "Hello, Solange," she said in a smooth, cultured voice, her eyes gently tracing Solange's features. "It's very nice to meet you."

Crandall said, "Tessa and I go quite a ways back, isn't that right, Tess?"

The woman nodded as she slowly released Solange's hand. "All the way back to grammar school," she murmured with a soft, nostalgic smile.

"Really?" Solange divided a surprised look between the two. "And you've kept in touch all these years?"

When they exchanged quietly amused glances, Solange realized her faux pas. "Not that I'm saying you're old or anything," she hastened to clarify. "I just meant...I mean, I think it's great that you've remained friends for so long."

With a gruff chuckle, Crandall came to her rescue. "It's all right, Miss Washington. We both understood what you meant the first time. And you're absolutely right," he added with a meaningful look at Tessa Philbin. "It is great that we've remained friends for so long."

Solange watched with interest as Tessa flushed and hastily withdrew her gaze from his. It was enough to make Solange wonder whether the couple shared more than a long history of friendship.

"I trust you found the ranch with no problem," Crandall said to Tessa. "It's been some years since you were last here."

"Yes, it has," she agreed. "But I had no trouble finding my way."

"Glad to hear it."

Tessa glanced down the walkway toward the large living room, where most of the guests had converged for champagne and exotic tidbits served on silver trays. "You have quite a gathering here," she said to Crandall with the barest hint of censure in her voice. "I was expecting something a bit...smaller."

Crandall gave a hearty laugh. "Tessa, darling. Compared to the fancy shindigs I used to throw, this *is* small. Now why don't you accompany me to the living room for some of those canapés you used to love so much? I had them specially prepared just for you."

For the second time since her arrival, Tessa blushed like a schoolgirl. "Why, thank you, Crandall. That was…awfully sweet of you."

"Nothing to it." He held out his arm with a gallant flourish. "Shall we?"

"All right," Tessa murmured, accepting his proffered arm with a trace of reluctance. As they started away, she glanced over her shoulder at Solange. "Aren't you coming, Miss Washington?"

"In a few minutes," Solange answered with a smile. "We're still expecting a couple more guests, then I need to check on the status of dinner."

"Of course." Tessa gave her a small, tentative smile. "I hope we'll have a chance to get better acquainted at dinner."

Deciding that the woman was just being polite, Solange responded in kind. "I'd like that very much, Mrs. Philbin."

After welcoming the last of the arrivals, Solange made her way to the large gourmet kitchen where Rita had been supervising dinner preparations—much to the obvious displeasure of Crandall's longtime personal chef Gloria Valdez, who felt she'd catered more than enough of her boss's headlining dinner parties over the years to not need someone looking over her shoulder.

When Solange appeared in the kitchen doorway—she didn't dare cross the threshold—the two women were arguing about something as inconsequential as whether or not a bowl of potato-and-leek soup needed more garnish.

Solange cleared her throat, hoping vainly to be heard above their bickering and the cacophony of clanging pots and pans, running water and shouted commands as members of the hired catering staff bustled about with last-minute dinner preparations.

Solange cleared her throat again, louder this time. Two pairs of eyes swung in her direction, and softened at once.

"Hey, baby," Rita cooed. "Don't you look pretty as a picture this evening."

"Absolutely gorgeous," Gloria agreed.

Solange grinned. "Thank you, ladies. I, uh, just wanted to make sure everything is on schedule."

"Of course," the two women chorused in unison, then turned to glare at each other.

"You tell Mr. Thorne that the first course will be served promptly—no thanks to his meddlesome housekeeper," Gloria groused.

Indignant, Rita demanded, "Who're you calling meddlesome?"

As they began quarreling again, Solange backed out of the doorway, chuckling softly to herself as she headed down the corridor to the living room.

Pausing at the entrance, she took in her surroundings—the soft music drifting through the spacious room; the lively din of conversation and laughter; the tinkle of wineglasses; the fragrance of expensive perfumes mingling with the inviting scents of apple wood and pine from a crackling fire in the hearth; and the festive beauty of the Christmas tree that soared fifteen feet high in front of the tall living room windows, aglow with lights and festooned with silver, porcelain and sparkling glass ornaments. Several people had gathered around the giant spruce, their murmurs of admiration making Solange's chest swell with pride and satisfaction.

She and Rita had decorated the tree last night in preparation for the dinner party. With Christmas hymns playing in the background and frothy mugs of hot chocolate cooling on the mantel as they worked, Solange had been transported back to her childhood, awash with memories of decorating the family tree with her mother while her father was busy outside, hanging lights on the farmhouse and setting up the nativity scene on the front lawn.

In the middle of sharing one of these reminiscences with Rita, Solange had glanced over and found Crandall framed in the doorway, watching her with an expression of such tender warmth she nearly dropped an ornament she'd been unwrapping. Seeing her reaction, he'd frowned, coughed into his hand then quickly retreated from the room, muttering something about an important phone call he had to make. It was the last she'd seen of him for the rest of the evening.

"I don't think my father's ever had a more beautiful tree in his home."

Solange turned her head to find Caleb Thorne standing beside her in the doorway, one hand thrust casually into his pocket as he gazed across the room at the brightly lit tree.

She smiled at him. "Thanks, but I can't take all the credit. Ms. Rita did as much work as I did."

Caleb chuckled softly. "She must really like you, then. Usually she just supervises the work."

Solange grinned. "Well, she *did* get a little bossy at times. She has very specific ideas about what should go where, and she's not afraid to say so."

"Not her fault. Her father was a career military man. Ms. Rita had a very regimented childhood."

"Yeah, she told me. Actually, we have a lot in common. We both grew up on a farm, but at least *she* had siblings to help with all the daily chores."

Caleb grinned down at her, and she was struck once again by how handsome he was. "I feel your pain. I grew up an only child, too, and I always prayed for a brother or a sister."

"To share the chores with?"

"Nah. To take the blame for stuff I broke around the house."

Solange laughed, shaking her head reproachfully at him. "In that case, maybe it's best that you remained an only child."

"Yeah. You're probably right." Sobering, he studied her face for a prolonged moment. "Have you had a chance to meet Tessa Philbin?"

Solange nodded, smiling. "She was very nice. Classy. She and your father go back pretty far, don't they?"

"A lifetime," Caleb murmured, his gaze settling on his father and the woman in question, who stood in a secluded corner of the crowded room, deep in conversation.

Solange swept another casual glance around, pretending not to look for anyone in particular—though she'd already discovered that Dane was nowhere to be found. Daniela, whom he'd escorted into the living room earlier, was sipping from a glass of sparkling cider while talking animatedly to a group of colleagues from the law firm. The women had arrived around the same time, Solange remembered. Three attorneys and two secretaries, among them a young, attractive brown-skinned woman in a killer red pantsuit and Prada pumps—who was now missing.

Along with Dane.

Where the hell is he? Solange thought with an unwelcome stab of irritation.

"Speaking from too many years of experience," Caleb said with a lazy glance at the gold watch peeking from beneath the snowy cuff of his shirt, "I think they're getting ready to serve the first course."

Solange gave him a blank look for a moment. "Who? Oh! Yes. Of course." *Idiot,* she mentally berated herself. *Stop worrying about Dane Roarke and do your damned job before you no longer have one!*

"Do you want to tell the guests to start heading into the dining room?" Caleb gently prompted.

"Right. That's exactly what I was about to do." But after a few unsuccessful attempts to get everyone's attention, she frowned ruefully. "I don't think my voice will carry over all the noise—unless I stand on a chair and yell like a banshee."

Caleb grinned. "Allow me." He put two fingertips in his mouth and whistled.

Instantly a hushed silence fell over the room. The assembled guests turned toward the doorway like spectators doing the wave at a football game. Mouth twitching, Caleb sketched a gallant bow, giving the floor to Solange.

Smothering a grin, she announced in her most formal tone, "Ladies and gentlemen, your presence is now requested in the dining room."

* * *

Halfway through the lavish five-course meal, Solange realized that ignoring Dane would be a lot harder than she'd led herself to believe.

While she sat directly to the left of Crandall, who'd taken his rightful place at the head of the long mahogany dinner table, Dane had been seated all the way at the opposite end, making it difficult, if not impossible, for them to speak to each other. The fact that Solange had to peer around the heads of several guests in order to catch a glimpse of him should have discouraged her from doing so, but she couldn't seem to help herself. She was acutely aware of him, almost to the exclusion of everything else. And it didn't help that every time she glanced down the table, he was laughing or engaged in conversation with the lovely woman in red, who was seated beside him.

She now realized it was no coincidence that Crandall had insisted upon handling the seating arrangements, a task he normally entrusted to Rita. He'd not only wanted to keep Dane and Solange apart; he'd invited the attractive young woman from his law firm to serve as a distraction, because he knew Dane would never be able to resist the lure of a new conquest.

"Is something wrong with your meal, Miss Washington?" Crandall inquired at that precise moment.

Solange glanced up from her plate to meet his bemused gaze. "No. Not at all. Everything is delicious." Which was true. She didn't have a single complaint about the prime rib, lobster, new red potatoes and exotic pasta dishes, all of which were to die for.

Crandall raised a dubious eyebrow. "One would never know that, given the way you've been picking at your food for the last half hour."

"I guess I'm not very hungry," Solange murmured. "Daniela and I had a big lunch at the mall."

"And yet," Crandall countered, inclining his head toward the opposite end of the table, where his daughter-in-law sat next to her husband, "that doesn't seem to have stopped Daniela from enjoying *her* dinner." He paused for a thoughtful moment, seeming to take pleasure in Solange's obvious discomfiture. "Perhaps you'd enjoy your meal better if you were seated somewhere else at the table. Closer to a certain someone."

Solange blushed furiously at the insinuation. Before she could formulate a response, Tessa, seated across from her, intervened. "Leave the poor girl alone, Crandall. You just never know when to quit, do you?" Without awaiting his reply, she turned and smiled ruefully at Solange. "I've never gotten used to these social gatherings myself, and I've attended—and hosted—plenty of them. There's so much pressure to make the right impression, whether you're the hostess or an invited guest."

"Solange is doing just fine," Crandall said gruffly, reaching for his glass of cabernet sauvignon. "She's already received plenty of compliments this evening for the way she's been handling herself."

"Really?" Solange asked, pleasantly surprised.

Crandall nodded, taking a sip of wine then stabbing a finger at her. "So don't ruin it by panting after Roarke."

"Crandall!" Tessa hissed, scandalized.

Solange could only laugh. It was either that or hide her face under the table.

Shaking her head, Tessa sent her an apologetic look. "Don't mind him. He's never quite grasped the concept of minding his own business. But enough about him. I want to hear more about you, Solange. Crandall tells me you're interested in becoming a lawyer."

Solange nodded, smiling. "Yes, I am."

For the next hour, she ate good food, drank fine wine and talked mostly about, well, herself. Not because she was self-absorbed, but because Tessa—and even Crandall, to an extent—seemed to have an endless supply of questions for her, and it felt good to realize that these two people, who were virtually strangers to her, seemed to genuinely care about her well-being. At one point, Solange found herself enjoying their company, as well as the banter of others seated around her, so much that she almost forgot about Dane at the opposite end of the table.

Almost.

When the meal was over and the guests had returned to the living room for coffee and after-dinner drinks, Solange slipped into the powder room to freshen her makeup and to check on the supply of toilet tissue and liquid soap, as suggested in an online article she'd read about hosting the perfect dinner party.

On her way back to the living room, she was unexpectedly captured around the waist and dragged into an empty corridor filled with moonlit shadows.

She squeaked in surprise. "What the h—!"

A big, warm hand was suddenly clamped over her mouth. "Shhh. Not so loud," Dane leaned down to whisper, his dark eyes gleaming with wicked amusement.

Solange glared up at him, even as her nerve endings responded to the intoxicating heat of his hard, muscled body pressed against hers. She tried to speak again, but the firm pressure of his hand muffled her words.

Dane chuckled low in his throat, the sound curling her toes. "You've been avoiding me all night," he murmured, gazing down at her. "What gives?"

She lowered her eyes, staring pointedly at his hand over her mouth. A slow smile curved his sensuous lips. "If I let you go, do you promise not to scream?"

Solange shot him an exasperated look, to which he merely smiled. "You have to promise, Angel Eyes."

She hesitated, then gave a jerky nod.

Slowly he released his hand and stepped back, and Solange instantly missed the delicious warmth of his body. In retaliation, she reached up and punched him on the shoulder. She might as well have punched a brick wall, for all the damage she inflicted.

"You scared me half to death!" she said accusingly.

His teeth flashed in a quick grin. "I've been trying to think of ways to get you alone all evening. When you went to the bathroom, I saw an opportunity and took it." The grin disappeared. "Why have you been ignoring me?"

"In case you haven't noticed," she said with icy hauteur, "I've been very busy."

"Bull."

"What?" she sputtered in indignation. "I *have* been—"

"I'm not denying that you've been busy. I'm saying that's not the reason you've been avoiding me."

"Why do *you* care?" she flung back. "Already bored with little what's-her-name?"

Dane scowled. "Hey, don't blame me for making friends! It's a dinner party. You're supposed to mingle with others—especially if the hostess has gone out of her damn way to make everyone feel welcome but you."

Solange felt a sharp pang of guilt. She started to say something, then stopped herself. She shook her head and dropped her gaze to the open collar of his shirt, where the strong column of his throat was revealed. She wanted to kiss him there, wanted to press her lips and tongue against his warm, velvety skin and tease the beating pulse at the hollow of his neck. And that was just the beginning of what she wanted to do to him, and with him.

"Take a ride with me, Solange," Dane said softly.

Her eyes flew to his face. "What?"

"Let's go for a ride. Just the two of us."

She swallowed convulsively. "I—I can't just leave the party." She shouldn't even be considering it!

"The party is practically over. You can sneak away for a little while."

She gave her head a vigorous shake. "I can't, Dane. Mr. Thorne will be looking for me."

Dane snorted. "The only woman on Crandall's mind tonight is Tessa Philbin, or haven't you noticed?"

She had, of course, but that was beside the point. "Look, we really need to talk."

"That's why you should go for a ride with me. We can talk…and do anything else you want," he added suggestively.

Solange held up a warning hand. "Just talk. That's all I'm interested in, Dane."

"Fine. We'll talk. All night long, if that's what you want. Let's just go."

"I can't leave now. I'm the hostess—I have to walk each guest to the door and say good night. We can leave when everyone else is gone."

He hesitated, looking as if he were debating whether or not to toss her over his shoulder and abduct her from the house.

After another moment, he nodded shortly. "Fine. We'll leave after the party. I'll ask Caleb and Daniela to keep the old man preoccupied so he won't notice you're missing."

Solange nodded. As she moved to leave, Dane reached out and caught her wrist. She looked back at him questioningly.

Big mistake.

His focused, smoldering gaze heated the blood in her veins and set off a sweet, pulsing ache between her legs. As she watched, transfixed, he raised his other hand and touched her cheek, skimming his fingertips down her jaw. She shivered.

In a low, compelling voice, he said, "It's been pure hell being under the same roof as you, walking around the same room as you, eating at the same damn table as you, and not being able to touch you." The pad of his thumb caressed the racing pulse in her wrist. "Don't keep me waiting too long, Solange. I don't know how much more hell I can take."

Solange swallowed. Not trusting her voice, she turned without a word and beat a hasty retreat.

Crandall was in a celebratory mood later that evening.

The dinner party had been a unanimous success. Gloria had delivered another top-notch culinary feast, justifying the generous salary and quarterly bonuses he paid her. The guests had enjoyed themselves immensely and would go back and tell all the naysayers that Crandall Thorne still knew how to throw the best damn party around. And Solange, that lovely granddaughter of his, had far exceeded his expectations in her capacity as hostess for the evening. Not only had she impressed his guests with her wholesome beauty, grace and hospitality, but she'd charmed the pants off Tessa simply by being herself. By the time dessert was served, she'd had Tessa eating out of the palm of her capable little hand.

When Crandall had escorted Tessa to her Mercedes at the end of the evening, she'd turned to him with tears of gratitude in her eyes and thanked him for arranging the introduction.

"She's ours, Crandall," she'd said in a soft, aching voice. "I don't need any private investigator to tell me what my heart already knows. That incredible young woman in there belongs to us. You know that, don't you?"

He'd pretended to hesitate for a moment before nodding slowly. "I knew you'd come to the same realization when you met her."

Tessa smiled, a quiet, winsome smile. "It wasn't just her uncanny resemblance to me that sent shivers down my spine. It was the way our spirits connected. Did you sense it, too, Crandall?"

Even if he hadn't, he wouldn't have had the heart to disagree with Tessa. Not when she was gazing at him like that, her eyes full of hope, longing, the sorrow of unfulfilled promises and dreams.

"I want to see her again, Crandall," she said in a tone that reminded him of the way she'd once begged him to skip their high school homecoming dance in favor of spending a quiet evening at the drive-in movie theater with her. If he had a quarter for every time he'd remembered, and lamented, his stupid decision to attend the dance without her, he'd be even richer than he already was.

"Do you think she'd like to join me for lunch sometime?" Tessa continued. "Next week I'm giving a speech to the League of Women Voters at the Oak Hills Country Club. I thought I'd invite Solange, then afterward we could sneak out and have lunch together. Do you think she'd say yes if I asked her, Crandall?"

He gave a low, indulgent chuckle. "Don't you think you're rushing things a bit, Tess?"

The look she leveled at him would have felled an African baobab tree. "She's twenty-nine years old, and tonight was the first time I've ever laid eyes on her. Rushing things? On the contrary. I'd say I have a lot of catching up to do, wouldn't you?"

Crandall laughed, holding up his hands in mock surrender. "I'm not arguing with you. All I'm saying is that we need to proceed carefully. There's still the possibility—"

"No, there isn't," Tessa cut in firmly. "She's our granddaughter, and we both know it. And she's not after your money, either. That girl doesn't have a scheming bone in her body. If she genuinely knew who you were, she would have told you up front. She has character, Crandall, the kind that was obviously shaped by the good, loving parents who raised her." Tessa paused as a fresh sheen of tears sprang to her eyes. Averting her gaze, she added in a choked whisper, "Thank God she was dealt a better hand than Melanie."

They shared a moment of somber reflection, forever bound by guilt and sorrow for the role they'd each played in the tragedy that became their daughter's life.

After another moment, Tessa turned to him with dark, imploring eyes. "When are you going to tell her the truth?"

As Crandall stared back at her, this woman he would love until his dying day, he reached a momentous decision. "Christmas. I'm going to tell her on Christmas Day." Remembering the sight of Solange laughing and sharing her favorite holiday memories with Rita as they'd decorated the tree last night, he smiled softly. "It'll be my gift to her. The gift of a new family."

Tessa beamed with pleasure and approval. Surprising him, she reached on tiptoe and kissed him gently on the cheek. "Thank you, Crandall," she whispered with feeling.

He could only nod, then stand and watch as she climbed into her silver Mercedes and drove off. Oblivious to the cold, he remained there, watching until her taillights disappeared behind a moonlit thicket of trees down the road before he returned to the house.

And now, as he stood in the entrance to the living room, staring at the sleeping faces of Caleb and Daniela—who had kicked off her shoes, curled up next to her husband on the sofa and laid her head upon his chest—Crandall felt a deep sense of pride and contentment wash over him.

He couldn't have asked for a more perfect evening.

Now where the hell was his granddaughter?

Chapter 19

"If you get me fired, Dane Roarke, I swear I will never forgive you."

Chuckling softly, Dane slid an amused glance at Solange in the shadowy interior of his Durango, which was parked in a small clearing down the road from the ranch. Close enough to get her back to the house in a timely manner, but obscure enough to give them privacy—which he intended to take full advantage of.

"Relax," he drawled. "You're not going to get fired."

"How do you know? We snuck out before the last guest had even left!"

"The last guest was Tessa Philbin, and she doesn't really count, since Crandall has the hots for her."

Solange paused. "You sensed that, too, huh?"

Dane snorted. "Hell, yeah. Everyone under that roof sensed it. And I think it's pretty safe to assume his feelings aren't one-sided."

"Yeah, I thought so, too." Solange frowned. "But Tessa Philbin is married."

"Hey, all's fair in love and war."

It was, apparently, the wrong thing to say.

Her dark, glittering eyes narrowed accusingly on his face. "Then I guess you also think it's okay to use any means to get what you want. Like the way you sweet-talked Rita into telling you I'd be at that meeting yesterday morning, so you could show up and pretend it was purely coincidental that we were both there."

Dane grinned sheepishly. "Oh, that."

"Yes, *that*."

"Hey, I didn't lie about Roarke Investigations belonging to the Alamo City Chamber of Commerce, and my cousins and I *do* take turns attending the monthly meetings. It's just that…well, this month wasn't exactly my turn…until Rita told me you'd be there. What's the problem?"

She stared at him. "Are you serious? You can't see how I might find that information just *a little* disconcerting? You played me for a fool, Dane!"

He scowled. "How? I wanted to see you again—badly, it so happens. When Rita called to let me know where you'd be that morning, I wasn't about to pass up the chance to see you and spend more time with you. I make no apologies for that."

She folded her arms across her chest, unconsciously drawing more attention to the enticing swell of her cleavage. "I suppose some women would be flattered by that explanation," she muttered mutinously.

Dane was too distracted to respond. She looked like an absolute goddess in that sexy little black dress he'd been itching to peel off her beautiful body all evening. It clung to every sublime curve and flared softly above her knees in a way that tempted him to lift the flirty hem and take a peek. He wondered if it was too much to hope that she wasn't wearing any panties.

"Hello? Did you just hear what I said?"

Dane blinked, feeling like a horny adolescent who'd been caught daydreaming about the big-breasted head cheerleader. Except *he'd* never had to settle for daydreaming. He'd always been given whatever he wanted.

He'd never wanted as much as he did now.

Leaning back against the headrest, he gazed at her from beneath his lashes. "Look, Solange, I didn't mean to offend you or make you think I was running game on you. I meant what I said when I told you I really enjoyed spending time with you yesterday." When she remained stubbornly silent, her face averted to the window, he sighed heavily. "What do I have to do to convince you that I'm serious about wanting to get to know you better?"

She turned to look at him. Her thick-lashed dark eyes, which were naturally wide and exotically slanted, were even more dramatic with the smoky eye shadow and mascara she'd applied that evening. Man, she was a knockout.

"Believe it or not, Dane, I want to get to know you better, too," she said softly. "As wonderful as our, uh, encounter was, there's still so much I don't know about you."

He turned slightly in the seat to face her. "Ask me anything, and I'll tell you."

"Anything?"

"Anything," he said, but with a little less gusto than before, because he suddenly realized she might ask him about the very thing he didn't want to discuss.

"What's your favorite pastime? *Besides* that," she added at the wolfish gleam that filled his eyes.

Dane chuckled, secretly relieved she'd started with an easy question. "Favorite pastime? I love playing basketball. Not necessarily as a competitive sport, although I grew up on a steady diet of street ball. I love to just go out by myself and shoot around. Gets the heart pumping and the juices flowing, and it helps me unwind after a long day. I don't have to think about anything deep or stressful. It's just me and the hoop. Very relaxing, therapeutic."

Solange nodded, smiling. "Where do you usually play?"

"Well, right now I'm renting out Daniela's house in the King William District. Historic town filled with a bunch of Victorian houses and antiques stores. Not really my scene, but hey, the rent is affordable and I'm helping out Daniela by letting her hold on to a house she really loves."

"Awww. Aren't you a sweetheart." Solange cooed.

Dane grinned. "That's what I keep trying to tell you, woman. Anyway, I described the neighborhood to give you some context, so you can understand how pleasantly surprised I was to find this hidden treasure right around the corner from Daniela's house."

"What hidden treasure?"

"A full basketball court, old but still in very good condition. I go there all the time, and it's almost always deserted."

She smiled. "Lucky you, then."

"Yep. Your turn. What's your favorite pastime?"

"Oh, that's easy. Reading a good mystery novel and watching football. I'm a huge Dallas Cowboys fan, along with everyone else in Haskell. Well, maybe not *everyone*," she amended, grinning. "When I grew up, I found out that my father had been a closet Redskins fan the whole time."

"Shameful," Dane pronounced in mock disgust.

Solange giggled. "I know, right? Anyway, any man I marry *must* be a bona fide Cowboys fan, or it can never work."

Dane grinned. "You drive a hard bargain, woman."

She sighed. "What can I say? I have my standards."

They exchanged teasing smiles, then lapsed into companionable silence for a few moments.

The diamond pendant nestled between Solange's plump breasts twinkled in the moonlight as she shifted in the passenger seat, turning her body to face him better. "There's something else I want to ask you about."

Dane stiffened. *Here it comes.* "Go ahead," he murmured.

She hesitated, biting her lush lower lip. "Why did you leave the FBI?"

"It's a long story."

"I'd like to hear it," she said quietly. "If you don't mind."

He minded very much, but not because he didn't want to confide in her. On the contrary. Talking to Solange was as easy and natural as breathing.

So he found himself opening up to her, telling her about the sports-bribery investigation and the resulting probe involving him and his former partner. She listened in rapt absorption, never interrupting, not speaking until he'd finished his account.

"Oh, Dane, I'm so sorry," she said almost tenderly. "I can't even imagine how terrible that must have been for you, to be wrongfully accused of a crime-and by someone you trusted. You must have been devastated."

"I was," he quietly admitted, gazing out the windshield. And for the first time in two years, he didn't want to put his fist through it at the memory of Rosalind's betrayal. What had changed? he wondered. Had confiding in Solange lessened the burden of anger and disillusionment he'd been carrying around all this time?

"Have you spoken to her…since then?"

Dane shook his head. "She got transferred to another field office and hasn't been heard from since." He didn't bother adding that Rosalind had called and e-mailed him several times over the last two years, but he'd never responded.

"I hope she got demoted," Solange grumbled under her breath.

Surprised by the cutting remark, Dane stared at her, then burst out laughing. Solange chuckled sheepishly.

Without thinking, he leaned over and kissed her forehead. "Thank you," he said simply.

She gazed up at him. "You're welcome."

His eyes lowered, drifting to her lips, and the next thing he knew they were kissing and tonguing each other like their very lives depended on it.

She didn't protest as he dragged her across the console and into his lap, her legs straddling him. He slid his hands beneath her short dress and discovered, to his everlasting delight, that she wore a garter and silk thigh-high stockings, which gave him easy access to what he desperately sought. With a low growl of approval at the convenience, he slid his hands over the curvy, delicious swell of her bottom and delved inside her lace panties, his fingers tangling in the soft nest of curls between her thighs. She shivered, arching against him with a trembling moan.

He slid his tongue along her parted lips while his fingers probed the wet, silky heat hidden in her soft folds. She whimpered uncontrollably, writhing against him.

"You like that?" he whispered against her mouth.

She nodded, licking her lips, teasing his tongue with the velvety tip of hers. It was enough to send a rush of blood straight to his groin.

He reached for the thin straps of her dress and yanked them down over her shoulders, dimly aware that the designer dress had probably cost Crandall a pretty penny. *Too damned bad,* Dane thought, too ravenous to be gentle. He tugged at the fitted bodice, then swore hoarsely as her magnificent breasts spilled out over the top, her nipples puckered with arousal. Greedily he reached for them, cupping their weight in his palms before using the pad of his thumbs to rasp her nipples. She sucked in a tiny breath, then moaned as he dipped his head and began suckling her left breast before moving to the other.

Unable to ignore his raging erection a second longer, he reached down and quickly unzipped his pants, freeing himself. Nudging aside the damp scrap of lace between Solange's thighs, he circled the swollen head of his penis around her clitoris, making her groan and quiver with anticipation.

He shifted in the seat, dislodging her a little as he dug his wallet out of his pocket and fished out a condom.

"Let me," Solange murmured, taking it from his hand.

She smoothed the condom over his rigid shaft with a slow, lingering caress that drove him out of his mind. Straddling his lap once again, she guided him into her body, sinking down on his engorged length with a shuddering moan of pleasure.

Dane grasped her waist, groaning as she rose above him and sank down again, taking more of him into her—deeper, bolder, fueling his hunger with her silken heat.

Soon he was thrusting hard and fast, driven by an insatiable thirst that demanded quenching. His breath was harsh and ragged against the scented hollow of her throat. He squeezed her buttocks and her shapely thighs, his fingers digging into her flesh as he surged in and out of her.

Throwing back her head, she gripped his shoulder with one hand, while the other was flattened against the closed window as she tried to keep her balance astride his bucking body. He watched her beautiful bouncing breasts, then exulted in the tremors that convulsed her body as she climaxed with a breathless cry, pulsing and contracting rapidly around his penis.

He shuddered as he came in a violent rush, wedged high and deep inside her. Time froze. Everything froze. The two of them were clenched together as tightly as a fist. They stared into each other's eyes, not speaking, barely breathing, as if afraid to shatter the exquisitely profound moment.

And Dane knew right then and there that he'd do whatever it took to keep this incredible woman in his life.

Chapter 20

"How was the dinner party?" Noah asked the next morning when he arrived at Roarke Investigations.

Dane glanced up from a report he'd been preparing for a client to find his cousin lounging in the open doorway of his office, a cup of steaming coffee in his hand. "Lousy," Dane retorted.

Noah lifted an eyebrow. "So why are you grinning like a cat with his face in a bowl of cream?"

"Because it's a beautiful day," Dane declared, setting aside the report and leaning back in his chair until it creaked. "The sun is shining, the birds are singing and there are still fifteen shopping days until Christmas."

Narrowing his eyes, Noah studied Dane as if searching for a sign that his body hadn't been commandeered by an extraterrestrial creature. After another moment, a slow, knowing grin spread across his face. "Oh, I get it. The dinner party was lousy, but the company of a certain 'very fetching' young woman made up for that."

"You could say that." Dane gave him a crooked smile. "I'm surprised Daniela didn't call you first thing this morning to fill you in on all the details."

Noah chuckled, stroking his chin between his thumb and forefinger. "If she did, I was, uh, otherwise occupied."

Dane shook his head in mock disgust. "You married people. Didn't any of you get the memo explaining how sex is supposed to become a chore after you've made the trip down the aisle?"

Noah grinned. "Riley and I *definitely* didn't get that memo. And if that's what you really believe happens to all couples after they get married, no wonder you've been running scared all these years."

Dane had to admit the notion of being confined to the same sexual partner for the rest of his life had scared him just a little.

That is, until he'd met Solange.

The sex between them was unlike anything he'd ever experienced with another woman. It was so hot, so explosive, that he couldn't imagine ever reaching a point where he wouldn't crave her as much as he did now. Just thinking about her, remembering the way she'd looked in that little black dress—and the way she'd looked *out* of it—aroused him to the point of pain.

But it wasn't just the incredible lovemaking with Solange that had him rethinking his views on the institution of marriage. It was the whole enticing package. The companionship and laughter, the sense of completion, the promise of unconditional love and support. In the short time he'd known Solange, she'd given him a rare glimpse of what the future could bring, the endless possibilities. It was enough to whet his appetite for more.

Noah's deep, amused voice pulled him back to the present. "I take it by the goofy grin you're still wearing that you and Miss Washington had a good time last night."

Dane nodded slowly. "Yeah. We did." *That* was an understatement if he'd ever heard one.

"Glad to hear it." Noah chuckled dryly. "Kenny was half convinced Crandall would greet you at the front door with the barrel of his hunting rifle pointed right between your eyes."

Dane gave a short, grim laugh. "I'm sure the thought crossed his mind more than once. He wouldn't let her out of his sight for most of the evening, and he made a point of seating me at the opposite end of the dinner table. Have you *seen* that damned table? He might as well have banished me to a foreign country— that's how far I was sitting from Solange."

"I guess the old man really means business."

Dane scowled. "Yeah, well, so do I."

"I know." Noah was watching him closely, a knowing smile playing about the corners of his mouth. "I can tell."

Afraid he'd revealed too much, Dane sat forward in his chair, cleared his throat briskly and reached for the report he'd been working on before his cousin interrupted. "I'm meeting with a client in an hour. Gotta get this paperwork done before then."

"Sure, no problem. We can talk later." Noah straightened from the doorjamb and turned to leave, then paused, glancing over his shoulder at Dane. "Remember last week when I told you that you can run, but you can't hide forever?"

Dane hesitated, then nodded.

A slow, satisfied grin curved Noah's mouth. "I didn't realize at the time how soon I'd get to say, 'I told you so.'"

Dane watched him leave, then whispered under his breath, "You and me both."

When Crandall summoned Solange to his library the next morning, she fully expected to receive an earful about staying out late with Dane, although Daniela had covered for her last night, telling Crandall that Solange had retired to her room to take a long-distance phone call from a friend.

She was immensely relieved when Crandall, instead of lecturing her about her midnight rendezvous, asked her to set him up for a scheduled videoconference with his board of directors that morning, then informed her she would be taking minutes in lieu of his secretary, who was on vacation.

As Solange went about the task of setting up the videoconferencing equipment, which she'd routinely done at her old law firm, Crandall openly appraised her blue cashmere sweater, pleated charcoal trousers and ankle-high Prada boots.

"That outfit is quite flattering on you," he announced after a moment. "You and Daniela did very well yesterday."

"Thank you, Mr. Thorne," Solange murmured. "I'm glad you approve."

When the meeting ended two hours later, at eleven, Crandall surprised her by saying, "Let's go for a walk before lunch. I need to get my daily exercise."

They left the house and started off down the gravel path that wound past more barns, outbuildings and a large roping arena that, according to Crandall, had been a beehive of activity just a few months earlier during branding season at the ranch. Now the land lay quiet, serene, with cattle and horses grazing peacefully in the vast fields under a gray winter sky.

"Do you like it here, Solange?" Crandall asked.

"Yes, very much. Everything is absolutely beautiful."

Crandall nodded, his dark eyes shining with pride as he surveyed his surroundings. "I bought the ranch as an investment property almost twenty-five years ago. Although law has always been my first love, I've always wanted to own and operate a cattle ranch. There's something so natural, so purposeful, about the life of a rancher. Waking up to the scent of freshly mown hay every morning as the sun rises over the mountains, roping, branding and driving a herd of cattle, fixing fences and checking pastures, soaking up the warm sun and fresh air as you and your horse race across the valley after a long, hard day's work. There's nothing like it, I tell you. And when I first saw this place, I imagined my grandchildren and great-grandchildren frolicking and chasing one another up and down these hills—God's playground."

Solange smiled. She didn't realize her boss could be so poetic. "I'm sure Caleb Junior will appreciate being the first to enjoy the land."

"Ahh, yes. And I hope he'll be the first of many grandchildren my son and Daniela give me."

Solange chuckled, adjusting her stride a little to accommodate Crandall's slower, more measured pace. They walked for a few minutes in companionable silence.

It didn't last.

"Did you enjoy yourself last night, Solange?" Crandall casually inquired. "You disappeared before I had a chance to ask you."

Automatically her stomach clenched. *Uh-oh,* she thought. *Here it comes.*

"I had a wonderful time," she answered truthfully. "I've never been to a real dinner party before, so I was a little nervous at first."

"No one could tell. You seemed very relaxed and in your element." Crandall gave her a bemused sidelong look. "The only time you seemed tense was whenever Dane Roarke was in the vicinity. May I be frank with you?"

As if he ever needed anyone's permission to speak his mind!

Nonetheless, Solange nodded her consent for him to continue.

"You may not think it's my place to advise you on your love life, but as you are an employee and a member of my household, I consider it my responsibility to look after your welfare and share my concerns with you."

"All right," Solange said evenly. "What about Dane concerns you?"

Crandall slowed to a stop, turning to face her. He was a tall man, almost as tall as his son and Dane, so once again she found herself tilting her head back to meet his solemn gaze.

"Let me preface my warning by admitting to you how much I actually like and respect Roarke. He's brash, tough, smart as a whip, a hard worker and he has little tolerance for pretentiousness. I watched him interacting with my guests last night, and he can command the attention of an entire room with little or no effort on his part. That's a quality not many people possess. Truth be told, Solange, he reminds me a lot of myself at that age—and therein lies the problem."

"I don't understand," she murmured.

Crandall's lips flattened into a grim line. "I was a lousy husband, and up until a few years ago, not much better as a father. I was incredibly selfish, and I put my career ahead of my family until it was too late."

Recalling the painful story from his past Dane had shared with her last night, Solange frowned. "That doesn't sound like Dane. He walked away from a career he loved when his integrity was wrongfully called into question."

"And that decision will haunt him for the rest of his life, rendering him incapable of completely giving himself to anyone who makes the mistake of falling in love with him," Crandall said emphatically. "Not only is he damaged goods, but he's a heartbreaker. Oh, I don't think he sets out intentionally to hurt the women he gets involved with, but he just can't seem to help himself. Roarke has a restless spirit, Solange, and while there are some men who can eventually be tamed into settling down with one woman, he isn't one of them. He loves the thrill of the chase, but once it's over, so is the affair."

Solange was surprised to feel emotion clogging her throat. Nothing Crandall was telling her came as a shock to her. She'd had the same misgivings about Dane from the very beginning, and even as recently as last night had decided not to pursue a relationship with him.

That is, until he'd taken her for a drive.

After the intimate things he'd shared with her and the way they'd connected—both physically and emotionally—all bets were off. What she'd experienced with Dane in the past week was unlike anything she'd ever known with Lamar in the three years they'd been together. Not only was Dane the perfect lover— intensely passionate and unselfish—but he was strong, caring and generous, and he made her feel fiercely protected. She enjoyed being with him, more than she could have ever imagined.

She knew the tremendous risk she was taking in getting involved with him, but she'd decided to take it anyway. If Dane broke her heart, she had no one to blame but herself.

Besides, what if Crandall is wrong about him? an inner voice challenged. *What if he has other motives for trying to keep the two of you apart? What if he simply doesn't like Dane?*

As if he'd intercepted her thoughts, Crandall gave her a pitying look. "I think you know, deep down inside, that what I'm sharing with you is the truth. But, as I always told Caleb when he was growing up, I can't live your life for you. You have to decide what's best for you, because ultimately, *you're* the one who has to live with the consequences of that decision—good or bad."

"I agree," Solange said mildly. "But I thank you for caring enough to share your concerns with me. Your honesty is appreciated."

He looked at her, his lips curved in a faintly mocking smile. "I may be getting old, Miss Washington, but I'm not dumb or deaf. I know when I've just been politely told to go to hell."

Solange said nothing. Their gazes locked in a silent battle of wills.

After another moment, Crandall let out a short bark of laughter, startling her. "You've got spunk, young lady," he said, shaking his head. "I may not agree with your taste in boyfriends, but I've gotta hand it to you. You don't back down from a fight."

Solange grinned. "And just for the record, I would never tell any employer of mine to go to hell."

"Oh, is that right?"

Her grin turned impish. "Not to his face, anyway."

Crandall threw back his head and roared with laughter.

When they got back to the house, Rita met them at the door as if she'd been awaiting their return. "You have a visitor," she told Solange with an odd, anxious expression.

"Me?" Solange asked in surprise. "Who is it?"

When Rita wavered for a moment, Crandall scowled. "Well? Who is it, woman?"

Before Rita could respond, Solange's gaze swept beyond her shoulder and came to rest on the handsome, uniformed man who'd appeared silently in the foyer.

Her eyes widened. She went limp with shock. *"Lamar?"*

"Hello, Solange." He offered a small, tentative smile. "Surprise."

"Man, you sure weren't lying about this place being so far away," exclaimed fifteen-year-old Jacob Tarrant, his face pressed to the passenger-side window of Dane's Durango as it hurtled up the rocky hill toward Crandall Thorne's ranch. "We're out here in the middle of nowhere!"

Dane chuckled, slanting an amused glance at the teenager.

"We definitely need to get you out of the city more often, kid. You were born and raised in Texas. How is it you've never seen a real horse before?"

Jake turned, giving him a look that said the answer should be obvious. "Ain't no horses in the middle of the East Side!"

"Really?" Dane feigned a look of exaggerated disbelief. "I could have sworn I saw one in your neighbor's backyard the other day."

Jake cracked up. "That wasn't a horse. That was mean ol' Mr. Wallace!"

Dane didn't laugh. "Now, Jacob," he said in his gravest I'm-disappointed-in-you tone, "what have your mother and I taught you about respecting your elders?"

The boy faltered, the dimpled grin fading from his smooth, chocolate-brown face. "Sorry," he mumbled.

Dane could hardly keep a straight face. "That's all right. I know you didn't mean to imply that Mr. Wallace looks like a horse." He paused a beat. "Even if it's true."

Jake's uproarious laughter filled the interior of the truck, drawing an answering chuckle from Dane. It was good to hear the kid laugh again, he thought. He hadn't been the same since his mother was diagnosed with breast cancer eight months ago. Although the cancer had been caught on time and she was now in remission, the stress of her illness, chemotherapy treatments and the growing stack of medical bills, along with the scary realization that they'd nearly lost their mother, had taken a serious toll on Jake and his two younger siblings. Jake, whom Dane had met earlier that year through the Big Brothers Big Sisters program, started skipping school and neglecting his responsibilities at home. After bailing him out of trouble a third time, Dane got in the boy's face and threatened to have him sent away to a military academy run by an old friend of his—a place that made Guantanamo Bay look like a tropical vacation destination.

The threat worked like a charm.

"Are you sure Mr. Thorne is gonna let me work in his stables?" Jake asked anxiously.

"Of course. I told you, kid, it's already a done deal." Last night at the dinner party, Dane had made a point of seeking out Wyome, the Native American foreman in charge of hiring all laborers at the ranch. After hearing about the bright, hardworking teenager who could use a part-time job to help support his struggling family and keep himself out of trouble, Wyome had instructed Dane to bring Jake to the ranch the following day so that Tomas could begin training him on how to clean the stables and take care of the horses. Jake had been thrilled at the opportunity to work on a real cattle ranch and couldn't get dressed fast enough. His mother had been overcome with gratitude, while his younger brother and sister had groaned with envy until Dane promised to pick them up one afternoon during their two-week Christmas break and take them horseback riding at the ranch.

"This place is off the chain." Jake breathed in awe as they approached the sprawling property. "Mr. Thorne must be seriously balling."

Dane grinned at the slang terms. "Oh, he's balling all right. The man is richer than King Midas." And probably just as arrogant, he refrained from adding.

After getting Jake situated at the stable with Tomas, who gladly welcomed the extra help as well as the company of another boy his age, Dane accompanied Wyome to the main house for a cup of coffee while he filled out some paperwork.

He was unprepared for the sight that greeted him when they entered the living room.

Seated next to Solange on the sofa was an attractive, clean-shaven man in full dress uniform, the silver oak-leaf cluster on his shoulder identifying his rank as a lieutenant colonel. He was carrying on an animated conversation with Crandall, who sat in an adjacent armchair while Rita, a courteous smile pasted onto her face, occupied a corner of the chintz-covered love seat.

It was a wonder Dane processed any of those minute details when a red haze was slowly settling over his brain. Who the hell was this chump? And, more to the point, why was his hand resting possessively on Solange's knee?

When Crandall glanced up and met his gaze, there was no mistaking the malicious gleam of satisfaction in his eyes. "Ah, Mr. Roarke," he said smoothly, standing. "You're just in time to meet our special guest."

There was a sudden flurry of movement as both Solange and Rita lunged to their feet and chorused awkward greetings to him, while the stranger rose more slowly. With his eyes locked on Solange, Dane watched the play of emotions that flitted across her face—embarrassment, annoyance, regret and guilt, the latter of which alarmed him the most.

What did she feel guilty about? Had she done something to feel guilty about?

In a voice like oiled silk, Crandall said, "Dane Roarke, allow me to introduce Lieutenant Colonel Lamar Rogers— Solange's fiancé."

Solange flushed, seeing the flash of shocked fury in Dane's eyes. "For the last time, Mr. Thorne, we're not engaged," she said with forced patience.

Lamar looked down at her with a proprietary little smile that set Dane's back teeth on edge. "Not yet, anyway."

She frowned. "Lamar—"

Ignoring her, he stepped forward to shake Dane's hand. "Nice to meet you, Dane."

Dane arranged the muscles in his face into a polite smile. "Same here," he said coolly, resisting the savage urge to crush the other man's smaller hand.

"Lamar was in San Antonio attending the promotion ceremony of a fellow officer," Crandall took the liberty of explaining. "Afterward he drove all the way out here to see Solange and take her out to lunch. I was just telling him that he's more than welcome to stay at the ranch until he returns home in a few days."

"And I was just taking him up on his generous offer." The two men exchanged meaningful smiles, like a pair of coconspirators.

Dane's gut clenched on a fresh wave of fury. He searched Solange's eyes, but this time her impassive expression gave nothing away.

Lamar eyed Dane curiously. "And how are you acquainted with my Solange?"

In more ways than you can ever imagine. And she's not yours, you smug bastard. She's mine!

Crandall interjected, "Dane works at a private-investigation firm owned by my daughter-in-law and her brothers." His lips curved in a mocking smile. "I made the mistake of allowing him to run the routine background check on Solange when I hired her, and I haven't been able to get rid of him since."

Lamar laughed, the sound loud and forced. "I'm not surprised. Solange has that effect on members of the opposite sex. Always has." He curved a possessive arm around her waist, drawing her closer to his side as he smiled into her eyes, which were almost at the same level as his. "I'm so lucky she gave me the time of day when we met at the county fair four years ago. I was wearing this very same uniform. Do you remember, sweetheart? You said I looked like a hero returning home from war."

And speaking of war, Dane thought darkly, if Lamar Rogers didn't get his damned hand off Solange in the next ten seconds, there was going to be some serious carnage in Thorne's expensively furnished living room.

Seeking to defuse the mounting tension in the air, Rita said with an overly bright smile, "There's no need for Solange and Lamar to eat out for lunch. Gloria always prepares more than enough food for extra guests. Dane, why don't you join us as well?"

Before he could unsnap his tightly clenched jaw to respond, Crandall said airily, "Nonsense, woman! Let the two lovebirds spend some time alone together. They haven't seen each other in almost a year."

"Yes," Solange murmured, looking at Lamar. "It *has* been a while. We really need to talk."

Dane stiffened. Hearing her utter the very same words she'd spoken to him last night, and remembering the way their "talk" had ended, was nearly his undoing.

Lamar smiled warmly at Solange. "You're right. We have a

lot of catching up to do. I passed a nice little Italian restaurant on the way up here. Shall we go?"

She nodded quickly. Stealing one last furtive glance at Dane, she slipped her arm through Lamar's proffered one and allowed herself to be escorted from the living room.

Crandall grinned after them. "What a fine couple! Does my heart proud to see young people in love. Ah, Wyome," he said, as if noticing his foreman standing there for the first time. He draped a companionable arm around the man's broad shoulders. "I'm glad you're here. I wanted to ask you about one of your ranch hands, a hardworking fella by the name of Chavez. I understand he and his wife are expecting their fourth child soon, and I was just wondering if…" His voice receded as he led Wyome out of the room and down the corridor, leaving Rita alone with a quietly seething Dane.

The look she gave him was full of maternal sympathy. "I'm so sorry, baby. He just showed up out of the clear blue, talking about how he drove all the way from Haskell to claim his woman." She gave a derisive snort. "The whole time he was here, he and Solange hardly spoke three words to each other. He spent more time trying to impress Crandall with all his fancy military credentials than trying to find out why his quote-unquote woman seemed less than pleased to see him."

Dane could scarcely hear what Rita was saying above the roar of blood pounding in his ears. Maybe if he'd actually heard the last part, he would have felt somewhat comforted. As it was, all he felt was murderous. And sick to his stomach.

Had he been wrong about Solange's feelings for him? Had she merely been passing the time with him until her lieutenant-colonel boyfriend returned to claim her, as he'd put it? After years of cavalierly playing the field, was Dane finally getting his comeuppance—just when he'd found the one?

"…You know I'd love to have your company," Rita was saying. "Do you want me to set an extra plate at the table for you, baby?"

Dane shook his head. Muttering an apology to the worried woman, he turned and strode purposefully from the house.

Chapter 21

He got halfway to the carport when he heard the rapid approach of footsteps behind him. He knew who it was even before Crandall opened his mouth and said tersely, "You're not welcome here anymore, Roarke. This is my last warning to you."

Dane stopped walking, but didn't turn around. When he spoke, his voice was flat and hard. "Go back inside the house, old man. I have nothing more to say to you."

"Did you just hear what I said? I don't want you hanging around here anymore. Wyome told me about the boy he just hired. I've arranged for him to have transportation to and from the ranch on the days he has to work, so your services won't be needed. Do you understand?"

Dane hesitated, then lifted his shoulder in a careless shrug. "Have it your way, Thorne, but don't expect me to stop seeing Solange."

"That's *exactly* what I expect you to do."

Something inside Dane finally snapped. His pride could only take so much battering in one afternoon.

He whirled on Crandall. "What gives you the right to interfere in her personal life?"

Crandall's face was suffused with rage. "I have every right!"

"Says who?" Dane snarled.

"*I* say!"

"Why? Because she's your employee?"

"No, because she's my granddaughter!"

It was the absolute last thing Dane had expected to hear. He staggered back a step, staring at Crandall with a dumbstruck expression. Surely he couldn't have understood him correctly. "Your *what?*"

"You heard me. Solange Washington is my granddaughter." Crandall looked visibly shaken, as if the admission had shocked him just as much as it had shocked Dane.

"I don't understand," Dane whispered hoarsely. "How can she be your granddaughter?"

Crandall glanced over his shoulder at the house, as if expecting to find Solange framed in a window, watching them with avid interest.

Turning his back on Dane, he started walking down the gravel path that led away from the house, knowing Dane would follow.

"Forty-three years ago," he began, his voice pitched low as Dane fell into step beside him, "I cheated on Caleb's mother with a married woman I had loved since my youth. The affair produced a child, a daughter we gave up for adoption to spare our spouses from the pain and humiliation of our betrayal. I'm not proud of the decision we made. It was selfish and downright cowardly, but at the time, it seemed like the best—and only—way to save our marriages. Marriages that, unbeknownst to us, were already beyond salvaging.

"Our daughter, Melanie, grew up in the foster-care system, bounced around from one dysfunctional home to the next. As you might imagine, such an upbringing didn't engender warm, fuzzy feelings about the parents who had once abandoned her. When she turned nineteen, she came looking for us. After tracking down her mother, she still wanted answers. But she had more in mind than seeking closure."

He paused, and Dane held his breath, instinctively bracing himself for the worst.

He wasn't disappointed.

"She showed up at my house with a gun," Crandall continued grimly. "She was nearly incoherent with rage, rage over the fact that she'd been forced to fend for herself on the streets while her mother and I were both living in the lap of luxury, as she called it. She threatened to kill me and my wife, then Caleb when he returned home from school. I was terrified—not so much for myself, but for my family. Why should they have to pay for the terrible mistake I'd made so many years ago? I couldn't let that happen. So, while Melanie was distracted, I went for the gun. We struggled, and I…I accidentally shot her." He swallowed hard. "She died in my arms."

Dane swore softly under his breath. He thought he'd heard it all, witnessed enough tragedies in his years as an FBI agent to have grown immune to them. He couldn't have been more wrong.

Crandall dragged in an unsteady breath, looking haggard and haunted. "When the police arrived, I told them I didn't know Melanie, that she was an armed intruder who'd forced her way into my home. They accepted my story, and that was the end of it." A muscle tightened in his jaw. "Until now."

Dane frowned, dread clenching in his gut. "How do you know Solange is Melanie's daughter?"

"I know."

"*How* do you know?" Dane barked impatiently.

Crandall turned to him, his face contorted with grief and outrage. "Because I hired a private investigator, and because she looks just like her grandmother!" he roared, spittle flying from his mouth. "And because every time I look at her, damn it, I feel as if God Almighty is playing a cruel joke on me, punishing me for my past sins! Do you have any idea what that's like? *Do you?*"

In the tense, ensuing silence Dane said nothing, staring at Crandall as if he'd never laid eyes on him before. And maybe he hadn't. The man who stood before him bore little resemblance to the brash, arrogant, powerful force of nature Dane had come to know over the last year. *That* Crandall Thorne had never displayed such naked fear and vulnerability. And in that moment,

Dane was struck by two jarring realizations. The first was that the woman Crandall had hired to be his personal assistant, the woman Dane had fallen so hard for, was actually the old man's long-lost granddaughter. The second, and perhaps more startling, realization was that Thorne had loved Melanie's mother, loved her with a fierce intensity that sank deep into a man's soul, took root and never, ever let go.

Thanks to Solange, Dane now knew a thing or two about that kind of love.

He said quietly to Crandall, "Who's her father?"

Crandall waved a dismissive hand. "Some lowlife punk Melanie met on the streets when she ran away from one of her foster homes. Last I heard, the man had OD'd on crack."

Dane closed his eyes for a moment, his heart squeezing painfully at the knowledge that Solange would never have the opportunity to meet her birth parents. The choice had been taken away from her a long, long time ago. "When?"

"When what? When did he die? I don't—"

Dane opened his eyes. "When were you going to tell her the truth about who she really is?"

Crandall flinched uncomfortably at Dane's harsh tone. "I was waiting."

"For what?"

"For the right time. I had to make sure—"

"What? You had to make sure she was worthy of your love and acceptance?" When Crandall said nothing, Dane stared at him, torn between disbelief and contempt. "How can you be such a heartless bastard? The moment you learned about her existence, your main concern should have been getting to know her, to at least *try* to make amends for what happened in the past!"

Crandall's face twisted with anger. "What happened to her mother that day at my house was an accident! And I didn't share that story with you to have it thrown back in my face, boy!"

They glared at each other for a long, charged moment before Dane, with a snort of disgust, turned and headed back toward the carport.

"Where are you going?" Crandall blustered after him. "We're not finished yet!"

"Oh, yes, we are," Dane bit off tersely without breaking stride. "I have better things to do with my time, old man."

"I don't want you talking to Solange! Do you hear me? I don't want you talking to her!"

"Hey, if you won't tell her the truth, I will."

"Like hell you will!" Crandall hurried to catch up with him. "This is none of your business, Roarke. Stay out of it."

Dane whirled on him. "I can't, damn it!"

Crandall drew up short, staring at him as if he were seeing a demonic apparition. "My God," he breathed. "You're in love with her, aren't you?"

Dane averted his gaze, a solitary muscle throbbing in his jaw. He could no more deny the accusation than he could deny what day of the week it was. He was in love with Solange, deeply and irrevocably. And God help him if she didn't feel the same way.

Crandall's mouth tightened with displeasure. "You're no good for her, Roarke. You and I both know it. You're going to break her heart."

"You don't know the first damn thing about me!" Dane thundered furiously. "How do you know whether or not I'm good enough for Solange? Just because your son happens to be married to my cousin doesn't make you an expert on my character!"

"No, son, years of training and experience make me an expert on your character!" Crandall gave a harsh, mirthless laugh. "I've been around a lot longer than you, Roarke. I've seen your kind. Hell, I've even *been* your kind. Oh, it's not your fault a cold-hearted, mercenary woman once betrayed your trust and hurt you. No, don't look surprised, son," he said when Dane's eyes narrowed. "Of course I know all about your past. I make it my business to know everything about the people who work for me, you know that. My personal contact at the FBI told me you were one of the best and the brightest, an extraordinary agent with a long, promising future ahead of him. Until you let that woman take it all away from you."

His hard, accusing gaze bored into Dane's. "Are you going to stand there and tell me you're not slowly dying inside, consumed by hatred for her and every other woman who crosses your path? Do you honestly believe you can make my granddaughter happy when you've spent the past two years punishing every female for the treachery of one? *Do you?*"

Dane stared into Crandall's eyes for so long the other man actually glanced away, then took a subtle step backward.

When Dane finally spoke, his voice was low and controlled. "Like I said before, old man, you don't know the first thing about me. I'm not a misogynist. I don't hate women, nor do I go around punishing them in some cruel, twisted attempt to get back at a silly, misguided female from my past. Maybe that's *your* baggage, but it sure as hell ain't mine. Let me assure you that I'm not going to spend the rest of my life regretting my decision to leave the Bureau. As it turns out, I don't have to. When—and if—I ever decide to return, I've been promised the sun, moon and stars on a silver platter, a promise signed in blood by the director himself. As for whether or not I can make your granddaughter happy, I sure as hell intend to try—with or without your permission." He paused, one corner of his mouth twisting cynically as he shook his head at Crandall. "You're not a psychologist, Thorne. You're a lawyer. So here's my advice to you. Stick to what you know—lying and keeping secrets—and leave the rest to the overpaid shrinks."

Crandall glared at him, looking as humiliated as if he'd been slapped across the mouth. "I'm going to tell her on Christmas day. I had already decided." His gaze hardened. "Don't ruin this for me, Roarke."

"This isn't about you, old man," Dane growled. "It's about Solange's right to know the truth." With that, he turned on his heel and stalked off again.

With a muffled oath, Crandall hurried after him. As he neared Dane's shadow, he reached out, seizing Dane's shoulder to halt his steps.

Dane jerked violently away, fists balled at his sides, half

praying he wouldn't be forced to thump Daniela's father-in-law on his own property. Good God. Hadn't he just reminded young Jake Tarrant to respect his elders?

Veins throbbed visibly in Crandall's temple, his face was flushed bright red and his nostrils flared as he struggled to catch his breath. If Dane hadn't been so incensed, he would have felt an actual twinge of alarm. Crandall Thorne had always been such an imposing figure—the picture of robust health and virility—that it was easy to forget he was a sixty-six-year-old man who'd suffered a major health crisis four years ago.

"Are you all right?" Dane asked through gritted teeth, his temper cooling to a slow simmer.

Crandall nodded quickly, looking slightly embarrassed. "Just a little winded," he admitted. "I'm not a young man anymore. I can't keep up with you when you storm off like that."

Dane felt an annoying pang of guilt. "You should go back to the house. You need to rest."

Crandall glowered at him. "Don't you dare treat me like an invalid, boy. And I'm not going anywhere until we've settled this matter. I'm asking you to give me a chance to tell Solange the truth. It should come from me, not you or anyone else."

Dane frowned. "That may be true, but do you really think it's a good idea to wait until Christmas?"

"I've waited this long. Twenty-four years, to be exact. What difference does fifteen more days make?"

Dane swore savagely. "*Twenty-four years?* You've known you had a granddaughter for *twenty-four years* and you did absolutely nothing about it?" he demanded incredulously.

Crandall grimaced. "She was healthy, she was happy. Her parents adored her. What more could I do for her?"

"Unbelievable," Dane muttered in disgust. "Un-freaking-be-lievable. If you ask me, Thorne, *you're* the one who needs therapy."

Crandall glared balefully at him. "Do I have your word that you won't tell Solange?"

Dane shook his head at him. "I don't understand you. Can't you see how it might be important to her to know that the man whose roof she's living under is actually the grandfather she never even knew she had?"

"Of course I realize that. I know how unfair I've been to her, how much I've deprived her of by keeping her identity a secret. That's why I chose Christmas to tell her. I want to make the holiday special for her. Tess and I already discussed—"

Dane's eyes narrowed on his face. "Tess? As in Tessa Philbin? Is that Solange's grandmother?"

Crandall hesitated, then nodded reluctantly. "Yes."

No wonder he'd only had eyes for her at last night's dinner party, Dane thought. After all they'd been through, he was still madly in love with her—another man's wife. And not just any man. The former mayor of San Antonio.

Good grief. What a tangled web.

Crandall was watching him intently. "Do I have your word, Roarke?" he asked quietly. "Will you give me a chance to tell Solange the truth?"

Dane scowled. "You're putting me in a very bad position, old man. I don't like lying to her. What am I supposed to say the next time I see her?"

"Say nothing. Or better yet, why don't you just wait until *after* Christmas to see or speak to her again? That way you won't have to worry about lying to her by omission."

A tight, grim smile curved Dane's mouth. "Spoken like a true lawyer. You've really perfected the art of lying and manipulating others, haven't you, Thorne?"

Pain, along with a dose of resentment, hardened the other man's eyes. "Don't ever judge a man until you've walked a mile in his heavy shoes, Roarke."

Dane stared at him for another moment, then gave a curt nod. "Fair enough." Without another word, he turned and made his way over to his Durango.

"Wait! Does that mean we have an understanding?" Crandall called after him, a note of desperation in his voice.

Dane slid behind the wheel of his truck, buzzed down the driver's-side window and started the engine.

Crandall appeared beside the Durango before Dane could pull off. "Do we have a deal, Roarke?"

Dane pushed out a deep, ragged breath, then pinned the old man with a steely look. "You have until Christmas to tell her the truth, Thorne. If you don't, so help me God, I will."

Crandall inclined his head. "Fair enough."

As Dane revved the engine—pointedly so—Crandall stepped away from the truck. "Oh, and before I forget. Wyome informed me that you asked for higher salaries for Tomas and the new stable boy. Consider it done."

Dane hesitated, then nodded tersely. "Thanks."

And as he drove away from the ranch—perched on the lush hilltop like a slice of heaven—he couldn't help feeling as if he'd just made a pact with the devil and sold his soul.

Chapter 22

Lightning arced across the night sky, illuminating the distant hulk of the mountains beyond Solange's bedroom window.

Lying in bed beneath a thick satin duvet, she gazed through the tall French doors leading out to the private terrace. It was almost midnight, and sleep had stubbornly eluded her.

Normally she was comforted by the sound of rainfall. On any other night, the soothing lash of rain against her bedroom window, combined with the lazy warmth of a crackling fire, would have lulled her right to sleep. But she was too keyed up for sleep tonight. Thoughts of Dane had dominated her mind ever since she'd left him standing in the middle of the living room, simmering with barely controlled fury as he watched her walk out the door on the arm of another man.

On the ride to the Italian restaurant, she'd spoken very little, only half listening as Lamar chattered about the weather in Haskell and about the promotion ceremony he'd attended that morning, and filled her in on what he'd been doing with himself over the past year. As soon as they were seated at a table in a secluded corner of the restaurant, she'd looked him square in the eye and told him she had no intention of taking him back. Ever.

He'd looked genuinely flabbergasted. "You're still mad at me for the way I ended things between us before."

"No, Lamar. I'm not mad anymore. Really, I'm not," she'd insisted at the disbelieving look he gave her.

"Then why aren't you willing to give us a second chance?" He reached across the linen-covered table and grasped her hand. "I love you, Solange. I never stopped."

"But I did." She regarded their joined hands on the table with a sad little smile. "A part of me will always care for you, Lamar, and appreciate the good times we shared together. But those days are long behind us. I've moved on with my life, and so should you."

He frowned. "Are you saying I've missed the window of opportunity for us? If I'd asked you to marry me back then, would you have said yes?"

"I honestly don't know, Lamar. I was a different person back then. There's no telling how I might have responded to a marriage proposal from you."

His mouth twisted bitterly. "Oh, *I* know how you would have responded. The same way you always did whenever I even hinted at marriage. You clammed up or changed the subject. Admit it, Solange. You *never* had any intention of marrying me."

She grew silent for several long moments, contemplating his hurt, angry words. When she spoke again, her voice was soft, reflective. "Maybe you're right, Lamar. Maybe I always knew deep down inside that we weren't really meant for each other. And if that's the case, aren't you glad you did us both a favor by ending the relationship before we wasted any more of each other's time?"

He scowled. "Do I *look* glad?"

She smothered a helpless laugh. "No. You look disappointed. But in time you *will* see that this was the best thing for both of us." She paused, gazing at him across the table, realizing she'd never loved him the way she should have.

The way she loved Dane.

She opened her mouth. "I hope—"

Lamar held up a warning hand. "Don't say it, Solange. Don't say you hope we can be friends. I came here *hoping* to convince you to return home with me as my fiancée. If you think I'm willing to settle for being your friend, you can just forget about it. I'm a soldier, not a saint. And don't even think about inviting me to your wedding with that guy back at the ranch. Unless you want me to show up at the ceremony and give *him* the same murderous looks he was giving me today." He snapped open his menu, effectively putting an end to the conversation.

As difficult as that experience had been, it paled in comparison to the agony Solange had felt that afternoon, trying to maintain her composure while Lamar did his level best to convince everyone in the room that their wedding was a foregone conclusion. And now, every time she closed her eyes, it was the look of wounded betrayal on Dane's face that she saw, not Lamar's dejected expression over lunch.

She tossed restlessly beneath the covers. God, what must Dane think of her? Not much, apparently. Since returning from the restaurant, she'd called him twice on his cell phone and once at the office, but he hadn't answered, and she'd been too much of a coward to leave any messages.

Pulling herself to a sitting position, she reached across the nightstand, picked up her cell phone and stared at the blank display screen, as if willing his number to suddenly materialize as an incoming call.

But the phone remained silent.

Heaving a deep sigh of frustration, she flopped back against the pillows and squeezed her eyes shut. It was too late to call Jill, and even if she did, what would she say? The last time they'd spoken, nearly a week ago, Solange had made it clear she had no plans whatsoever to get involved with Dane. How quickly things had changed! In less than a week, she'd made love to Dane and had fallen hopelessly in love with him. At the rate she was going, the next time she spoke to her best friend, she and Dane would be married with two-point-five kids!

Assuming he doesn't hate your guts.

Groaning miserably, Solange punched her pillow and rolled fitfully onto her side.

When another streak of lightning zigzagged across the dark sky, she bolted upright, wondering if her eyes were deceiving her.

There, standing on the terrace in the pouring rain, was Dane.

For a moment she just sat there, frozen, convinced her tortured imagination had conjured him up, and in the very next flash of lightning he would be gone, like a wraith.

But, no, she realized a moment later. He was still there. Not a figment of her overwrought imagination. Dane was really there. In the flesh.

With a soft cry, Solange flung back the covers and raced across the room to the pair of French doors, fumbling with the lock in her haste to open the door.

He stepped in from the gusting wind and rain, his untucked white shirt plastered to the hard muscles of his chest, shoulders and upper arms. Rainwater dripped from his long black eyelashes, turning them spiky. His eyes were smoldering pools of onyx.

He was so incredibly appealing, so dangerously male, he took her breath away.

She stared up at him, her heart knocking against her ribs. "Dane—"

Without uttering a single word, he kicked the door shut behind him, then cupped her face in his large hands and crushed his mouth to hers, his tongue plunging inside and stroking deep.

Solange eagerly responded, wrapping her arms around his neck and reaching on tiptoe to press herself more fully against his body, not caring that he was soaked to the bone, and that she wore only a thin gossamer nightgown. All she cared about was the wondrous feel of him in her arms and the sweet taste of him in her mouth—coffee, peppermint and his own uniquely delicious flavor.

His arms banded around her waist as he lifted her from the floor, holding her so tightly against him she couldn't tell where his body ended and hers began. They shared a hard, deep, open-mouthed kiss that left her moaning and trembling uncontrollably.

Setting her back down, he raised his head and gazed into her eyes with such fierce intensity her throat constricted. "Don't marry him," he whispered raggedly. *"Please don't marry him."*

Solange reached up, tenderly cradling his cheek in her hand. "I'm not, darling. I promise."

He made a strangled sound deep in his throat. A sound of tortured relief.

And then he bent and swept her into his arms. Completely by-passing the rumpled bed, he carried her over to the separate seating area, where a sedate fire glowed invitingly. He set her down gently on the chaise longue, then stepped back to divest himself of his wet clothing.

Held captive by the intoxicating heat of his gaze, Solange watched as he peeled the white shirt off his wide, beautifully sculpted torso and flung the garment away. Next he toed off his boots and socks, kicking them in the vicinity of his discarded shirt. As he unbuckled his belt and reached for the zipper of his dark pants, Solange licked her lips.

"Come here," she said, her voice husky with arousal.

He moved toward her with that slow, pantherlike grace she'd admired from day one. When he stopped in front of her, she lifted her eyes to his sexy face, then reached for his zipper, easing it down ever so slowly and deliberately. As she slid off his trousers and briefs, the thick, swollen length of his shaft sprang free, jutting enticingly toward her.

Holding his eyes, she leaned down and took him deep inside her mouth. He groaned, throwing back his head with a guttural oath that made her feel immensely powerful, like a beautiful sex goddess who'd been sent down to earth to grant his every wicked desire.

"Solange…" he uttered thickly, sinking his hands deep into her hair, his fingertips digging into her scalp.

She explored every delicious inch of him, suckling and flicking and swirling her tongue, wanting to drive him crazy with need. She wrapped her fingers around the smooth, engorged base of his penis and simultaneously massaged his testicles, un-bearably stimulated by the hoarse groans of pleasure that erupted from his throat. With her other hand she grasped one firm, muscled buttock, pulling him closer still, and he responded by rocking his hips and thrusting deeper into her mouth.

Just as she tasted a slippery saltiness on her tongue, he drew back from her, his chest heaving. His dark eyes glittered in the firelight, fierce with arousal.

He pulled her to her feet and slanted his mouth over hers in a hot, demanding kiss that electrified her senses and liquefied her bones. His erection throbbed against her belly through the sheer layer of her nightgown. He reached down, grabbed a fistful of gossamer and tugged the gown up and over her head, then tossed it onto the chaise. When he saw that she was naked beneath, he swore softly, his eyes sweeping hungrily across her quivering body.

"Beautiful," he whispered reverently.

Taking her hand, he led her over to the fireplace, and together they sank to their knees on the floor. He cradled her face between his hands, and she let her head fall back as he trailed his mouth down her throat, nipping and raining seductive kisses that ignited frissons of sensation along her nerve endings. His hands slid down to her bottom and gently cupped her, and she moaned and ground her hips against him in mindless need.

His probing fingers slipped between her legs and glided along the delicate folds of her sex, sending blissfully sensual tremors through her. She moved against his hand, seeking deeper contact. He obliged her, sliding his thumb around her pulsing clitoris until she writhed against him with a sob of eagerness, desperate to have him inside her.

He lay down on the thick hearth rug and pulled her on top of him, arranging her legs on either side of his hips. Their gazes locked, powerfully intimate. Her breath escaped from her on a soft hiss as he impaled her, stretching her deeply. A hard, delicious shiver swept through her. He lifted her by the waist and eased her back down on him slowly, inch by exquisite inch. She inhaled sharply, biting her bottom lip so hard she tasted blood. Bracing her palms on his taut abdomen, she began to move on him, slowly at first, and then with increasing vigor as an erotic pressure built inside her, taking her higher and higher. Suddenly she felt savage and hungry, full of fierce, primal yearning.

Arching into him, she pushed her breasts into his face, and his hot mouth covered one sensitized nipple, suckling greedily and nearly driving her over the edge. She threw back her head, panting his name as she rode him, as he fondled her bouncing breasts. She moved faster and faster until they were both breathless, until the heat between them condensed to a slick gloss of sweat on their skin.

With a rough, inarticulate sound, Dane rolled her onto her back and she tightened her damp thighs around him, clasping him eagerly to her body. Planting his hands on either side of her head, he thrust deep and hard, his body slapping noisily against hers. She raised her hips to meet him, stroke for greedy stroke, frightened at the intensity of the explosion gathering like a storm inside her.

He plunged rhythmically inside her, his face above hers hard and dark with passion as he whispered erotic promises to her. She gazed up at him through heavy-lidded eyes, wondering just when and how he had become so important to her, as vital to her survival as breathing. She loved him so much she couldn't remember what her life had been like before him, and couldn't imagine her life without him.

Dane lowered his head to hers, and they kissed with the hungry desperation of two lovers who feared the world was coming to an end.

Her throat was vibrating—her whole body was vibrating, as if she were about to shatter apart. And then she did, her head falling back on a soundless cry as she hurtled headlong into an orgasm of such mind-blowing proportions tears sprang to her eyes. His hips pumped furiously against hers until he dropped his head, then shuddered and groaned with the force of his own powerful release.

She lay beneath him, limp and exhausted with pleasure as he hung over her for several moments, his chest heaving as he gasped for breath, his muscled arms quivering slightly as he supported himself rather than letting his weight down onto her. After another moment, he eased his penis from the snug clasp of her body and collapsed onto the rug beside her, then gathered her against him. She breathed deeply as he stroked her hair and her shoulders, and hugged her tightly.

For several minutes they lay without speaking, gazing into the fire as the logs burned and hissed, the heat from the flames spreading like a slow, thick liquid over their cooling bodies. Outside, the rain continued falling, punctuated by an intermittent rumble of thunder.

"Solange, Solange," Dane murmured huskily, his soft lips nuzzling the nape of her neck. "What have you done to me?"

"Mmmm." She turned in the circle of his arms and nestled against his warm, solid chest, wishing she could stay there forever. "I was just about to ask you the same thing."

He angled his head to stare down at her with a fiercely possessive expression. "I've been going out of my mind all day, trying not to imagine you with that smug bastard. I don't know what I would've done if I'd pulled up tonight and found his car still parked here."

She grinned up at him. "He left a long time ago. Right after we returned from lunch, as a matter of fact."

Dane arched an amused eyebrow. "That was a quick visit."

"I think he secretly feared for his life. You *were* a little menacing, Dane. No, make that terrifying. Downright terrifying. Even *I* was afraid."

Dane chuckled softly, leaning down to brush his lips across her temple. "I've never been so damned jealous in my life. It turned me into a bloodthirsty, territorial animal."

She made a face. "Well, Crandall didn't help matters any, introducing Lamar as my fiancé when I'd already corrected him about that several times before you even arrived."

Sobering, Dane searched her eyes with his own. "What really happened between you and Rogers?" he gently probed.

Solange blew out a long, deep breath that stirred her already disheveled bangs. "We were together for three years, and then one night out of the clear blue, he broke up with me, telling me he needed space. Naturally I was hurt and confused. And then my parents died, and my relationship with Lamar, or lack thereof, got pushed to the back burner. Saturday night was the first time I'd spoken to him since the funeral. He called to tell me he'd made a mistake in letting me go, and he asked me to marry him."

"Saturday night," Dane murmured thoughtfully. "No wonder. When I saw you at breakfast the next morning, I automatically knew something had changed. That's why you were so grouchy when we went horseback riding."

Solange muffled a laugh against his throat. "I was grouchy because I wanted to jump your bones, and I was fighting my feelings for you."

Dane smiled a little. "But you were also considering Lamar's offer." It was a statement, not a question.

She hesitated, then nodded. "My parents adored him. I was feeling a little vulnerable and lonely, being in a new place, embarking on a new life. I knew my parents would have approved of my decision to marry Lamar. I wouldn't give him an answer right away, so I guess he came here to demand one."

"Can't say I blame him. I would've done the same thing if I'd let you slip out of my life the first time."

Solange, warming with pleasure at his words, gave him a teasing smile. "If that's the case, then why didn't you cut Lamar some slack?"

Dane scowled darkly. "Any man who's dumb enough to let you go doesn't deserve any slack. Did you let him down easy?"

Remembering Lamar's sullen mood throughout lunch and during the long drive back to the ranch, Solange grimaced. "Let's just say we reached an understanding both of us can live with."

Dane reached out, trailing a finger lightly down the length of her spine from the top of her neck to the small of her back. She shivered in response.

"Do you still love him?" he asked quietly.

She met his dark, penetrating gaze. "No. Not anymore." She wanted to tell Dane she loved him, but fear held her back. What if he didn't feel the same way? What if her confession sent him fleeing for the hills?

Dane pulled her against him and kissed her forehead and nose before reaching her parted lips. She felt an intoxicating rush as his tongue delved inside her mouth and took hungry possession of hers. Heat and need flared instantly between them.

She moaned as his strong fingers swept down her back and grasped her buttocks, holding her tightly against his rigid erection. Her nipples hardened against his chest, and her thighs trembled.

"Spend the night with me," she breathed against his mouth.

"What about Thorne?" Dane murmured.

"I don't care if he finds out you're here. I'm a mature, responsible— *Ohhh*," she moaned as Dane's wicked fingers reached between her thighs and began stroking the swollen folds of her sex in an unbearably arousing caress.

"What were you saying?" he prompted between deep, silky kisses.

At that moment Solange could hardly remember her own name, let alone the declaration of independence she'd been making. "I was, uh, saying that I'm a mature, responsible adult," she mumbled, her voice slightly slurred. "And although I'm, uh, living under Crandall's roof, I expect him to treat me like one. A mature, responsible adult, that is." As Dane slipped a finger inside her, she gasped sharply and arched her hips, and the rest of her words came out in a high, breathless rush. "Besides, it's not as if he's my father or anything!"

Dane tensed against her, and for a moment his marauding fingers stilled. Lifting his mouth from hers—they'd been kissing and talking the whole time—he stared down at her with a sudden alertness she didn't know how to interpret.

In any case, it was unimportant at the moment.

She gave him a slow, sultry smile. "So you'll stay?"

When he hesitated, she reached for his hand between her legs. As he gazed at her, she drew his fingers into her mouth and tasted herself, deliberately reminding him of the way he'd licked fudge from her own fingers two days ago. In satisfaction she watched as his nostrils flared and his eyes grew hooded with desire.

"Stay," she whispered.

He gave her a smoldering look. "Just try to make me leave."

Rising from the floor and sweeping her into his arms, he strode purposefully toward the bed, and was buried deep inside her before their bodies hit the mattress.

Chapter 23

The next two weeks passed in a dizzying procession of activities and social outings. With Christmas right around the corner, Solange bravely consented to another shopping excursion with Daniela—this time, thankfully, to buy gifts for others. They were joined by Daniela's sister-in-law Riley Roarke, an award-winning reporter for the *San Antonio Express-News*. Almost from the moment Riley swerved to a stop in front of Daniela's apartment building, narrowly missing the fender of Crandall's Rolls Royce limousine parked at the curb, Solange had liked the beautiful, spirited woman. Spilling from her car, she'd apologized for being late, smiled warmly at Solange and issued a warning to her sister-in-law that she would not be dragged into every store at the mall simply to satisfy Daniela's crazy shopping addiction. After hearing that, how could Solange *not* have liked the woman?

She also had an unexpected opportunity to bond with Tessa Philbin, who'd invited Solange to hear her speak at a luncheon sponsored by the League of Women Voters. They'd snuck out immediately afterward, choosing to stuff themselves on fried catfish and candied yams at a local soul-food restaurant rather than suffer through the bland fare served at the posh country club. If anyone had ever told Solange she would someday find herself

sharing a bowl of collard greens with the elegant, well-bred wife
of a former mayor, she wouldn't have believed it. Yet there she
was, laughing and talking with Tessa Philbin as if they'd been
acquainted for years. Although the older woman had sacrificed
her own career in order to support her husband's, Solange knew
she could learn a lot from Tessa. When they parted ways at the
end of the afternoon, she'd eagerly accepted Tessa's invitation
to join her for the opening of an art exhibit the following week.

Another highlight of the month was attending a holiday mixer
at St. Mary's University with Daniela and Caleb, who took her
around the room and introduced her to many of his colleagues, describing Solange as an "up-and-coming law student to watch for."
Afterward, when she'd tried to thank him for providing the wonderful networking opportunity, he'd laughed and told her that he and
Daniela would gladly accept free babysitting services as repayment.

Solange's active social calendar kept her too busy to do any
real work for Crandall—not that he seemed to mind. Other than
to set up his weekly videoconferences and run an occasional
errand for him, she didn't have many responsibilities, which left
her wondering whether he really needed a personal assistant. She
spent more time assisting Rita around the house, accompanying
her to the flea market and baking apple cobblers to be delivered
to the battered women's shelter.

On the Saturday before Christmas, Dane brought Jacob
Tarrant's siblings to the ranch for a promised afternoon of horseback riding followed by a picnic. As an added bonus, they got to
watch their cocky older brother hard at work repairing horse-
shoes, shoveling manure and mucking out stalls.

After taking the three siblings home, Solange and Dane
returned to the ranch. Finding the house silent and empty, they
hurried to her bedroom like a pair of horny teenagers, hoping to
get in a quickie before Crandall and Rita came home.

"Let's do it out on the terrace," Dane suggested, his eyes
glinting with mischief as he led Solange toward the French doors.
"I don't want you holding back if you need to scream once or
twice over the next hour."

She gave a throaty laugh. "My, my, what a naughty boy you are, Dane Roarke. An hour? We're supposed to be having a quickie."

He sent her a sexy, wolfish grin. "We'll call this the extended version."

Outside on the private terrace, with its breathtaking view of the surrounding valley, Solange melted into Dane's arms and surrendered to the slow, drugging sensuality of his kiss.

The moment was interrupted by a burst of loud, angry voices that reached them from the nearby courtyard outside Crandall's library.

"When are you going to wake up, woman? He doesn't give a damn about you, and I know you don't love him! What's it gonna take to convince you to finally leave the worthless bastard?"

"It's not that simple, Crandall!" cried Tessa Philbin. "We've been married for more than forty years! We've built a life together, made friends—"

"Some friends," Crandall said scornfully. "They smile in your face, then tear you apart behind your back because they know you don't belong in their world of white privilege. And how can you stand there and defend that man after what he said to you today? He practically called you a whore and accused you of cheating on him!"

Tessa gave a low, bitter laugh. "Considering our history, Crandall, can you honestly blame Hoyt for having those suspicions after hearing that I attended a dinner party at your house while he was out of town? And while we're on the subject, you told me it was going to be a very small gathering, and you assured me that none of your guests would go back and run their mouths about my presence at the party!"

Solange and Dane exchanged uncomfortable glances. "Let's go back inside," he murmured. "We shouldn't be hearing this."

Solange nodded in agreement. But as they turned and started from the terrace, she heard her name—and froze.

"So are you saying that you regret coming that night?" Crandall demanded. "Are you saying you regret the opportunity to meet Solange?"

"Of course not!" Tessa cried tearfully. "How could you even suggest such a thing? How could I regret something as important as meeting our precious granddaughter?"

Solange stopped breathing.

What was Tessa saying? That Solange was their...*granddaughter?*

She must be mistaken. She *had* to be!

But when her stunned gaze flew to Dane's face, he was already watching her with a quiet, grim expression that could only mean one thing.

"You *knew?*" she whispered faintly.

He hesitated, his jaw tightly clenched as he stared at her for what seemed an eternity. Finally he nodded. "I knew."

The blood drained from Solange's head. The ground tilted beneath her feet and she swayed on the balcony. With a guttural oath, Dane reached out and caught her in his arms, hauling her roughly against him.

"I'm sorry," he whispered hoarsely, burying his face in her hair. "You weren't supposed to find out this way."

Solange shoved blindly against his chest. "Let me go!"

He reluctantly released her and took a step back, gazing at her with an expression of deep sorrow and regret. "Solange—"

She was shaking so hard she feared she might collapse at any moment. "You knew Crandall was my grandfather and you never told me? How could you keep something like that from me? *How could you?*"

"You have to understand—"

"How long have you known?" she demanded.

Dane hesitated, a solitary muscle ticking in his jaw. "Two weeks."

Solange gasped.

Over the last two weeks he'd made love to her countless times, cooked dinner for her and escorted her to the movies and the symphony. He'd taken her home to meet his family and to attend the game in which her beloved Dallas Cowboys had wrapped up their season by beating the Houston Texans. As if that trip weren't memorable enough, he'd even surprised her with an incredibly romantic overnight rendezvous at the River-walk hotel where it all began.

And not once had he felt it necessary to tell her she was Crandall Thorne's granddaughter.

Dane took a slow step forward. "Solange—"

"Get out."

Pain filled his dark eyes. "I love you," he said, his voice achingly husky. "I've been too scared to say it before now, but it's true. I love you so damned much, Solange."

Closing her eyes, she steeled herself against his words, the naked vulnerability in his gaze and the terrible anguish clawing at her heart, threatening to rip her apart from the inside out.

"Get out," she said again, several degrees frostier. "Now."

When she opened her eyes again, he was gone.

Choking back a sob, she drew several deep, calming breaths, then turned and went inside the house. She marched purposefully through her bedroom suite and down the corridor to Crandall's library. Without bothering to knock on the closed door, she barged into the room and crossed to the French doors.

Crandall and Tessa stood in the middle of the small courtyard. They were locked in a passionate kiss, their arms banded tightly around each other like they would never let go.

When Solange cleared her throat, they sprang apart guiltily and stared at her in dazed confusion.

"I hate to interrupt this touching little reunion," Solange said, bitingly mocking. "But I have a burning question for both of you that couldn't wait another minute."

They exchanged wary glances. Crandall looked like a convicted prisoner waiting for the judge to pronounce the death sentence.

Tessa stepped forward with a gentle, tentative smile. "What is it, Solange?"

She glared at each of them in turn. "Just when were you planning to give me permission to start calling you Grandma and Grandpa?"

* * *

Later that evening, Solange stood at the window in the spare bedroom of Caleb and Daniela's downtown penthouse. With her arms folded tightly across her chest to ward off a chill that radiated from deep within, she stared down at the rain-washed street below, where holiday shoppers bustled along the sidewalks, their arms laden with last-minute gift purchases. A yellow cab hurtling around a corner nearly struck a pedestrian who'd darted out into the intersection, and a trio of festively attired mariachi singers serenaded passersby from the covered doorway of an old Mexican restaurant.

Solange saw nothing.

How could she, when her whole world had been turned upside down in a matter of minutes?

Four hours after her emotional showdown with Crandall and Tessa, her pain, confusion and shocked fury had finally given way to a feeling of numb resignation. She was no longer an orphan, as she'd come to think of herself in the year since her parents had died. She had family. Two grandparents, an aunt and uncle, and a cousin on the way, not to mention a bevy of other faceless relatives.

But the parents she'd never known and had secretly hoped to find someday were hopelessly beyond her reach. And her troubled young mother, in search of the truth about her own identity, had died at the hands of the man who'd deserted her so long ago.

It was like something out of a Greek tragedy—except it wasn't.

It was Solange's history.

Her new reality.

A gentle knock sounded at the bedroom door. She glanced over her shoulder. "Come in," she said tonelessly.

The door opened, and Caleb—*Uncle* Caleb—stepped into the room. He tucked his hands into the pockets of his low-rise jeans, propped one shoulder on the doorjamb and regarded her in thoughtful silence for several moments.

Solange knew she must look a sight, her eyes red and puffy from crying, her hair still damp and matted from her mad dash through the rain to escape the ranch house earlier. She'd been running and stumbling along the gravel path, with no particular destination in mind, when the Rolls had pulled up alongside her, and old Mr. Bailey had buzzed down the window to peer worriedly at her. She'd been so shocked by the uncharacteristic display of emotion on his face that when he told her he'd been instructed by Caleb and Daniela to bring her to their downtown apartment, she'd climbed into the limo without argument.

Turning from the bedroom window, she reached up self-consciously and combed her fingers through her hair. "Thanks for letting me crash at your place for the night, Caleb," she mumbled dispiritedly. "I had to get out of there."

"You can stay as long as you like," he said gently. "That's what family is for."

She met his concerned gaze, then glanced away. After another moment, she walked over to the queen-size bed and sat down on the edge.

"Daniela and I were going to order takeout from somewhere on the Riverwalk," Caleb said. "Any particular requests?"

Solange shook her head. "No, thanks. I'm not very hungry."

"That's understandable. I didn't have an appetite for weeks after learning about my sister."

My mother.

Solange lifted her troubled eyes to his. "What did you do when you found out?"

"Resigned from the law firm. Stopped speaking to the old man for five years." Caleb lifted one broad shoulder in a shrug. "At the end of the day, though, no amount of running or hiding could change the past or bring Melanie back. So I did the only thing I could to get back some of my sanity. I forgave him."

"How?" Solange cried. "How could you forgive him for lying to you all those years, for not telling you that the dead homeless girl on your living-room floor was really your half sister?" Tears bit beneath her eyelids, and she blinked them angrily away.

Caleb straightened from the doorway, crossed to the bed and sat down. "It wasn't easy to forgive my father, believe me. I wanted to spend the rest of my life hating him for the way he'd betrayed not only me and Melanie, but my mother as well." He paused, staring out the window at the softly falling rain. "It took me a while to realize that in hating him and blaming him for the past, I was actually punishing myself. Hatred takes a lot of energy, Solange, more than I was willing to expend. So I decided to liberate myself and forgive him. Of course," he added dryly, "it only took me five years. Better late than never, I suppose."

"And what about now?" Solange demanded. "Now that you've just found out that he lied to you about me, are you willing to just give him a pass?"

"Not quite," Caleb drawled, a glint of steel in the dark eyes that met hers. "I've already given the old man a piece of my mind. I let him know that if he even thinks about keeping any more secrets from me, it will be a very long time before he lays eyes on his unborn grandson." He paused, his mouth curving sardonically. "I think he knew I wasn't bluffing."

Solange didn't doubt it. As hurt and angry as she was, even *she* couldn't imagine shunning Crandall for five whole years. Yet Caleb had done just that. But somehow, some way, he'd found the strength and courage to forgive his father and forge a new relationship, a relationship so strong Solange found it hard to believe they'd ever been estranged.

Was she capable of that kind of forgiveness?

"At the risk of sounding like an apologist," Caleb said, watching her with a solemn expression, "I'm glad my father finally did the right thing and sent for you. I don't approve of the way he deceived everyone and manipulated you, but I'm grateful to have you here, in our lives." His voice softened with emotion. "I never had the opportunity to get to know my sister. I hope you won't deprive me of the pleasure of getting to know my niece."

Tears blurred Solange's vision. Averting her gaze, she gave a shaky little laugh. "You're not making this very easy for me, Caleb. I'm trying really hard here to be bitter, angry and hostile."

He chuckled softly. "Go ahead. You've more than earned the right. But just remember what I said. It takes a lot of energy, and

I think you can find far better uses for your time. Like applying to law school for next fall, getting involved with the Court Appointed Special Advocates program like you've always wanted. Making up with Dane." At her startled look, he grinned ruefully. "Thanks to my lovely wife, I know about a lot of things that go on in this family. In some cases, more than I'd ever *want* to know."

Solange bit her bottom lip. "Did…did he call Daniela?"

"Nope. He didn't have to. Since she, Dane and Noah are so close, she's always had this weird sixth sense that lets her know when something's wrong with one of them. When she called Dane on his cell phone this afternoon, she could tell by his voice that something bad had happened, but she couldn't pry it out of him. So she hung up and called Rita. That's how we knew you'd just run off."

Solange dropped her eyes to her lap. "I wasn't thinking straight," she murmured. "Too much had happened. First I found out my boss was really my long-lost grandfather, which explained why he'd never really treated me like an employee. And then I found out that my so-called boyfriend had known for weeks and kept the truth from me. How am I supposed to forgive him for that?"

"The same way I forgave Daniela for entering my life under false pretenses," Caleb said quietly.

When Solange looked up, her eyes searching his curiously, he shook his head. "It's a long, complicated story that we can rehash another time. All I'll say is that I almost made the biggest mistake of my life by letting Daniela go, simply because I couldn't forgive her. I was miserable as hell without her, but I was bound and determined to make her pay for what she'd done." A small, self-deprecating smile curved his mouth. "Do you know who finally talked some sense into me?"

Solange shook her head.

"My father, of all people. He told me that if I didn't go and make things right with Daniela, I'd spend the rest of my life alone and bitter, or worse, I'd end up married to some woman I didn't even love, and I'd spend my days and nights wondering about the one that got away." Caleb paused, smiling sadly. "Now that you've met Tessa, I think you can understand the depths from which my father was speaking that day."

Solange nodded, remembering the scene she'd stumbled upon in the courtyard. "I can't imagine what it must be like to spend over half your life loving someone you've convinced yourself you can never have."

"I don't know. Fortunately," Caleb said, giving her a meaningful look, "if you decide to forgive Dane, you'll never have to know, either."

Solange hesitated, her throat clogged with unshed tears. After another moment she nodded slowly, decisively. "You're right."

Caleb grinned, bumping her playfully on the shoulder. "Of course I'm right. I'm nine years older than you—I'll *always* be right, baby girl."

Solange gave a teary laugh, then suddenly groaned, slapping her hand to her forehead. "Oh, God. I just remembered something."

"What?"

"The first time I met you, I thought you were a hottie. And now I find out you're my uncle. Ewww."

Caleb threw back his head and laughed.

At that moment Daniela appeared in the doorway with a pleased grin. "If you two are finished bonding, I'm starving and would like to have my dinner now. I'm eating for two, you know."

"Yeah," Caleb and Solange said in unison, "we *all* know."

They looked at each other, then dissolved into another round of laughter.

Chapter 24

She found him just where she thought he'd be.

Shooting hoops alone at the old blacktop basketball court around the corner from his house. She stood quietly in the lengthening shadows of dusk, watching as he skillfully executed a series of layups and hook shots, the metal rim of the basket vibrating from the force of his hard dunks. He had discarded his shirt in the grass and wore a pair of long black sweat shorts that left his strong, toned calf muscles exposed to her admiring gaze. A fine sheen of sweat clung to his beautiful mahogany skin and made her remember what it was like to feel his body quiver beneath her touch, to brace her palms on the taut surface of his abdomen and ride him through one earth-shattering climax after another.

"Hey, you," she called out before her imagination could take over.

Poised to shoot the basketball, Dane whipped around and saw her standing beneath the large oak tree that guarded the court. His eyes widened in surprise. "Solange?"

She stepped from the shadows and started toward him on legs that felt like rubber. "Hasn't anyone ever told you it's bad luck to be alone on Christmas Eve?"

Dane tucked the ball underneath one arm, watching her approach with an unreadable expression. "Never heard that one."

"O-kay," she said, drawing out the word. "How about the fact that it's sixty degrees out here and you're running around with no shirt on? Trying to catch your death of cold or something?"

"Or something," he murmured. "What're you doing here, Solange? It's Christmas Eve. Why aren't you having dinner at the ranch with the rest of the family?"

She came to a stop in front of him, and although she wore a pair of four-inch stiletto boots, he still had the superior vantage point. She angled her head slightly to look up at him, her heart drumming wildly from his sudden nearness, after four days of deprivation. "I was there, but then I left."

"Why?"

"Because *you* weren't there."

When he said nothing, she continued, "I kept expecting you to show up, but every time the door opened, someone else walked through. And then Daniela mentioned that you might be leaving for Houston tonight to spend Christmas with your family. I rushed over here as fast as I could, and when I saw your truck still parked in the driveway, I nearly passed out with relief. I knew where to find you."

Dane nodded slowly. "You found me." Stepping back from her, he began dribbling the basketball in place, quiet and controlled.

So he wasn't going to make this easy for her.

Solange took a deep breath and buried her moist palms inside the pockets of her belted leather trench. "Crandall says he owes you an apology for the way he mistreated you and interfered in our relationship. And he says it was his fault that you didn't tell me the truth sooner. He says he practically begged you not to, and you took pity on him. He told me that's when he finally realized what an extraordinary man you are. Not that I needed *him* to tell me what I've known all along."

Dane remained silent, continuing to dribble in place. Up and down, down and up. Solange curled her hands into fists inside her pockets, resisting the urge to smack the ball away. "He's really eager to make amends."

"That won't be necessary," Dane said in a low, even voice. "I knew I was wrong for agreeing to keep his secret. I take full responsibility for my own actions."

"Then why do I get the feeling you're angry with me?" Solange asked, frustrated.

Dane caught the basketball in midair, palming it easily in his large hand. His dark, searing eyes met hers. "It's been four days, Solange. Four days is like a damned eternity when you're left wondering whether the woman you love will ever find it in her heart to forgive you for the stupid lapse in judgment you made. I called you twice, but you never answered the phone or returned my messages. Is that what you did to poor little Lamar before you finally put him out of his misery?"

"You're not Lamar!" Solange cried out. "And I needed time, damn it! I needed time to sort through my feelings and wrap my mind around everything that had just happened. I never meant to hurt you by sending you away. I was so angry and confused. I felt betrayed by everyone in my life at that moment!" Her voice hitched, and she glanced quickly away before adding in a choked whisper, "Truth be told, I've been scared, just like you were, to tell you what I've known for a while."

Dane grew very still. "What are you saying, Solange?"

She lifted her eyes, met the searching intensity of his gaze and took the final plunge. "I'm saying that I love you, Dane. It probably happened the very first time you called me Angel Eyes, the day we went horseback riding and had our first kiss. I was a goner after that, even though I knew it was risky to get involved with you."

"Why?" he demanded, tossing aside the ball and stepping toward her. "Because you thought I wouldn't be faithful to you?"

"No." A soft smile trembled at the corner of her lips. "Because I thought any man who made me feel the way you do had to be too good to be true."

His eyes traced her features in the fluorescent light that illuminated the basketball court at nighttime. "And now?" he prompted softly. "Do you still think I'm too good to be true?"

"You might be." Her smile deepened. "But that's a risk I'm willing to take."

"Atta girl," he whispered, and bending his head, he covered her mouth with his. She reached up at once, curving her arms around his neck and kissing him back with all the love she felt in her heart.

At length Dane lifted his head, his heavy-lidded eyes roaming hungrily across her face. "Marry me, Solange," he said huskily.

Her heart swam into her eyes, filling them with tears. She thought her ears were deceiving her. "Dane…?"

He lifted her hand to his warm lips. "Be my wife."

An elated sob rose in her throat. Solange slid her arms around his neck, buried her face against his bare chest and held him fiercely to her.

Dane chuckled, nuzzling the top of her head. "Is that a *yes?*"

Laughing, Solange drew back to look at him. "Yes! One hundred percent yes!"

He touched his tongue to the tear that had rolled down her cheek, kissing it away. "I love you," he said thickly. "I can't wait to spend the rest of my life with you. Making love to you every night, waking up to the sight of you every morning. Meeting you for quickies during lunch, curling up on the sofa together to watch football games on lazy Sunday afternoons."

"Hmmm, sounds good to me," Solange murmured, grinning so hard her cheeks hurt. "But you have to become a Cowboys fan, or there'll be no peace in our home."

Dane chuckled dryly. "We'll talk about that later."

Solange leaned forward, covering his mouth fully with hers. They shared a deep, lingering kiss.

"Come on," Dane whispered. "Let's go back to the house before the nosy neighbors start talking."

As they made their way back through the quiet, tree-lined neighborhood filled with old Victorian houses and quaint clapboards bedecked with holiday lights, Solange told Dane about her long, heartfelt conversation with Crandall and Tessa, and about Tessa's momentous decision to finally leave her husband in order to be with Crandall, the only man she'd ever loved. She was willing to let go of the painful past and forgive him, even though he'd deceived her about how long he'd actually known about Solange, and about the fact that *he* was the one who'd sealed Solange's birth records to keep her existence a secret from Tessa's vengeful husband, who would have used the knowledge as a battering ram against her. In the end, Tessa had decided that if Crandall could forgive *her* for breaking his heart and marrying another man, she could forgive him for the terrible lies he'd perpetrated.

Love, she'd told Solange, *is the great equalizer.*

When Solange and Dane arrived at the little beige bungalow he'd been renting from Daniela, he unlocked the front door and gestured her inside. She glanced briefly around, taking in the dark, masculine furnishings arranged around the cozy living room, before turning back to him.

"You haven't set up the little tree we bought." They'd gotten sidetracked the last time, spending the rest of the romantic evening in bed, then in the shower—and then back in bed.

"I didn't want to. Not without you." His hand curved around her nape, sliding into her hair and tilting her face up to meet his smoldering gaze. "Nothing is the same without you, Solange."

Her heart soared. She sighed in relief, closed her eyes and took a moment to savor his words. "I was so afraid you'd decide you never wanted to see me again."

"Not a chance." Dane scooped an arm around her waist and brought her firmly against him. Her eyes fluttered open, settling on the sensuous curve of his mouth. Her body stirred with hunger.

She wreathed her arms around his neck and leaned close, kissing him softly, tenderly. "We can decorate the tree tonight, if you'd like," she whispered.

"Later, Angel Eyes," he promised, his voice low and silky. He bent and swept her effortlessly into his arms. "We've got all night."

Solange shook her head slowly. "Not just all night," she corrected as he carried her toward the bedroom, his eyes never leaving hers. "We've got the rest of our lives."

Two GROOMS and a Wedding

Award-winning author
Adrianne Byrd

For one forbidden night, ambitious attorney
Isabella Kane indulged her deepest passions.
Now she can't get Derrick Knight out of her mind…
and Derrick is equally obsessed. The problem is,
Isabella's engaged to his old college rival.
But Derrick's determined to make Isabella his.

"A humorous, passionate love story."
—*Romantic Times BOOKreviews*
on *Comfort of a Man* (4 stars)

Coming the first week of March, wherever books are sold.

KIMANI™
ROMANCE

"Ms. Craft is a master at storytelling…"
—*Romantic Times BOOKreviews* on *Star Crossed*

Author favorite

Francine Craft

Designed
for
PASSION

Second chances never looked so good…

When Melodye Carter's husband's mysterious death is linked
to another shooting, Detective Jim Ryman must protect
Melodye and her twin boys. Jim shut down his heart after
losing his wife, but proud, vulnerable Melodye makes him
remember what it means to be a man in love.

Coming the first week of March, wherever books are sold.

KIMANI™
ROMANCE

*He was the best thing
that had ever happened to her…*

The
FOREIGNER'S
CARESS

Favorite author

Kim Shaw

Determined to change her wild ways, Madison Daniels finds
the man of her dreams in handsome Jamaican billionaire
Stevenson Elliott. But when her past indiscretions earn the
disapproval of Stevenson's family, she must convince him that
a lifetime with her is worth more than his family's billions.

Coming the first week of March, wherever books are sold.

KIMANI™
ROMANCE

www.kimanipress.com   KPKS0580308

WHEN LOVE Calls

National bestselling author

CELESTE O. NORFLEET

Washington lobbyist Alyssa Wingate is tired of all the
double-talk surrounding the plight of the elderly, and is
determined to do something about it. So she sets her
sights on obtaining the help of Senator Randolph Kingsley,
a man of enormous popularity and power. But will their
mutual attraction get in the way of advancing her cause...
and his career?

"Norfleet's latest is sinfully sexy reading with a
hint of mystery and a dash of humor."
—*Romantic Times BOOKreviews* on *Only You*

***Coming the first week of March,
wherever books are sold.***

ARABESQUE®

www.kimanipress.com

KPCON1110308

From acclaimed author

Dwight Fryer

The evocative prequel to *The Legend of Quito Road...*

The Knees of
Gullah
Island

A beautifully rendered novel that explores the
complex racial dynamics that shaped the South
through one family's extraordinary journey to
freedom. Born to free parents, Gillam Hale realizes
he can never be truly free until he finds his lost loved
ones and faces the legacy of his own rash decisions.

"Dwight Fryer's debut novel is a scintillating mixture
of love, betrayal, hope and redemption disguised
in the incredible human condition of a sleepy little
1930s Tennessee town."
—*Rawsistaz Reviewers* on *The Legend of Quito Road*

*Coming the first week of March
wherever books are sold.*

sepia™

www.kimanipress.com   KPDF1190308

These women are about to discover that every passion
has a price…and some secrets are impossible to keep.

NATIONAL BESTSELLING AUTHOR

ROCHELLE ALERS

After Hours

A deliciously scandalous novel that brings together
three very different women, united by the secret lives
they lead. Adina, Sybil and Karla all lead seemingly
charmed, luxurious lives, yet each also harbors a
surprising secret that is about to spin out of control.

"Alers paints such vivid descriptions that when Jolene
becomes the target of a murderer, you almost feel
as though someone you know is in great danger."
—*Library Journal* on *No Compromise*

**Coming the first week of March
wherever books are sold.**

sepia™

www.kimanipress.com   KPRA1220308

A compelling short story collection...

New York Times Bestselling Author

CONNIE BRISCOE

&

ESSENCE Bestselling Authors

LOLITA FILES
ANITA BUNKLEY

YOU ONLY GET *Better*

Three successful women find themselves on
the road to redemption and self-discovery as
they realize that happiness comes from within...
and that life doesn't end at forty.

"This wonderful anthology presents very human
characters, sometimes flawed but always
heartwarmingly developed and sympathetic.
Each heroine makes changes for the better that
demonstrate the power of love. Don't miss this book."
—*Romantic Times BOOKreviews* Top Pick on
You Only Get Better

*Coming the first week of February
wherever books are sold.*

KIMANI PRESS™

www.kimanipress.com   KPYOGB1540208